# Also Sherri Hayes

***Hidden Threat*** - Cali Stanton has always wanted to be a doctor. But when her father is injured, she finds herself behind his desk at Stanton Enterprises.

Matthew Andersen's only priority is keeping the company and its CEO safe. That is easier said than done when someone starts making threats.

Things get personal when Cali becomes the latest target. Can Cali and Matthew put aside what lies between them long enough to find the *Hidden Threat* before it's too late?

***Slave (Finding Anna, Book 1)*** - As president of a not-for-profit foundation, Stephan knows what his future holds and what he wants out of life. All that changes when a simple lunch with his college friend and Mentor, Darren, leads him to buying a slave.

Brianna knows only one thing, she is a slave. She has nothing. She is nothing.

Can Stephan help Brianna realize that she is much more than just a Slave?

***Truth (Finding Anna, Book 3)*** - Things are going good for Stephan and Brianna, until her father shows up and sends her world into a tailspin. His presence forces her to face the reality of her past and what happened to her in order to move forward with her life. Will Stephan's love be enough to see her through or will outside forces tear them apart?

***Behind Closed Doors (Daniels Brothers, Book 1)*** - Six months ago Elizabeth Marshall's world came crashing down. Her husband dead and her friends gone, Elizabeth moves to the small town of Springfield, Ohio to start a new life for herself where no one knows who she is or about her past.

After his divorce three years ago, Christopher Daniels swore off women. They are nothing but trouble by his estimation. He has no desire to change that philosophy.

When Elizabeth Marshall moves into the apartment below his, he is determined to resist her charms. But when someone starts sending threatening messages to her, he finds himself in the role of protector. Can he protect Elizabeth and still resist the pull she has on his body and his heart?

***Red Zone (Daniels Brothers, Book 2)*** - The only thing Rebecca Carson ever wanted was to join the FBI, but now her career is in danger because of a situation over which she'd had little control. As she waits to be reinstated, her ex-partner offers her a job, and she jumps at the chance. Now Rebecca must work to protect a star quarterback from a stalker, while staving off his advances.

# Sherri Hayes

# Need

## Finding Anna Book Two

First published by The Writer's Coffee Shop, 2012

The Writer's Coffee Shop
(Australia)   PO Box 447 Cherrybrook NSW 2126
(USA)   PO Box 2116 Waxahachie TX 75168


Paperback ISBN- 978-1-61213-304-1
E-book ISBN- 978-1-61213-098-9



A CIP catalogue record for this book is available from the US Congress Library.


Cover image by: © Monkey Business Images Ltd
Cover design by: Jeff Bracke


www.thewriterscoffeeshop.com/shayes

This book is dedicated to all the wonderful people I've met so far on this journey. Thank you for all your help and support, and your love of Stephan and Brianna.

# Chapter 1

**Brianna**

*I stood, looking at myself in the mirror, the events of last night running* through my head. It wouldn't stop. I couldn't believe what he'd told me. For nearly a year, I had lived my life as a slave, as someone else's property. Now I . . . *wasn't?*

*"I didn't buy you to own you. Not like you think I did."*

*"If . . . if you didn't want to . . . own me, then why did you . . . why would you buy me?"*

*"There are people out there who enjoy what Ian does. Alex, for example, but if you weren't that type of person . . . well, I couldn't just not do something. I had the means to help you. I couldn't just walk away, and leave you there, if that wasn't what you wanted."*

His next words rang in my ears as if he were standing right beside me saying them again. *"I was selfish, though. When I brought you into my home, I knew that I wanted to keep you. Not as my slave, Brianna."*

He'd gone on to tell me that he wanted me as his submissive. I'd heard that word before, with some of Ian's friends, but I didn't know how it was different from being a slave. He'd said he was different from Ian, but the same. I had so many questions, and yet no idea where to begin.

What did it all mean? Was I no longer his?

I fingered the metal collar still in place around my neck. As he'd held me, I still felt like I was his. There, in his arms, no one could hurt me. I felt safe. Maybe that was stupid, but it was true. The moment I sat down in his lap, his arms came around me, and I instantly felt better. All the uncertainty no longer mattered because he was there.

Nothing could come and take that feeling away. Not even me. He caressed me ever so softly over my arms and back. Every now and then, I'd felt his lips graze my hair or my temple, but he said nothing and neither did

I.

From the moment he began explaining to me why he'd bought me from Ian, I knew that I should be asking him questions and demanding answers, but again, I couldn't. I had thought I would spend the rest of my life owned by someone, to be used and abused as they saw fit. And now . . . I was . . . not.

I clung to his shirt with my right hand while my left lay close to my side. Nothing had felt right in my life for the last eleven months. Not until this.

We'd sat there for a long time, neither speaking, with the television playing in the background. Eventually, Ma . . . Ste . . . Mast . . . he moved to turn it off.

He arose fluidly from his chair with me in his arms, and carried me to my bedroom. It had only made me hold on tighter.

He sat me gently on the bed and began to move away. I wouldn't let go.

He pried my small fingers from his shirt. "I'm just going to get you a change of clothes, Brianna. I'll be right back." I wanted to beg him to stay, but I let him walk away.

Just as he'd promised, he was only gone for a minute. He returned with some clothes, but I didn't pay much attention to what they were. Gently, he began undressing me.

His movements were unhurried. Never once did he try to do anything. He never had. I'd been in his home for more than a month, and yet he'd never had sex with me.

He scooped me up again in his warm arms and laid me down in my bed. My eyes found his as he hovered over me. They were filled with concern.

He brushed the hair away from my face. "I'll just be in my room. If you need me or want to talk, come wake me."

I didn't respond to his request. He watched me for several more minutes before standing once again to his full height and turning to leave. Again, I wanted to ask him to stay, but I didn't. Instead, I watched him leave.

I'd lain in bed for hours just thinking until I'd finally drifted off into a fitful sleep. I woke several times during the night. Once, I thought I'd seen him standing in the doorway, but I couldn't be sure.

Light was streaming in through my bedroom windows, leaking into the bathroom through the open doorway as I continued to look in the mirror. It was after eight; I'd glanced at the clock before getting up. He would have already left for work by now. I had no idea what I was waiting for. The mirror held no answers.

Instead of going out into the main room as I usually did, I climbed back into bed. On my side, I pulled my knees up to my chest, hugging myself.

I was alone all the time when he went to work, but for some reason today it brought with it an overwhelming sense of . . . well, not exactly fear, but uncertainty. What was I supposed to do with myself? Did I get up and do what I always did? Was that what he wanted?

However, did that matter anymore? I mean, I wasn't his slave. He'd said so himself.

I could be Anna again.

*Anna.*

I felt the moisture well up in my eyes and spill over. Who was Anna? Did she even exist anymore?

Suddenly, I felt comforting arms wrap around me. I thought I might have drifted off to sleep again until I heard his voice in my ear, his breath against my hair. He was here. Really, truly here.

I snuggled back against him, and he held me tighter. My tears ran freely down my cheeks, and he silently brushed them away until I drifted off to sleep again.

The next time I woke up the sun was higher in the sky, and I knew it had to be close to noon. I was alone in my bed again, but when I rolled over I saw him sitting in a chair just off to the side. He had a laptop resting on his legs, but looked up in response to my movement.

His eyes roamed my face as if searching for something. "Hi," I squeaked. My throat was dry, probably from crying.

"Hello," he replied in a steady, even voice. As if he knew what I was thinking, he picked up a glass of water that was on the nightstand beside my bed and handed it to me. I hadn't even noticed it. "Drink."

I brought the glass up to my lips and felt the liquid coat my dry throat. Only after the contents were completely gone did I lower the glass and look up at him again. His eyes were still on me. Watching.

"Thank you," I whispered.

"You're welcome," he responded. "Are you feeling better?"

I nodded.

"Are you hungry?" he asked.

I hadn't even thought of food until he mentioned it, but my stomach grumbled in response. He smiled. "I guess that answers my question."

He arose from his chair and set his laptop aside. His hand reached out to me. "Join me?"

It was a question. He was asking me again. I was free to refuse.

My hand reached out and found his. He helped me up, and we walked in silence into the kitchen.

"Would you like breakfast or lunch?"

"Um," I mumbled, looking down out of habit. His finger came up under my chin, making me look at him. He didn't say anything, just quirked an eyebrow. "Breakfast?" I said as more of a question than an answer.

He nodded and motioned for me to take a seat at the island. I slid onto the stool without comment. It had been a while since we'd eaten at the island. We usually ate breakfast together at the table. The change made me slightly nervous.

I watched as he made ham and cheese omelet for us, just as he had over a month ago. The differences between then and now struck me. Then, I had been worried about what was expected of me by my new Master. Now, I was just as concerned over what to expect, but for very different reasons.

After splitting the large omelet onto two plates, he set one in front of me, and placed the other to my left before coming around to sit down. He was silent as he ate, only glancing up at me once when he noticed I hadn't started eating immediately.

I was almost finished when he said, "Tell me what you're thinking, Brianna."

My fork stopped midway to my mouth. This was it.

I laid my fork down and placed my hands in my lap. "I'm wondering . . . what happens now?" I said without confidence.

"What do you want to happen now?" he asked.

I clenched my hands into fists in frustration. "I don't know," I said somewhere between a sigh and a sob.

His right hand covered both of mine before he spoke again. "This decision is yours, Brianna. I can't make it for you."

"I know, Mas—" Was I supposed to call him Master? Did he want me to?

He sighed. "Maybe we should start with names."

"Names?" I asked, bringing my head up to look at him hesitantly.

"Yes," he said more confidently. "You may call me Stephan, or Sir, if you prefer."

I knew my eyes were wide with shock. He was giving me permission to call him by his given name.

"Also, I was curious as to which name you prefer?"

"You know my name," I whispered.

He nodded. "This is true." He paused as if thinking through something. Then, seeming to finish his thought, he began talking again as if he hadn't stopped. "When I purchased you from Ian, he told me your name was Brianna Reeves. He called you Brianna, and you've never said any different or given me any reason to think you preferred to be addressed in any other way."

Now I was more confused. If he knew my name was Brianna, what was he getting at?

I didn't have to wait long. "I had a meeting with Brad this past week to see how things were going with your workout routine. He called you Anna," he said, searching my face for a reaction. He got one. I sucked in a breath at hearing the name my family and friends had called me before this nightmare began.

Brad did call me that, but for some reason it was different. Hearing him . . . Stephan . . . say my name again brought back the memory of the phone call with my father that Saturday afternoon when he told me that a car would be picking me up. I felt my heart rate pick up along with my breathing, but I was okay. I was okay.

"I was called Anna. Before," I whispered, knowing he'd hear me.

He waited until I looked at him again before asking in that calming voice of his, "Do you wish to be called Anna?"

I didn't know how to answer him because I truly didn't know. I wasn't sure I was that girl anymore, or if I ever could be again. "I don't . . . know?" Again, it came out sounding like a question.

He nodded again. "All right. We'll stick to Brianna for now."

Without another word, he slid from his seat and went to the sink with his plate. After rinsing it off and putting it in the dishwasher, he turned back to me. "You should finish your breakfast. I need to get some work done, but I'd like to talk again in a few hours."

"Okay," I answered without emotion.

His face dropped a little, but he quickly recovered. "I'm going to get my laptop from your room, and then I'll be upstairs in the library if you need me."

He paused to watch me for a minute and then walked out of the room, leaving me to finish my omelet.


## Stephan

At least she was still talking. That was good.

After her restless night, I'd been concerned that she'd completely retreat into her shell. Although she hadn't woken up screaming as she had those first few nights, she'd rarely stopped moving. Her arms, legs, and head had thrashed about causing the sheets and blankets to bunch and tangle in her limbs. Moans, both loud and soft, were constant visitors until the sun had started to rise in the sky.

I retrieved my laptop from the chair in her room and headed upstairs. She was still in the kitchen when I passed by, eating—or rather picking at— what was left of her food. The urge to go to her was strong, but I knew that I couldn't. I wanted her to have time to gather her thoughts before we talked later, and that was something she needed to do without me hovering.

It was hard to concentrate on work, but somehow, I managed to get through the e-mails that needed my attention. The clock read three thirty by the time I was finished, and Brianna had yet to come upstairs. I'd heard her moving around downstairs, but not enough for me to decipher what she could be doing.

Figuring I needed a little moral support, I called Logan's number. Thankfully, he picked up on the third ring. After the pleasantries were out of the way, he got down to business and asked me how the talk with Brianna went.

"She's got more strength than she gives herself credit for," he said once I'd brought him up to date on both our conversations last night and the one this morning.

"Yes, she does. I wish she would trust me more. There are still so many things that she keeps to herself."

"Have you told her that?"

"What? Well, of course . . ." The more I thought about it, the more I realized that although I had told Brianna she could talk to me, told her that she could trust me, I had always tried to keep my feelings and wants under control. Maybe Logan was right and I needed to tell her specifically what I wanted from her. She hadn't reacted badly when I'd told her I wanted her to stay last night. It might not be so bad.

"Thank you, Logan."

"What are friends for?" he said, and I could hear his amusement through the phone.

"There is one more thing. If Brianna decides to consider becoming my submissive—"

"She should talk to Lily," he said, before I could finish my sentence.

"Yes. I can answer her questions, but I think it would help having another submissive to talk with." I paused, and then added, "I don't know if I could handle it if she agreed, and then rejected me."

"You need to be prepared, Stephan. She may not want what you want, or like what you do."

I ran my hand through my hair in frustration. "I know that, Logan," I said through gritted teeth. "Do you think I don't *know* that?" Realizing I was raising my voice, I took a deep breath to calm myself down. "I know. Believe me, I know. I just . . ." I couldn't explain it other than to say, "She's different."

He didn't say anything for a long time. I knew he was weighing his response. Finally, he spoke. "I know this is different for you, Stephan, but you can't allow that to color your judgment or influence her. She has to want this or it won't work. Not for the long term anyway. And I know you well enough to know that is what you want."

Now it was my turn not to say anything. Logan knew me better than anyone else did. He'd stuck by me during my rebellious teenage years, and kept me out of the kind of trouble that would have ended up with me in Juvenile Hall. We'd experienced so many firsts together in our adolescence. I trusted him. He trusted me. Time and life experience had done nothing but strengthen that.

By the time I hung up with Logan, it was after four and I could hear Brianna moving around in the kitchen. I smiled to myself. She'd be starting dinner for us.

I decided to give her a little more uninterrupted time and called my assistant, Jamie. She assured me that although Karl Walker, the foundation's CFO, had been looking for me, it didn't appear to be urgent. Missing work was not something I liked to do, but I hadn't wanted to leave her alone today.

After hanging up with Jamie, I closed down my computer and opened the lower left drawer of my desk. There in the back was what I had been looking for: an empty journal.

As I walked back downstairs, the sounds in the kitchen got louder and then suddenly stopped. When I rounded the corner, Brianna was standing frozen in the center of my kitchen.

I walked over to her. "Is everything all right?"

She nodded.

"Brianna, please talk to me. Why are you standing in the middle of the kitchen? Do you need something?"

Again she didn't speak, just shook her head no.

This time, I reached out and brought her head up. Her eyes held uncertainty again. "Tell me."

"I don't . . . know what to do."

"About?"

She pressed her lips tightly together, and I was beginning to get frustrated. I tried very hard to remember what Logan had said just before hanging up with me:

*"Whatever you do, Stephan, don't lose your temper with her."*

I took a deep breath and refocused on her. She shifted her feet several times before she said, "I don't know what you want me to do. How you want me to . . . act."

"How do you want to act?"

That was when the tears started. I knew she was confused. This could not be easy for her. She had just begun to accept that she belonged to me, and now I had once again destroyed her reality. I only hoped she would let me help her build a new and better one.

I brushed the tears from her cheeks with my thumbs and stepped forward to bring us closer together. She took the invitation and laid her head on my chest. I wrapped my arms around her and rubbed my lips against her hair. "You can tell me anything, Brianna. Anything. I don't want you to keep things to yourself. I want you to trust me."

She nodded against my chest.

I noticed there was water boiling on the stove, so I reached over and turned the burner off. She started to step away and apologize, but I pulled her back against me. "No. Dinner will wait. I think we need to talk first."

Brianna nodded and stayed close to my side as I led us to the living room. I walked to my chair and sat down, holding my hand out in offering to her. She placed her fingers in my grasp and lowered herself onto my lap.

Once she was settled and my arms were around her, I said, "Now, tell me what is bothering you."

She took several minutes to answer, but finally said, "I don't know how I'm supposed to act . . . what I'm supposed to do now."

I took a deep breath and said, "Let's start with the first one, shall we?"

Her face was full of anxiety, but she nodded.

"This is my house, so I expect you to treat me and my things with respect. You are free to come and go. If you aren't going to be home when I am, then I expect you to either call me or leave a note. My bedroom is still off limits to you unless I give you permission to go in there. I would still like for you to continue working with Brad. I think it will help you not only physically, but mentally as well. It doesn't matter what you decide to do, but it is your decision. You may stop if you wish."

I let that set in for a minute before I continued. "As I told you last night, I'd still like to see you go back to school. Again, it will be a benefit to you no matter what path you end up choosing." Pausing, I made sure she was looking at me before calmly saying, "Everything else is up to you."

She just watched me, not saying anything for two hundred and four seconds. Then she said, "So, if I decide I don't . . . want to stay?"

I felt a deep pain in my chest unlike any I'd ever known. It took me a few seconds to find my voice. "I won't stop you."

Brianna didn't respond. Her eyes roamed my face and then fell to her lap. Once again, she pressed her lips together.

I decided to take Logan's advice and tell her exactly what I wanted. "I would like for you to stay. How do you feel about that?"

She shifted on my lap a little. "Scared."

"Why do you feel scared?"

"You want me to be your . . . submissive," she whispered.

"Yes," I answered.

"I don't," she said, and then stopped herself. "What would I have to do?"

The fact that she didn't say no outright gave me some hope. I smiled, tucked her hair behind her ear with one hand, and reached over to retrieve the new journal with the other. Her fingers touched it reverently when I placed it in her lap. "This is a journal. It's yours. I'd like for you to put your thoughts and feelings down in it every day."

She opened it, flipping through the blank pages. "I used to have a journal when I was with my mom," she said absently. "Thank you."

"You're welcome."

I waited until she closed the book and cradled it to her chest. Brianna seemed very pleased with her new journal. "We need to communicate. I need to know what you are thinking and feeling, Brianna. I want to help you so that you're not afraid anymore, but you have to help me. You have to talk to me. Will you do that?"

"Yes."

I cupped her face with both of my hands. "You don't have to make any decisions right now, Brianna. I won't force you into this. It has to be your choice."

She closed her eyes briefly. When they opened again, they were glistening, and a single tear fell down her cheek. My mouth opened and pressed against her skin, capturing the moisture. The salty taste lingered on my tongue.

Brianna's lips parted as she sucked in a deep breath. My senses registered her reaction, and I felt the pull I had felt so many times before. Tilting her face up with the pads of my thumbs, I moved my lips down to within a breath of her own. "I want to kiss you, Brianna."

She didn't answer me so I remained where I was. She tilted her head, bringing her mouth closer to mine almost unconsciously.

"Do you want me to kiss you?" I whispered.

"Yes," she said, her breath ghosting across my lips.

A second after the word left her mouth my lips were covering hers. My fingers wrapped around her scalp, moving her head to give me the best access. Her lips parted and I took advantage.

The taste of her against my tongue drove me on. Ever so slowly, I explored every inch of her mouth. The mouth of the woman I hoped to one day make completely and solely mine.

Brianna's hands came up to rest lightly on my chest. My hands increased their grip on her hair as I pulled back enough to say, "Touch me," before going back to my delicious exploration.

Slowly her hands moved up my torso to my neck. Feeling her touch my bare skin sent a shiver down my spine, and I pulled her closer. I wanted to devour her.

My body shifted and I put my left hand on her waist, pressing her closer. She was too desirable for her own good.

I forced myself to push her away. My forehead rested against hers as our harsh breath mingled together. Her expressive blue eyes fluttered open. For a moment, they weren't afraid. Then, I saw it again as she registered the want I knew was reflected in my own eyes.

With great reluctance, I leaned back and cleared my face of my desire. "I have one more request," I said once I'd regained my voice.

"What?" she asked, still not fully in control of herself.

"I want you to talk to Lily."

# Chapter 2

**Stephan**

*The rest of Monday night was uneventful. I joined Brianna in the kitchen* to help her finish making dinner. She was still a little hesitant, but I could tell that she was trying not to be.

Tuesday morning, she joined me for a very quiet breakfast before I left for the office. I beat Jamie in and was already in the middle of a grant proposal by the time she knocked on my door. "Good morning, Mr. Coleman."

"Morning, Jamie. Come in."

She walked into my office and took a seat in front of my desk. "It's good to have you back."

"Thank you," I smiled.

My assistant was very loyal, and one of the nicest people I had ever met. "I brought you some phone messages," she said, handing them to me. I flipped through them quickly. There was nothing overly important there other than a call from my lawyer. "Oh, and Miss Adams called just before five yesterday as well, but she said she would just track you down today. Should I call her and set something up?"

"Yes. I do believe I have lunch available today. Why don't you see if she is able to join me and order us something from the deli across the street?"

She nodded. "Is there anything else, sir?"

"I think that's all for now, Jamie. Thanks."

Less than five seconds passed after my door clicked shut before I picked up the phone and dialed my lawyer. "Davis and Associates. How may I help you?"

"Good morning. This is Stephan Coleman."

"Oh yes, Mr. Coleman. Mr. Davis is expecting your call. One moment, please."

The phone clicked and the line filled with hold music I'd heard more times than I could count. Luckily, I didn't have to listen for long before Oscar picked up the line. We exchanged brief pleasantries before he cut to the chase.

"My office received another phone call asking about Brianna Reeves. It was the same guy, I think. Anyway, after last time I put a tracer on the receptionist's phone and instructed her to use it if he called again." He paused for what seemed like several minutes, but was in fact only a few seconds. "The phone call originated from the Lake County Minnesota Sheriff's Office."

Any doubt I had in my mind that Jonathan Reeves was looking for his daughter went out the window. I had known it in my gut, but now I had proof.

"Stephan, what's going on? Is this girl running from the law or something?"

I debated for half a second whether to tell Oscar what was going on, but it was clearly information he should have. There was no way I could know what having someone in law enforcement actively coming after Brianna would do. "Oscar, there are some things you need to know."

"Whatever it is, I'll do my best."

I decided to stick to the basics. "After a phone call from her father, a car picked Brianna up from her home in Two Harbors. She ended up being held by a man named Ian Pierce for ten months until I was able to get her out." I conveniently left out the part of 'how' I got her away from him.

It didn't take Oscar long to draw the same conclusions I had. "Do you really think a county sheriff would do that to his own daughter?" he asked.

"As much as I would like to think otherwise, yes."

"I'll see what I can find out about Sheriff Reeves without drawing too much attention. It might not be a bad idea to look at Mr. Pierce either. See if maybe we can find a link between the two."

"Everything has to be below the radar. Nothing can tie this to me. Or you."

The conversation ended shortly after that with a promise from Oscar to contact me as soon as he obtained any information.

The rest of the morning went quickly. It was amazing how much work could pile up after only a day's absence this time of year.

At eleven thirty there was a knock on my door. Jamie peeked her head in. "Mr. Walker is here to see you," she said, reluctantly.

I set the papers I had been looking at aside. "Show him in."

Jamie took a step back and motioned for Karl Walker to enter my office. The man looked at her with annoyance. He never liked having to go through Jamie to see me.

"Good morning, Karl," I said as Jamie closed the door behind her.

Karl just smiled at me and took a seat in front of my desk. His eyes scanned over the wood surface as if he was looking for something, but he didn't speak. "Is there something I can help you with? I do have work to do," I said, pointing out the obvious.

His smile took a slightly rueful turn for just a second. It was so quick that if I had not been so used to watching for subtle reactions, I would have missed it. "Just wanted to make sure your secretary gave you the final grant proposals for your signature. They need to get out this week."

"She did," I said in a tone that I hoped made clear that I did not appreciate him second-guessing my assistant and her ability to do her job.

He continued to sit there, and his eyes began taking in my office as a whole. It was quite apparent that he was looking for something. I just had no idea what. Karl had been in my office many times before, yet he had never scrutinized it so closely.

"Is there something else you needed?"

That seemed to snap him out of whatever trance he'd been in. "Um. No. No. I'll just . . ."

He stood fluidly from the chair and headed toward the door. I lowered my head back down to my paperwork in clear dismissal.

I heard the knob turn and the door begin to open slightly. "One more thing," he said.

My frustration rising, I raised my gaze to meet his across the room. An all-too-innocent expression crossed his face. "I was wondering if you were planning on bringing that girl with you Saturday night. What was her name?" He paused. "Oh yes, Brianna."

It took a great deal of effort to keep my face from showing the emotion I was feeling, but I managed. I had not had a chance to talk to Brianna about Saturday. She was still leery of people, but I was hoping she would accompany me. Karl, however, did not need to have any doubts as to Brianna's availability.

"Yes," I said, keeping it simple.

His mouth pulled down in a false frown. "Pity," he said, then turned his back on me and left.

I hadn't realized just how much rage I was feeling at Karl's show of interest in Brianna until I heard the pen I'd been holding snap in half. He'd be there Saturday night. North Memorial was where it had all started for The Coleman Foundation. It was an important event for not only the hospital, but for us as well.

After throwing my now-useless pen in the trash, I tried to pick up where I'd left off, but couldn't. The only thing I could think about was Brianna. Before I could second-guess myself too much, I picked up the phone and dialed her cell phone.

She answered on the second ring. "Hello—" She paused. "Hello."

Brianna was still having trouble figuring out what to call me. She hadn't actually called me anything since we'd talked about names yesterday.

"Hello, Brianna. How's your morning so far?"

"Good, Um . . ."

I decided to address the point directly. "You may call me whatever you wish, you know."

"I know," she said shyly. "It just doesn't feel right to call you by your name."

"Try it."

"What?" she gasped.

I couldn't help the chuckle that escaped my lips. "Say my name."

"I . . . I . . ."

"Don't say you can't, because I know that you can. You are capable of so much, Brianna. You just have to push beyond your fear."

She was quiet for so long that I thought she wasn't going to respond. Then, I heard my name spoken in what barely qualified as a whisper.

"Again," I said.

"Ste . . . phan," she squeaked.

It was louder, but she could do better. "Again, Brianna."

She paused and I could almost see her pressing her lips together on the other end of the line. "Stephan."

My name was still foreign on her lips, but it was progress. "Thank you."

"You're welcome." Her response the shy whisper I often received from her.

I looked over at my computer and saw that Lily would arrive in a few minutes. "I was calling to see if you would be available to have lunch with Lily tomorrow."

"Yes," she whispered.

"Good. I'm meeting with her in a few minutes, and I'll let her know to swing by and pick you up. Maybe you two could go out."

"I don't . . ."

"If you want to go to school this fall, Brianna, you're going to have to get used to being around people. Lily will keep you safe."

"I know," she said. "Okay."

There was a knock on my door. Lily peeked in, her arms holding the food Jamie ordered for us. "I need to go," I told Brianna. "I'll see you tonight when I get home."

She said a shy goodbye and hung up.

Lily walked into the room and placed the food on the small table between two chairs I had set up in the corner of my office. I stood up from behind my desk and made my way over to sit opposite her. "How are you, Lily?"

Her eyes met mine for a second longer than normal before she said, "Fine." She paused for a few moments before giving me a rueful smile. "I'd be better if you'd get rid of Karl."

I reached down and picked up a sandwich. Lily did the same. "Causing problems again?"

"He's just annoying. Hovering. It's like he feels he has to double-check everything I do." Then she waved me off. "I'm just complaining," she said. "Don't mind me."

I trusted Lily to tell me if there really was an issue. "You were looking for me yesterday," I said, giving her an opening.

"I wanted to know how Brianna was doing."

"She's confused, which is to be expected."

"Was she upset?" Lily asked.

I thought about that for a minute. "No. She wasn't upset. Scared, yes, but not upset."

We continued to eat our lunch in silence for a few minutes before I started speaking again. "I told her I'd like for her to be my submissive." Lily stopped eating. "I'd like you to talk to her. Tell her what it's like. Answer her questions."

"Of course," she answered. "Whatever she needs."

"I was hoping you'd say that," I said and smiled at her. "Are you free for lunch tomorrow? I thought that maybe you two could go out. She needs to be around people more."

"Lunch is perfect. I need to stop at the hotel that's hosting the foundation's fall fundraiser anyway. I'll pick her up on the way and we can eat there. It will be perfect!"

"What time should I tell her to expect you?"

She hummed as she mentally went through her schedule for the next day. "Have her ready by eleven forty-five. The hotel is only about ten minutes from your place."

We finished our food and Lily stood to leave. "Were you able to find a dress for Brianna?" I asked.

"I did," she beamed. "I'll bring it with me and she can try it on. I can't wait to see what she thinks."

"Just go easy, Lily. Saturday is going to be a big step for her."

"You know me," she said and winked.

"Yes," I said dryly as she sauntered from my office. "That would be the point."


**Brianna**

My day had been filled with trivial things. The morning was spent reading and thinking over what . . . Stephan . . . had told me over the last two days. He wanted me to stay with him, but staying meant being his submissive. I didn't want to go, but I didn't know if I could do what he wanted.

He called just as I was beginning to make something for lunch. Seeing his name on my phone made me smile.

Our conversation had been short, as it usually was when he called from work, but it had also been different from the many other times we'd talked. He'd made me say his name.

As I sat down to eat my food, and for the rest of the day, I thought about how it felt to call him Stephan. It felt wrong on some level. Like I was breaking some rule, but I also found that I liked it. It was a very strange mix of feelings.

I did some laundry and cleaned the house before going back into the kitchen to start dinner for us.

The minutes ticked away on the clock, bringing it closer to the time I knew he would be home. I was . . . happy? Excited? Neither word really fit what I was feeling. All I knew was that I wanted to see him again.

Like clockwork, I heard footsteps just seconds before the door started to open. I started to move to take my usual place, but then I froze.

My brain was at war with my body. Therefore, instead of moving or reacting in any way, I just stood there.

He took a few steps inside, his eyes searching the room before landing on me. His smile faltered and changed into a look of concern. I tried to make myself move. Obviously, I'd made the wrong decision.

Before I could get my limbs working again, he was there in front of me. His hands came up and cradled my face. The change was almost instantaneous.

My body sank into his warm comfort. He pressed my head against his chest as he threaded his fingers through my hair. I felt . . . right again.

We stood there for several minutes until the timer let me know it was time to take the meat out of the oven. He pulled back and looked deep into my eyes before leaning down and placing a soft kiss to my lips.

When I opened my eyes again, his back was toward me as he walked across the space between his bedroom and me. He was so fluid when he moved; every step seemed to know its destination before it started.

Only when he disappeared into his room did I realize that I was staring. I felt my face heat up with embarrassment and quickly went to get the chicken out of the oven.

Dinner was quiet. I saw him watching me several times and wondered if he was waiting for me to speak. Questions swirled in my mind for both him and Lily, and I tried to get them in order while I ate.

After dinner, he helped me take the plates back into the kitchen before going to sit in his chair. I finished putting things away and then went in to join him. This time, I went directly to him, waiting for him to open his arms before I sat down.

He wrapped his arms around me, and I leaned against him. I rested my head on his shoulder, and my hand came up to play with a button on the front of his shirt. "Did you have a good afternoon?" he asked.

I shrugged. "It was okay. I cleaned the house mostly."

He was quiet for a few minutes, probably waiting to see if I was going to add anything. I wasn't.

"I spoke with Lily. She'll be here tomorrow around eleven forty-five to pick you up for lunch. I suggest you be ready early. Lily doesn't like to be late."

"I'll be ready," I said with only the slightest hesitation. It was too much to hope that he wouldn't notice.

His arms tightened around me a little and his lips brushed my brow. "You have nothing to be worried about, Brianna. Lily wants to help. She'll answer any questions you have."

I nodded and pressed myself closer to him. He said I could ask him anything. "Was Lily . . . ?"

When I didn't continue, he leaned back so that he could see my face. "Was Lily what?"

Did I really want to know this? What if he said yes? I went back and forth before I finally decided that I needed to be brave. "Was Lily your . . . submissive, too?" Then I hurried to add, "I know you said she is Logan's now, but was she ever yours?" I let the last word trail off into almost a whisper.

He took a deep breath, which made me nervous. "Lily and I met at a party. We hit it off. After seeing each other a few more times at various things we discussed doing a scene together."

"A scene?" I asked when he paused for a moment.

He took my right hand in his and began idly playing with my fingers. "Do you remember when I blindfolded you in the woods?"

"Yes."

"That was a scene of sorts. There are many different types of scenes, but in all of them, the goal is to teach something."

"So, you taught Lily something?"

"Yes," he smiled and then shook his head as if remembering. "And although technically everything went fine, it just didn't feel quite right." Then he looked me straight in the eye and let out a small chuckle. "It almost felt like she was my sister." His face sobered. "Not funny at the time, mind you, but looking back I can now find humor in the situation."

I was trying to process what he was telling me. He had taught Lily something like he had taught me. That had to mean that she'd allowed him to do things to her. Did I want to know more?

Whether I wanted to know was irrelevant. I *needed* to know. "Did you have sex with her?" Although Stephan had said he'd not have sex with me until I asked him, clearly Lily had been a willing participant in whatever they'd done together. Did that mean they'd had sex as well?

"No," he said. "As you saw in the woods, not every scene involves a sexual act. Many do, but not all."

"So . . . ," I said, hoping he'd finish the story.

"So . . . ," he said, smiling again. I loved it when he smiled. "We stayed friends and it came to my attention a few months later that she was looking for a new job. I had an opening at the foundation and thought she'd be perfect."

"And . . ." I paused, wondering if this was something that I would be better off asking Lily. "And Logan?"

"Logan has been my best friend since we were fourteen. He's in charge of public relations over at North Memorial Hospital. As part of her job, Lily attends events that benefit the foundation around town, just as I do. She was at the dinner they host every year when she saw him. They talked and instantly clicked," he said. "There was only one problem."

"What?" I asked, interested to hear the rest.

"Lily was a submissive and had been living the lifestyle since she was eighteen. Logan, on the other hand, was not involved in the lifestyle and never had been."

I was beyond interested. This is what I needed to know.

He continued. "When she found out that we were friends, she enlisted my help." Stephan shifted in his seat and pulled me back against him once again, this time taking both hands and lacing his fingers with mine. "It took some time and a lot of talking. I taught him what I knew and gave him material to read." Then, with a certain finality he said, "They've been together ever since."

I asked a few more questions about Lily and Logan before he said, "Saturday is the annual dinner for North Memorial."

At first, I sat waiting for him to continue. When he didn't, I turned a little to see his face. His eyes were soft. So soft, I wanted to melt into them. Him.

"Would you accompany me as my date, Miss Reeves?"

The first thing I felt was fear, but there was also another feeling. One I couldn't remember feeling before.

I pressed my lips together until it was almost painful. There was no pretense here. He was asking me to go with him, and I was free to refuse.

I couldn't refuse him, though. "Yes," I nodded. He smiled and it made it all worth it.

Before I knew what was happening, he turned me in his lap, and his mouth was on mine. As his lips took control, my fear of Saturday and the dinner disappeared.

# Chapter 3

**Brianna**

*He smiled warmly as he turned to leave for work Wednesday morning. I* blushed as he grazed my cheek with his fingers and he told me to have fun with Lily. As I watched him leave, I traced my lips with my index finger. I could still feel the ghost of his pressing against them.

I closed my eyes as I leaned against the back of the couch and remembered last night. It had started out to be a kiss just like all the others, but then he somehow managed to turn me so that my legs were on either side of his. I was straddling him.

He'd encouraged me to touch him. Touch him in any way I wanted. My hands found their way into his hair.

I was unsure. While he'd never had a problem with me touching him, it was something that was very new to me. Ian hadn't allowed much touching unless it was to service him. A few of the men he'd given me to had liked to be touched, but they always told me where to touch them and what to do. Ste . . . Stephan hadn't given me instructions.

I remembered my hands in his hair as his fingers traveled up and down my back over my shirt. It was amazing how wonderful it had felt. How wonderful it always felt when I was in his arms.

My breath caught as I remembered how his hands had held tightly to my hips before he pressed me hard against him. I'd felt his arousal through the thin layer of his dress pants.

The moment I felt that unmistakable bulge of want and lust, I'd frozen. I'd felt the panic begin to take over.

He abruptly pulled away from my lips and he made me look at him. I could still hear his voice. Still feel his breath against my lips. "Not until you ask me, Brianna. Not until you ask."

He'd held us both perfectly still until I'd calmed down. Then, he told me that he needed me to understand how much he wanted me and that he hoped one day I'd let him show me.

I hadn't known how to respond, but he didn't seem to need one. Instead, he proceeded to place soft kisses all over my face and then down my neck to a spot just behind my ear.

His mouth kept moving at an unhurried pace over every inch of exposed skin on my face and neck.

My face flushed just remembering it.

After a few minutes, I had started to forget about the part of his anatomy I could feel between my legs. The only things that I could think about were his lips. His tongue. And what they were doing to me. He always seemed to be able to make me feel things. *Good* things.

The problem was that even now, remembering, I had no idea what it all meant. Everything was very new. Although I liked it, I was scared.

No matter how hard I tried, my thoughts about the previous night continued throughout the morning. I tried to read, but after spending an hour looking at the same page, I stopped and set it aside.

There on the nightstand was the journal he'd given me. My journal.

I reluctantly picked it up. Its pages were fresh and new, just waiting to be filled, so I began to write.

Surprisingly, the words spilled out onto the page. Everything I'd been feeling. My fears. The strange reactions I had when he kissed me. How just having him there with me calmed me down. How different he was from Ian.

I was so caught up in my writing that I didn't notice the time passing. When I looked up, the clock read eleven thirty. Lily would arrive in fifteen minutes. I threw the journal down on the bed and rushed to my closet to find something to wear.

He was right. Lily arrived five minutes early and was giddy with excitement. She was completely different from the last time I'd seen her at Dr. Cooper's house - quiet, subdued. Before I knew it, we were out in front of the building and Lily was flagging down a cab.

Once we were in the vehicle, Lily could not stop talking about the hotel where we were going to have lunch. The Four Seasons.

When we pulled up in front, I felt my nerves start to get the best of me. Lily reached over and squeezed my hand. "I'll keep you safe," she whispered before getting out of the cab. Swallowing, I made my limbs move. I could do this.

Lily walked up to the front desk and introduced herself to the man standing there. He seemed small behind the massive wooden structure, but then he stood to his full height, and I cautiously took a step back.

He said something to Lily and then disappeared. I moved in the opposite direction, and pressed my back against the wall. The lobby was huge as I took in my surroundings. Everything was sleek and elegant. Not a single thing was out of place. Even the walls looked like fancy furniture.

My head whipped back around when I noticed an older man in a suit walking toward us. I tried to act invisible as the man came to greet Lily.

"Hello, Ms. Adams. It's so nice to see you again." Then the man seemed to notice me. "And who do we have here?"

Lily took a step toward me and reached out her hand, encouraging me to come closer. I hesitated for a moment before I took that first step. I felt safe with Lily, but not the same as I did with Stephan.

"This is Brianna, Al. She's going to be joining us today."

"It's a pleasure to meet you, Brianna." Thankfully, he turned his attention back to Lily after that.

Al guided us to a large elevator along the far wall of the lobby. The inside of the elevator matched the lobby with its warm neutral colors, but the walls were smooth.

The doors opened again, and we were looking into a huge room. The walls were a rich, tan color, and the carpet beneath our feet was like nothing I'd seen before. It was brown, green, and gold with lots of swirls. Chandeliers hung from the ceiling, making it feel even more overwhelming. I stayed close to Lily and tried to be as unnoticeable as possible. Al looked at me a few times, but other than that, he'd left me alone.

After Lily inspected every inch of the room, and asked many questions, I lost track of all her questions and his answers. We rode the elevator back downstairs to the restaurant. It was simple and elegant, just like the rest of the hotel. I'd never been in a place like it before. It was nicer than the restaurant where he'd taken me. The servers looked as if they'd come clean and pressed off an assembly line.

A woman dressed in a black skirt and cream blouse that matched the servers walking around took us to a table in the corner and handed us menus. I took it quickly before lying it down in front of me. Once she walked away, Lily asked, "What do you like? They have excellent fish here."

"Fish is good," I whispered.

Lily set her menu down and took hold of my hand. "You can order whatever you want. I was just making a suggestion."

"Okay," I nodded. She released my hand and picked her menu back up. I did the same.

Many things sounded very fancy on the menu. Then I saw they had duck and remembered how much I'd liked the bite he'd let me try. The server returned, and I gave her my order without much difficulty.

"Duck?" Lily asked when we were alone again.

I looked down. "Was that not all right?"

She laughed. "No. It was perfectly fine. I just didn't expect you to be the type of person who ate duck. I personally find it too greasy," she added.

I shifted in my chair before taking a deep calming breath. "I tasted . . ." I paused. This was harder than I thought. "Ste . . . phan had duck," I said lowering my head. I just couldn't look at her. "At a . . . restaurant. I . . .

liked it."

Lily nearly jumped out of her seat, startling me. "You called him Stephan!"

People were staring. I knew they had to be. My shoulders slumped, and I slid down in my chair hoping no one would see me.

Finally, Lily seemed to notice me again and stopped moving. Her eyes were huge when I looked up. "I'm sorry, Brianna. I didn't mean to make you uncomfortable."

"It's okay," I whispered.

"No," she said. "It's not. And I am sorry. I will try to control myself."

I slowly sat back up in my chair, making sure my hair was shielding most of my face. Lily just watched me as if she was trying to judge my mood. "I'm all right," I tried to assure her.

Her mouth turned down into a frown. She didn't look convinced. I knew I needed to distract her, so I began trying to think of something to ask. That was why I was here, right?

Lily moved just a little to the left and the sunlight reflected off her necklace. It was silver, like mine, but much thicker. Not something a woman would normally wear.

My hand rose to the collar Stephan had given me. The metal felt good under my fingertips. It was strange, now that I thought about it. I wasn't a slave anymore. I wasn't owned by anyone. Why did knowing that I still had this piece of him around my neck make me feel better?

I closed my eyes and gathered my thoughts. It was now or never. "Lily?" I started.

Before I was able to get my question out, the server came with our salads. After she checked to make sure we had everything we needed, we were once again left alone. Too much time had passed, and I wondered if I should even bring it up.

"What is it?" Lily asked.

It was only then that I noticed I was just moving the lettuce around my plate. I hadn't even taken a bite.

Once again, I closed my eyes and gave myself a pep talk. "Is your necklace . . . I mean, is it . . . ?"

"You mean is it a collar?"

I nodded.

"Yes," she answered as if she were talking about the weather. She didn't miss a beat of eating her salad. "It's one of them. I have several, but this is the one I usually wear to work."

One of them? "Why?" I swallowed nervously. "Why do you have more than one?"

"Well, I have ones I wear every day, and then ones that are only for the playroom."

"Play . . . room?" No matter how much I wished it weren't so, I could hear my voice shake.

"Yes, the playroom." She cocked her head to the side. "What's wrong?"

"I don't like playrooms," I whispered.

"Why not?" she asked. This time, I could hear the concern in her voice.

I bit my lip and closed my eyes. My heart was hammering in my chest. I was trying not to remember. "Pain," I choked out the word.

"Oh, Brianna," she cried. "I'm so sorry."

Her hand reached out to take mine across the table again. I didn't pull away. "I don't . . . I mean, I can't . . ." Lily seemed to be at a loss for words. That was rare. "Playrooms can be fun. I promise you. It isn't all about pain."

"But there is some pain?" I asked, my voice cracking.

"Yes," she said. "Every Dom is different, but I know you're most concerned with how Stephan is."

I nodded again and tried to keep my mind in the present. The last thing I needed was to fall into a memory. This was information I needed to know.

"Stephan is always fair with his punishments. I've never known him to be overly harsh, but they are still punishments."

Lily grabbed my hand again. I realized it was shaking. "Are you all right, Brianna?"

I heard her, but I didn't know how to answer her. Was I all right?

Her grip on my hand tightened. "Brianna?"

I registered movement around us, but not what it was. There was Lily's hand, keeping me from slipping from reality.

"Brianna? Say something. Please?"

"I'm . . ." I was trying hard. "I don't . . . I don't know . . . if I can . . . do it . . . Lily."

The next thing I knew, Lily had her arms wrapped around me in a hug. I leaned into her. "What is it that you don't think you can do?" she asked.

"Be his submissive. I don't think I . . . can," I said almost choking. The thought of leaving him was painful, but I would have to if I couldn't give him what he wanted. I'd have no choice.

Lily just held me. It was nice, but it wasn't the same. I wanted it to be his arms instead of hers.

As soon as that thought crossed my mind, I began sobbing again. She tried to soothe me and eventually, I did calm down.

I looked down and noticed our untouched meals. Lily didn't seem bothered by this at all, as she began talking again. "I know you're scared, Brianna, but you shouldn't be."

We were now both sitting up in our seats again, and she encouraged me to start eating. I took a few bites of the duck. It was good, so I ate more.

"Do you like sitting in Stephan's lap?"

I nodded, but she seemed frustrated.

"How do you feel about kneeling? I know you do that when he comes home."

I stopped eating and thought about it. How did I feel? It was something

I'd done out of habit. Something I'd not really thought about before.

When I didn't answer, she continued. "Do you like it? Does it make you feel anything?"

"It . . ." I stopped and thought about it for a minute. "I like when he touches my hair," I whispered, thinking back to how his hand would feel running through my hair. How he'd say 'Good evening, Brianna' in that voice of his that made me feel safe and secure.

Lily smiled. "So you don't hate it. How do you feel about serving him? Doing things for him?"

Again, I thought about it. When he was happy, I was happy. It was very hard to explain, but I tried.

"What is it about being a submissive that scares you so much? Aside from the pain, of course," she asked.

Here it goes. "I'm not sure if I can be what he wants. I mean, I'd have to do everything he says, right?"

Lily took a few bites of her fish before answering. "That's partially true. I mean you do have to do what he tells you when you're playing, but you always have your safewords if you feel you need them."

"What do you mean when we're playing?"

When I asked that question, her eyes lit up. "Well, not every couple plays all the time. Logan and I are pretty much like a normal couple during the week. It's only on weekends that he is my Master," she said.

"Is that what Stephan will want?"

She shrugged. "I don't know. That's something you'll have to discuss with him. He's only had two collared submissives though, and with those, they only played on weekends, too. During the week, they would go out. Date. One would never know what they did on the weekends." Lily smirked.

"You said you and . . . Logan, were pretty much like a normal couple during the week. What . . . ?"

"What did I mean by that?" she asked the question for me. "There are certain things that I am responsible for and if I fail to do them, I will suffer punishment no matter what day it is."

I shivered. She noticed.

"Don't get me wrong, Brianna. Punishments aren't pleasant. They aren't meant to be, but they are bearable. And it's not like you don't know it's coming. You broke a rule, after all."

"So he wouldn't just . . . hurt me?" I asked.

She finished her food before answering me. "I'm not saying that there aren't Dominants out there that would, but we're talking about Stephan. He doesn't like handing out punishments, but he will if his rules aren't followed. Stephan likes submission and being in control of things. He likes knowing that someone's pleasure comes only from him." She paused for a moment and then got that smirk on her face again. "Of course, that's pretty much consistent no matter the Dominant."

I was trying to take this all in. It was a complete contradiction to what I had in my mind. I kept picturing him standing over me. One minute his face would be that of the Stephan I'd come to know over the past month and a half, the next it would be just as cold and hard as Ian's had been. What was the truth?

The server came to remove our plates and she asked if we wanted dessert. We both declined, and Lily handed her a credit card. When the woman walked away, Lily went back to watching me once more.

"I know you're scared, and you have every right to be. I can't tell you what decision to make, but I will tell you that Stephan is a good man, and that he cares about you."

I didn't respond, and the server came back with the receipt. Lily signed the slip and then got up to leave. I followed her out.

The ride back to Stephan's condo was quiet. She seemed to know that I needed time to think. Every time I thought about being his submissive, I felt myself break out into a sweat. When I would think about leaving him, my chest would tighten and it was almost painful to breathe.

Once we were at Stephan's building, Lily took a detour to the garage and her car. She pulled out a garment bag and threw it over her arm before hooking her elbow with mine and dragging me back into the elevator.

The ride up was quick. It was the middle of the day and most other tenants were at work. Lily couldn't seem to stand still. I could tell she was excited about something.

I let us into the condo just seconds before Lily grabbed my hand and dragged me into my room. It was useless to resist, and I figured at least this way, I'd be able to find out what all her excitement was regarding.

She didn't make me wait long. Lily hung the garment bag on a hook by my bathroom door and opened it up to reveal a long purple dress. "Do you like it?" she asked.

"What?" I stuttered, not sure what she was talking about, or why she was showing me the most unbelievable dress.

"For the dinner, silly." When I still looked confused, she added, "Saturday. Stephan said you needed a dress."

Oh. Yes. The dinner. Saturday. The dinner I'd told Stephan I'd accompany him to as his date.

I felt the blood rushing out of my face and dizziness began to take over. Hands guided me to the bed and pushed my head between my knees.

My world was spinning less, but the panic was still just below the surface. I knew what I'd agreed to, but seeing the dress made it all too real. How was I going to do this?

I felt something being pressed against my ear and then I heard his voice.

"Brianna? Are you there?"

"Yes," I breathed.

"Concentrate. Listen to my voice. You're fine. Nothing is going to hurt you," he said in that voice that you just couldn't argue with.

I nodded even though I knew he couldn't see.

"Now, tell me what's wrong."

"I saw . . . the . . . dress," I squeaked.

"You don't like it?" he asked.

The fog was beginning to lift as I talked to him. "It's beautiful."

"Then what's the problem? Why did you start to panic?"

"I don't know if I can do it."

"Do you want to go to the dinner with me?"

It was so much harder when he wasn't here in front of me, but the memory of him asking still lingered. "Yes."

"Do you doubt my ability to keep you safe?"

"No," I quickly assured him.

"Then I see no problem. Try on your dress with Lily and we'll talk about this more when I get home. Can you do that?"

"Yes, Sir. I can do that."

"Good," he said, and I could tell he was happy with my response. It made me smile. "I'll see you tonight."

Then he was gone, and I was left with Lily. She was less excited now and worry crossed her features. I tried to give her a little smile to let her know I was okay. The look on her face told me she didn't buy it. Nevertheless, Lily held out her hand for me. She helped me put on the dress and guided me over to a long mirror in the corner. It was tight around my breasts and waist before it flowed to the floor. The way the dress touched the carpet made it look like I was floating. I couldn't see my feet.

"Will he . . . ?" I paused. "I mean . . ."

Lily's head peeked around my shoulder, and she moved my hair out of the way so that my neck was fully exposed except for Stephan's collar. "Yes," she smiled. "I think Stephan will like it very much."


## Stephan

The day could not end quickly enough. I wanted to get home to Brianna. I needed to see her. Speak to her. Feel her. It was the only thing on my mind.

When I'd seen Lily's name on my caller ID earlier it had taken great restraint not to bolt from my office and rush home. I knew there could only be one reason why she would be calling me; there had to be something wrong with Brianna.

When I stepped off the elevator, I felt the pressure in my chest begin to change. She was only yards away, just behind the door that was now in plain view. Both my body and my mind knew what it wanted. *Her.*

I turned the doorknob and walked into my condo. My eyes immediately began to search for Brianna.

She was right where I thought she'd be, just outside the kitchen waiting for me as she had been yesterday. The difference today was that she was looking up at me and smiling. I dropped my keys on the table beside the door and went to her.

I circled my arms around her, bringing her close. I heard a small sigh escape her as my hands traveled up her back and into her hair. "How are you feeling?" I whispered before pulling back to look into her eyes.

"Better," she said, looking just as relieved as I felt.

I wondered if she felt any of the same pull I felt toward her. Even if she did, would it be enough for her to stay? Would she give a relationship between the two of us an opportunity to develop? Or would fear from her past block any chance we had? I didn't know the answer, and I'm not sure she did either.

With that thought, I closed my eyes and let my lips find hers. She opened up to me and kissed me back. It was not full of heat like our kiss the night before, but it was just as full of emotion. At least, it was for me. I had no idea what Brianna was feeling. Although she was getting better every day, she was still reluctant to share her true feelings with me. I was hoping that would change soon. More than anything, I wanted to know what she was thinking.

We ate dinner—a delicious pasta dish with shrimp—and cleaned up. I went to my chair, and once she was finished she came to sit with me. I figured I would get right to the point and see where the conversation took us. "Tell me what happened with Lily." I didn't need to elaborate. She knew what I was talking about.

Brianna's hands began to twist nervously in her lap. I covered them tightly with mine, which made her stop and look up. She wasn't getting out of this. I wanted answers.

"What if I can't . . . I mean, all those people. What if they know . . . what will they think of me? What if I . . . can't . . . act right?"

I lifted my hand to brush the hair away from her face. It wasn't a practical gesture since her hair wasn't obstructing my view in any way. I just wanted to touch her. "You'll be fine. It will be fine. I will hold your hand the entire night if you need me to."

She nodded, but that wasn't good enough. I needed her to talk this through.

"I need more than a nod, Brianna."

"I . . . know." She sighed. "Part of me knows that you will stay with me. That you wouldn't let anything happen to me." She pressed her lips together before she continued. "But there is this little voice inside that tells me to be afraid. That people are going to hurt me. I don't know how to turn it off." Her voice trailed off into a whisper.

"You lack confidence. It's understandable. I can help you with that if you'll let me," I told her, holding her gaze so that she understood what I was talking about. "But even if you don't, Brianna, I've made a commitment to you," I said, my finger grazing her collar. "Until you tell me you do not wish to be with me. Until you remove this collar . . . I will do everything in my power to keep you safe."

She started to nod again, but caught herself. "I believe you," she said, but it lacked the confidence I'd hoped for.

Instead of pursuing it, though, I moved on. "How did your lunch with Lily go? Did she answer your questions?"

I felt her stiffen under my hands, but I decided to wait it out. It took just over a minute for her to squeak out, "Yes."

"Tell me."

And she did. It was slow going for a while, but then everything just kept tumbling out. I didn't stop her, even though I knew we would need to talk about things in more detail.

Once she appeared to be finished, Brianna sagged against me, exhausted. I held her closer while my lips brushed lovingly against her temple. "Is it the pain that scares you the most?"

"Yes," she said, but there was hesitation.

"You need to tell me. Communication, remember."

She huddled closer, burrowing her face in my neck. "You'd want to have sex with me?"

"Sex scares you."

"Yes," she whispered.

"Brianna, did you ever have sex before you lived with Ian?" She shook her head. "So, you've never had sexual contact with a man willingly?"

"No," she said softly.

"Sex can be an amazing thing, full of unbelievable sensations. I would love to show that world to you, but only if you would allow me. I told you before that I would not take it from you."

She was quiet except for her breathing. Her right hand played with a button on my shirt, and she appeared to be deep in thought.

"Will you let me show you, Brianna? Will you let me teach you how wonderful it can be? Let me give you a glimpse into the pleasures of my world."

Again, she said nothing. I started to wonder if I had pushed her too far, too fast. Then she whispered, "You won't hurt me? You'll keep me safe?"

"Yes," I said with no hint of doubt.

For the next forty-seven seconds, I waited as if my entire future depended on it. In a way it did. I wanted my future to include her, and if she turned down my offer, the chances of that future ever becoming a reality were slim. Then I heard the most beautiful word in the world.

"Yes."

# Chapter 4

**Brianna**

*Yes. I'd actually said yes. What in the world, had I been thinking?*

Although that question lingered, I knew exactly what had been going through my mind. Stephan.

The thought of leaving him, the idea of not having him in my life anymore, scared me more than anything. He was like a light in the sea of darkness I'd been living in for so long. I just needed to find a way to do this for him.

I was lost in my thoughts, trying to figure out how I was going to do what I'd just agreed to, when I felt his arms circle me tighter. He pressed his forehead against mine and I could feel his breath on my face.

"Open your eyes, Brianna."

I hadn't realized I'd closed them, but I did what he asked and found his hazel ones staring back at me.

"Are you all right?"

"Yes," I whispered.

"What number?"

It had been a while since he'd asked me that, but after a moment, I answered, "Six."

"Tell me why." I started to avert my eyes, but his hand came up to hold my head in place. "No," he said firmly.

It was so hard to look at him, but I did. "I'm scared," I said. "I know you said . . ." I took a deep breath. "I know you said you wouldn't hurt me, but . . ."

"But the fear doesn't just go away," he said, finishing the sentence for me.

I nodded.

He leaned back in his chair and pulled me with him. He guided my head to rest against his shoulder as he began slowly running his fingers through my hair. I loved this. When he touched me as he was doing now, I felt so safe. So cared for.

"Brianna, nothing is going to happen tonight."

*What?* "But I thought . . . ?"

"That as soon as you gave me the green light I would be dragging you into my bedroom to have my way with you?"

My only reaction was to push my body even closer to his. He was my only calm.

He responded by placing a kiss to my temple. "All I want to do tonight is talk. I know this is scary for you. I promise that I will push you, but I want this to be a positive experience. I want you to want this just as much as I do."

His lips continued to move along my hairline as he spoke, sending a warm feeling down to my toes. "I don't know if I can," I said honestly.

"*I* know you can," he said with confidence. It made me want to believe him. "It's only your fear that holds you back. I've known that since the first week you were with me. I want to help you overcome that fear." He paused before continuing. "Is that what you want? Do you want to chase those demons that haunt you away?"

I knew what he was asking. Did I want to live in fear my entire life? Did I trust him enough to help me work through the fear, and have a chance to be normal again? "I . . . want . . . to."

"Good," he said. "And do you trust me, Brianna?"

This time I didn't have to think about it. "I trust you more than anyone else."

I felt him nod. "That's good, but I want more than that. I want you to be able to trust me completely, and I know that isn't the case right now."

As much as I wanted to tell him that I did trust him completely, I knew that he was right. There was still that little voice inside my head that told me I needed to be careful. That if I gave him what he wanted, he would hurt me.

We just sat there in a charged silence for several minutes before he said, "Your safewords will be very important as we go forward. I will be watching you closely, but I'm going to be pushing, and I need to know from you when you reach a certain point."

The rest of the night was spent going over safewords again, and discussing what he expected of me in regard to communication in general. By the end of the evening, I felt relaxed. The fear I'd had at the beginning was pushed to the back of my mind, and I felt for the first time that I might actually be able to do this.

Before we went to our separate bedrooms, he leaned down and kissed me. The kiss had a new edge to it that I'd never felt before, and it sent my pulse quickening.

"Goodnight, Brianna," he said before leaving me standing at my bedroom door staring at his retreating figure.

Thursday morning, as I was making breakfast, he disappeared upstairs for almost twenty minutes. I was putting everything on the table when he came back down.

As we were eating, I kept eyeing the paper he'd brought down with him that was lying at the other side of his plate. He waited until he was finished eating before handing it to me.

"I want you to read this and write your thoughts about it in your journal. We'll talk about it when I get home."

I nodded my agreement, and he smiled at me while getting up to complete his morning ritual before leaving for work.

The paper he'd given me talked about trust. It explained trust in a way that I'd never thought of before. I not only put that in my journal, but also told him that night as we were sitting in his chair. Although trusting someone did make me vulnerable, it also created a feeling of safety. Something I was already feeling when it came to him.

On Friday morning, Stephan did the same thing. He disappeared while I was cooking and brought another paper down with him. He left once again, giving me the same instructions as the day before.

This time, the paper talked about submission and what it meant. I found I had many questions after reading it and wrote them all down in my journal so that I wouldn't forget. That night was the first time I let him read my journal.

He read in silence through the pages I'd written, not commenting until he was finished. "You express yourself well in writing, Brianna."

"Thank you, Sir," I said.

One of the questions I had was about kneeling. I was amazed to learn just how much he liked it when he would come home and I'd be there waiting for him. He told me how it felt to stand over me and greet me.

We talked for hours before it turned into something else. He moved his hands more freely over my body as his mouth covered mine. Everything was slow and almost comforting. This was Stephan. He said he wouldn't hurt me, and I trusted him. Plus, I had my safewords.

By Saturday morning, I'd almost forgotten later that evening, I'd be in a room full of a hundred strangers. Almost, but not quite.

I tried to keep myself busy so I wouldn't think about it too much, but it kept creeping into my mind. My worst fear was that something would happen, and I would embarrass him. He'd tried to reassure me every time the subject came up, but I knew he could tell how nervous I was.

By one o'clock, I'd cooked two full meals and cleaned the entire downstairs, with the exception of his bedroom and bath. I was just getting ready to head upstairs when the phone rang.

Stephan's voice floated to where I was in the dining room. From his comments, I could tell someone was here to see us. I just didn't know whom.

## Stephan

The last thing I expected on this day was a visit from my aunt. It wasn't that she never came to see me at my condo, more that it was rare. Usually, she would just pick up the phone and call, or ask me to stop by.

When I hung up with security downstairs, I glanced over at Brianna to find her watching me. She quickly averted her eyes, but I knew she would have heard enough to know that we had a visitor. I walked over to her. She still wasn't looking at me.

"Diane's here. Why don't you go freshen up while I get the door?"

Brianna nodded and went to her room. She disappeared just as my aunt's knock sounded.

Diane was dressed in a light blue pantsuit. Her hair pulled back so that it was off her shoulders but cascading down her back. She was beautiful and classy, as always.

"Hello, Diane. Come in."

"Thank you," she said as she walked through the door.

I didn't miss her eyes darting around the room in search of Brianna. "Would you like something to drink?"

"Oh, no thank you, dear." Diane took a seat on the couch. I followed her lead and sat in my chair across from her. "I'm sure you're wondering why I'm here," she said before I could comment.

"Well, yes, the thought did cross my mind."

She looked around again. "Is Brianna here?"

"Yes," I answered. "She just went to her room to get something. I'm sure she'll be out shortly."

"Oh. Well, good," she said shifting in her seat slightly. My aunt was a very composed woman and for her to be nervous, I knew it had to be something serious she wanted to discuss.

It would be better to find the underlying cause of this quickly. "What is it, Diane?"

"Stephan, I don't know what happened Sunday between you and your uncle. He's extremely upset about it. I may not know what's going on, but I'm not stupid. I know whatever it is, it has to do with Brianna. Maybe if the two of you talked . . . ?"

"No," I said, making it clear that I was not about to budge.

She looked at me almost pleading. "It *is* about Brianna, isn't it?"

"Yes."

"She's seems to be a sweet girl. I don't see why . . ."

I had no idea what my uncle had told her, but I figured there was no sense in sugarcoating this for her. She may not need to know about my lifestyle, but as far as I was concerned, Brianna was going to be a permanent fixture in my life. "Richard doesn't approve of my relationship with Brianna."

"Stephan, that doesn't make any sense. I know your uncle—"

"He doesn't like me," Brianna whispered.

Diane's head whipped around to see the woman who had come into the room unnoticed. Brianna's eyes were guarded as she looked from my aunt to me. I reached out my hand and she came to me.

My aunt watched with curious eyes as Brianna sat down in my lap. "I don't know what happened, but I'm sure that isn't it."

Leaning in, I whispered to Brianna that it was okay to talk. I felt a shiver run through her before she took a deep breath. She held on tight to my hand as she answered Diane. "He said he doesn't think being with Stephan is what's best for me."

My aunt was rarely at a loss for words, but this was one of those times. I could tell she was trying to think of something to say. Before she could manage to get anything out, I decided to speak up.

"I appreciate you coming today and trying to smooth things over between Richard and myself. However, I will not put Brianna in that position again. So, as long as Richard disapproves of our relationship, I'm afraid we will not be joining you for Sunday dinners."

Diane sat for a few minutes more before standing to leave. I patted Brianna's leg, indicating that I wanted her to stand. We both followed my aunt to the door.

"I don't know what's going on, Stephan," she said, turning to me with her hand on the doorknob. "I will speak to your uncle. You are like a son to me. I don't like this separation."

"You're more than welcome to come visit us anytime, Diane. We would be glad to have you." My aunt didn't miss that I had included Brianna as a resident of my home.

"Thank you," she said before turning to Brianna. I saw her hesitate for a split second before reaching out and giving her a hug. "I *am* sorry," she said in a soft voice just barely loud enough for me to hear. "Please don't let whatever this is bring you down."

Then Diane turned to me. She reached out and gripped both my hands in hers. "I'll talk to Richard, but you should, too. I know he doesn't want this anymore than you do." She rose on her toes and placed a kiss on my cheek before walking out the door.

Brianna was very still beside me. I turned and took her in my arms. "Talk to me."

She circled her arms around my waist and she huddled close to me. "I'm sorry I'm causing problems with you and your family." She paused, and I felt her stiffen. I knew I wasn't going to like what she said next. "Maybe I *should* leave."

"No," I snapped. Taking a deep breath, I got a hold of myself. "No," I said in a much calmer voice. "You leaving would not solve anything between my uncle and me."

As much as I didn't want to talk about Tami, I knew that it was time

Brianna knew the whole story. I led her over to the couch and sat down beside her. Taking her hands, I began to explain.

Where to start? I wanted to get through this as quickly as possible. "Tami and I met through Lily. They'd met and talked at a few events, and Lily thought we'd make a good match. At first, I said no, but Lily can be persistent when she wants something. Eventually, I relented and allowed her to set up a meeting. I wasn't seeing anyone at the time, so I figured why not?"

Brianna had been staring at our linked hands while I talked. Now that I'd paused, she looked up, her gaze meeting mine. I squeezed her hands in reassurance and continued.

"It was good at first. We both seemed to like many of the same things, and she was already a trained submissive. She'd left her last Dom a year before, and was looking for another."

Now came the difficult part.

"We'd been dating and playing for almost five months when she started hinting that she wanted more. I made it clear that I was happy with how things were and didn't want to change." I shook my head, remembering. "She wanted to move in with me, have a full-time relationship. I didn't."

"But I live with you," Brianna commented.

"Yes. You do." I smiled, wondering if she would ask me to elaborate. She didn't, so I continued. "Things began to get worse between us. Every time the opportunity presented itself, she would make a comment about how much easier it would be if we were just living together already. Eventually it became too much, and I ended things."

It was a very polite way of stating the end of our relationship, but Brianna didn't need to know the details. To say things got ugly was putting it mildly. She had gotten so angry that she'd thrown a vase at my head.

"The next day, I received a call from Richard saying he needed to speak with me. When I arrived at their home, my aunt was nowhere to be seen, which turned out to be a very good thing. The door was barely closed behind me when the yelling began."

Brianna's hands gripped mine tighter, and I looked her over to make sure she was still all right. What I found made my heart almost sing. Her face was full of concern for me. I gave her hands a comforting pat and went back to my story.

"I was there for about two hours. It took almost an hour for him to let me speak one full sentence, and even then, I rarely got out much more before he would interrupt me. She'd told him about being my submissive, however, she made it seem like she had not participated willingly. As if it was something I was forcing her to do . . . essentially, abusing her."

Brianna stiffened. I shifted our hands so that one of mine was holding both of hers and used my now-free fingers to raise her chin. She kept her eyes lowered, so I put some pressure behind my grip. Her gaze came up to meet mine as if a switch had been flipped.

"I didn't abuse her, Brianna."

She didn't answer or respond in any way.

I sighed and dropped my hand. "What did I tell you Wednesday night about using your safewords?"

"That if . . . whatever we were doing got to be . . . too much or started to overwhelm me, I was to use them without hesitation," she said unsure, but accurately.

"She had safewords, too, Brianna. She could have used them anytime she wanted. Also, if I was so abusive, why did she wait until I broke things off to go to Richard?"

Her mind was trying to process this information while it fought with her fear. I waited.

"She was trying to hurt you," she whispered.

"Yes."

There was still that look of uncertainty on her face. I opened my arms and she came to me. And just like always, I felt her relax against me. I breathed deep as I brushed my lips against her temple.

"I would never betray your trust, Brianna. This is why communication is so important. Remember what I had you read? What we talked about?"

She nodded.

I kissed every part of her skin that I could access. I was wearing a fitted T-shirt today, and her right hand had taken hold on a spot about four inches above my waist. Her free hand lay unmoving on her lap, and I picked it up, interlacing our fingers.

I shifted us slightly so that I could get more access to her face and neck. Time was passing more quickly than I would have liked, but I wanted to take advantage of what we had.

Her skin was so soft, but nowhere more so than her neck. I moved her hair out of the way as I continued placing gentle kisses from her jaw to her collarbone.

Brianna's breathing started to change, and I took advantage of the opportunity. I tilted her head away from me with a little more force than necessary, and began a slightly more aggressive pursuit of the skin within my reach. Her grip on my shirt tightened, and her mouth opened slightly as her breathing continued to escalate.

I removed my hand from her hair and trailed down her back to the hem of her shirt. The shirt she was wearing today ended just below the waistband of her shorts so it didn't take much to slip my fingers underneath.

Her reaction was golden. She sucked in a deep breath as I traced patterns on her lower back, occasionally dipping below the thin elastic band of her shorts. I was going to enjoy pushing those reactions in the future.

As much as I wanted to continue, we needed to stop and get ready for tonight. It was already after four.

I sat back and dropped my hands from her body. Brianna's eyes flew open and the look on her face was priceless. It was a mixture of surprise, arousal, and embarrassment.

Taking her face in my hands, I gave her a quick kiss and then sat back once again. "We have to get ready. I'm sure you would like a shower before you go."

"Oh." She blushed. "Yes."

Brianna got up and walked into her room. I stood and made my way to mine.

As I strolled into my bathroom, I heard the shower turn on in the other room. That was all it took for me to want to be in there with her, and I began thinking of how to make that happen. Soon.

By five thirty, I was waiting in the living room for Brianna. I'd let her know to come out when she was ready. We would have to be leaving soon. I was just about to go in and check on her when she walked into the room.

The dress she wore was perfect on her. Its deep purple color brought out the blue in her eyes and the rich brown of her hair. For the first time in my life, I was at a loss for words. It was strapless, which was a favorite of mine, and she had her hair pulled up and back. There was just something about her neck being bare of everything but my collar. The dress hugged her in all the right places, leaving hints of what lay underneath. It was elegant and sophisticated.

She walked over to me, and I could tell she was a little apprehensive. That would not do. Brianna had to know how beautiful she was. This was a date, after all.

I took her right hand, bringing it up to my mouth for a kiss. "You look stunning, sweetheart."

Her cheeks turned that delightful pink color I loved so much. "Thank you."

"Are you ready to go?" I asked.

"Yes," she said, her voice shaking slightly from her nerves.

I reached behind me, picked up a black wrap I'd gotten from Lily the day before, and placed it around her shoulders, but didn't let go of the ends. Instead, I pulled her flush against me and looked down into her wide, blue eyes.

"I'm very proud to have you on my arm tonight, Brianna," I whispered before lowering my mouth to hers for a slow kiss.

It wasn't long before we headed out. When we pulled up in front of Hotel 1000, Brianna's eyes grew wide as she took everything in. One of the valets opened my door, and I handed him the keys before going to join her on the other side of the car.

Brianna was nervous, but no more than she usually was when confronted by a new situation. I reached out and took her hand. She leaned into me, and I felt her relax a little. I brought our linked fingers up to my mouth and kissed the back of her hand before tucking her arm under mine.

"You'll be fine. I'm right here."

She looked up at me and I saw something on her face that I never had before. Complete trust. "I know."

I couldn't resist leaning down and placing another kiss on her lips before we walked into the hotel, and were surrounded by people.

# Chapter 5

**Stephan**

***The minute we walked inside, cameras started flashing and a reporter I*** recognized from the *Star Tribune* made a beeline for me. I knew exactly what he was going to ask before the words came out of his mouth. "Is this your new girlfriend, Mr. Coleman? What's her name?"

I smiled because that was what was expected of me. "Hello, Mitch." Following behind him was a small woman holding a professional-looking camera. "Beth," I said, nodding at her. As much as I didn't want to deal with this tonight, the press came in handy when promoting the foundation. It was good to have them on your side.

Beth lowered the camera from her face and smiled shyly at me. "Evening, Mr. Coleman."

"So come on, Coleman, spill. Who's the lovely lady?"

Brianna held tighter to my hand at the unwanted attention. I glanced over at her and gave her a reassuring smile before turning back to the reporter. "Ms. Reeves. Mitch. Mitch. Ms. Reeves."

"Nice to meet you, Ms. Reeves. Have you and Mr. Coleman been dating long?"

Brianna became stiff beside me. I knew I needed to get us out of there. "Stop harassing my date," I said to Mitch with a smirk before turning my attention to Brianna. "And now, if you'll excuse us, we have a party to attend." I nodded to Beth before guiding Brianna to the elevator that a hotel employee was holding open for us.

Once the doors closed, I pulled Brianna into my arms and kissed her temple. "Are you all right?"

She nodded.

"There shouldn't be any reporters in the ballroom."

Brianna leaned into me, but stepped back when the doors suddenly opened. I could tell she was somewhat startled. It was probably just her nerves, but I felt the need to remind her to be alert tonight. So before we stepped out and around the corner into the sea of people, I lifted her chin and waited until her eyes met mine.

"You must pay attention to your surroundings tonight. No daydreaming."

She swallowed and nodded.

I smiled to let her know that I wasn't upset, took her hand, and led her out of the elevator and into the ballroom.

The ballroom was filled with people mingling about. I scanned the room until they found Logan. He was on the opposite side of the room talking with a group of people I knew well. Lily was nowhere to be seen, although I knew she was in attendance. I wrapped my arm securely around Brianna's waist and began leading her in Logan's general direction. It was a good plan in theory, but we didn't manage to get farther than a few yards before Mr. and Mrs. Jensen waylaid us.

After introductions were made, they wanted to know about the foundation. The conversation was pleasant, and Brianna did surprisingly well. She was nervous, yes, but she kept herself focused on the conversation occurring in front of her.

Mrs. Jensen tried to ask Brianna a few questions to include her in the conversation, but soon realized how uncomfortable she was and thankfully quit. I'd known the Jensen's for years, since before my parents died. They were good people and very charitable.

A few other couples came up to say hello and we never did make it over to Logan before we had to take our seats.

Emily, the hospital's events coordinator, stood on the small stage to welcome all the guests. She gave a brief overview of the agenda and then took her own seat so that the wait staff could start serving.

There were six other people at our table. Brianna sat quietly beside me as the servers wove through the tables to set the first course in front of each person. Conversation began with idle pleasantries, as it normally did at these types of functions. I made sure to keep hold of Brianna's hand so she would feel as comfortable as possible.

Things continued in much the same way as we moved through each of the seven courses. If someone asked Brianna a direct question, she would answer. Other than that, however, she remained silent. She was doing very well.

The servers came around to remove the desserts, and I noticed a few of the ladies getting up, heading toward the restrooms. I was just turning to ask Brianna if she needed anything when I noticed a woman with long, dark brown hair get up. I recognized Gina instantly. If Gina was here, that meant so was Daren. I wasn't sure how that would go over with Brianna.

**Brianna**

There were so many people. All the men were in tuxedos, just like Stephan. The women wore beautiful gowns like mine. They were all moving and talking around me. The servers were also weaving in and out of the tables holding trays of food and drinks. Every time one came close, I cringed. I was trying to stay calm, even though it would have been so easy to panic.

Everyone he had introduced me to so far seemed nice enough. Even the reporter downstairs had been pleasant, albeit pushy to find out who I was.

Some of the other guests sitting at the table with us had tried to talk to me during dinner, but I really didn't know what to say. I knew they were curious about me, just like the reporter, but it wasn't something Stephan and I had discussed. He wanted me to be his submissive, that was clear to me, but what I was to be to him in public was a mystery.

The servers had just come to remove the dessert plates from the table when, out of the corner of my eye, I noticed that a few people were beginning to get up and move around. I wondered if that meant we would once again be getting up to mingle. As I turned slightly in my chair to face Stephan, I noticed his posture had stiffened and I immediately went on alert. Something was wrong.

Stephan's eyes were locked on something on the other side of the room. Every muscle in my body wanted to get up and run. Or hide under the table, at least. I knew that if he was anxious, then I should be as well.

Somehow, my thoughts had gotten the better of me, and I must have lost my focus. I felt strong hands on either side of my face. His warm breath was at my ear. "Calm down, Brianna. Everything is fine," he soothed.

I closed my eyes and concentrated on him. His warm body was so close to mine. It felt nice.

My eyelashes fluttered back open, and I found his heated gaze upon me. I'd seen that look before from him, but never in public. It was the look he had so many times when we were sitting in his chair after a long and involved talk. Although, I hadn't comprehended the look for what it was in the past, I was beginning to understand it. He wanted me. Not just sexually, but in every way.

It should have frightened me. It *did* frighten me, but this was Stephan. I trusted him more than I had ever trusted another person.

We sat frozen in that position for what seemed like hours. It was Emily walking behind the microphone again that broke the spell, or whatever it was, between us.

For a very long time, everyone sat at the large round tables and listened to a man by the name of Robert Carmichael. He talked about the hospital, and what had happened over the last year. I tried my best to follow what he was saying in case Stephan wanted to talk about it afterward, but it was rather hard to follow when he started talking about statistics I didn't understand. Finally, Mr. Carmichael took his seat and a group of musicians gathered in the far corner.

There was movement all around us, and I noticed that Stephan was anxious again. His eyes were searching the room. It was obvious there was someone here he did not want to talk to, or maybe he didn't want them to see him at all. Or was it . . . me? I had no way of knowing.

Stephan turned to me and took hold of my hands. "Do you need anything? Lily is coming this way and she can escort you to the ladies' room if you wish?"

I thought about it for a moment. Since I had no idea how long we would be staying, I nodded. "Yes. I would like that."

Just then, Lily appeared between us. "Wasn't the food just delicious? Oh, Brianna! You look beautiful. That dress is perfect. Isn't it perfect, Stephan?" She beamed.

"Good evening, Lily," Stephan smiled. When he looked back at me, it was with an intensity that made me a little nervous. "Yes. Brianna is breathtaking in her dress." He paused and turned back to Lily. "You have amazing taste. Thank you."

I looked up at Lily then. She was practically bouncing on the balls of her feet. "You shouldn't doubt me," she said with a sly smile on her face.

"Never," he said with a smile of his own. I knew they had a friendship, and a kind of history, but I didn't like the feeling I got in my chest when I saw them talking like this. It was the same feeling I'd gotten when I saw them holding hands in the living room.

Before I could dwell on my thoughts any longer, Stephan asked Lily if she would mind escorting me to the ladies' room. She agreed with a level of excitement that didn't fit the situation.

I stood, not really wanting to leave him, but knowing that I should. He reached out and brushed his fingers against my arm, sending little prickles across my skin where he'd touched. Then the next thing I knew, Lily's hand was in mine and we were weaving through tables.

The bathroom was tucked into a corner not far from where we'd entered the big ballroom. It was huge. All the walls had a very subtle design on them. There were fresh flowers on the counters. It looked more like a private bathroom in someone's home rather than something you'd find in public.

Lily gave me instructions to wait for her just outside the entrance when I was done, before she disappeared into a stall. There were a few other women there but I didn't know any of them, so I found an open door and quickly shut it behind me.

It didn't take me long, and it didn't feel right to linger around the sinks waiting for Lily, so I did as she instructed and walked out to wait in the hallway. There were people out there, too, but none of them seemed to notice me, which, in my book, was a good thing. I didn't like it when people stared at me.

As I stood there waiting, I started to think again about Stephan. I couldn't explain, even to myself, how I felt when I was near him. Or when I wasn't near him, for that matter. Like now, all I wanted to do was see him. Touch him. Have him touch me.

It made no sense. Why did I feel this way? What did it mean?

Then there was my fear of all those same things. I knew he wanted to do things to me. Even though I knew that would include sex—which scared me on a level all its own—I also knew there would be more to it than that. How much more I didn't know, but more.

I felt like I must be insane to even consider giving him what he wanted. However, I'd tried more than once to imagine leaving him, and I couldn't. And although the thought of him doing those same things to me made me want to cry, what Ian had done to me had not killed me. I'd survived. It couldn't be worse, could it?

Moisture began pooling in my eyes. I tried to will the tears away. It would not look good if I returned to him like this. He'd know I'd been crying. I didn't want to have to explain why.

I briefly wondered where Lily was, but I knew I hadn't missed her and she wouldn't have gone back to the table without me. Suddenly, I felt hands grab my arms. I could feel the aggression in them, and I froze. Air rushed past my ears as I was pulled around a corner and then pushed up against a wall.

When I looked up, I saw the same man who had been in Lily's office. Karl.

Karl was dressed in a tuxedo just like Stephan. The look on his face was anything but friendly. He wore what could be considered a smile, but was more like a sneer. His body leaned into mine. I tried to stay perfectly still.

Hot breath hit my face as he closed all polite space between us. "Finally, I get you alone. I've been waiting all night for just the right moment."

Panic was seeping through my limbs. I was trying to fight it, trying to push it down and away so I could think. That would be what Stephan would want me to do.

But, I couldn't. Already it was harder to breathe.

Desperate, I tried to turn my head to the side, hoping that someone might see me and come to my rescue. There was no one.

Karl grabbed my chin and jerked it back into place, so I had no choice but to face him. His hands were cold. Hard. They reminded me of Ian's hands. Stephan had never touched me like this.

"No one is going to save you," he said matter-of-factly. He leaned in and ran his tongue from my jaw to my temple. "Besides, this is what you like, right? You like a man that takes control. Hurts you." His hand let go of my chin only to clasp my neck, pushing Stephan's collar against me so hard that I was sure it would leave a mark.

"Please," I gasped. "Please."

I could feel the tears streaming down my face, but it only excited him more. He pushed me up against the wall with his body while his other hand came to my hair and jerked my head back. His mouth was on mine with brutal force.

Then he was gone.

At some point, I must have closed my eyes. When I opened them again, I saw two men who obviously worked for the hotel pulling Karl to his feet. Instead of releasing him, they were practically carrying him against his will to the elevators on the other side of the lobby. It was only then that I noticed the man kneeling on my other side.

The man was handsome, although currently he looked very concerned. "Are you all right, ma'am?" he asked.

My throat hurt and I reached up to touch it. I couldn't see the damage he'd done; the only thing I could feel was Stephan's collar.

The man—the one I now realized must have saved me from Karl—reached out to me with a hesitant hand. "It looks like he gripped you pretty hard. Maybe we should take off your necklace," he said, reaching for my collar.

"No!"

He backed off immediately. "Sorry. I was just trying . . ." He looked around the hallway. "I'm Cal Ross."

I knew the polite thing to do would be to tell him my name as well, "Brianna," I choked out. My throat really didn't feel right.

He nodded. "Do you have a last name, Brianna?"

"Reeves."

Cal Ross was quiet for too long. He had a strange look on his face. "Anna?" he asked.

I couldn't speak. I just looked at him.

"Anna Reeves?"

When I didn't answer him right away, he continued on. "You used to come spend the summers in Two Harbors with your dad, right? We used to play together."

Then it came rushing back to me. Cal's father, Neil, and my dad, John, had been best friends when I was little. That had been a long time ago, though. If I remembered correctly, Neil and Cal had moved to St. Paul when I was ten. I hadn't seen them after that. I hoped that they weren't still in contact with John.

"I remember," I whispered even though it hurt.

He must have noticed something was wrong. "I'm sorry. Are you here with someone?"

I nodded, although that hurt, too.

"Can I . . . ?"

He didn't get to finish. There was a squeal off to my right seconds before I saw Lily.

As she got closer, I saw her face change. I knew she'd seen my neck.

She knelt down beside me. "I came out of the bathroom and couldn't find you anywhere. Are you okay?"

"Yes."

It would take a while for my voice to return to normal. I obviously hadn't fooled Lily.

"And what do you have to do with this, Ross?" she demanded.

I saw his back stiffen and he glared back at her. "I managed to get your sleazy CFO off her before he did any more damage."

"Karl?" The look on Cal's face was enough of an answer. She stood. "I need to get Stephan." He didn't respond. "Will you stay with her until we get back?"

"I'm not leaving her," he said as though that was a foregone conclusion.

She gave me one last look and then she was gone. I knew I had to say one more thing to Cal before Stephan got there. "May I . . . ask a . . . favor?"

"Of course you can, Anna."

"Don't tell . . . anyone . . . about me." He looked confused. "I don't . . . want John . . ."

However, that was all I got out before I saw Stephan rushing toward me. He'd had a very similar reaction to Lily's, but after a slightly hostile look at Cal, he knelt beside me and hugged me. "Did Karl really do this?"

I nodded. "Yes."

I felt him cringe at hearing my raspy voice. He placed several small kisses on my head before resting his cheek on my temple and turning to face Cal. "I owe you a thank you, Ross."

"I didn't do it for you, Coleman."

I felt Stephan nod and then he was helping me to my feet. He held me in front of him and took in all the changes in my appearance. His finger gently touched my neck and I knew he must have been tracing the mark Karl had left.

Two men from the hotel suddenly appeared behind Stephan, and I took a step closer to him. One of them whispered something in Stephan's ear, but I didn't hear. I was too busy trying to make myself invisible. He said something back to the man, and he nodded. They walked away as quickly as they'd arrived.

Stephan turned to Lily. "Would you mind retrieving Brianna's wrap? We're going home."

Suddenly, I felt a hand that wasn't Stephan's on mine. I looked over to see Cal. His face was hard. "You live with *him*, Anna?"

Stephan's body was rigid. I felt his hold on me tighten. I felt worn out. I just wanted to go home. "Yes," I answered him.

Lily returned with my wrap before anything more could be said. She looked like she wanted to hug me, but since Stephan wouldn't let go of me she instead said, "I'll call you tomorrow."

She went back inside the ballroom, but glanced at us once before disappearing inside. Lily was here with Logan. This was his big night. She had to stay.

Stephan placed the wrap over my shoulders and tucked me under his arm. He surprised me by extending a hand to Cal. "Thank you," he said simply.

After only a moment's hesitation, Cal took the hand that was offered.

"You're welcome."

Stephan gave Cal a final nod and guided us toward the elevators. The relief I felt to be going home was almost more overwhelming than those few minutes with Karl. All I wanted to do was curl up in Stephan's lap. It was where I felt most safe.

There wasn't a lot of activity by the elevators, but there were a few other couples waiting with us.

The elevator dinged, but before the doors opened, I heard someone call Stephan's name. He turned us toward the sound.

The person I saw sent me into a panic faster than I had remembered possible.

I felt Stephan hold me tighter. The man was close enough to touch me! My mind screamed, *Yellow!* But I couldn't form the words.

"Stephan, I'm so glad I caught you."

Then it wasn't yellow anymore. It was red. They knew each other!

"Hello, Daren."

# Chapter 6

**Stephan**

***Brianna's leaving my side with Lily, even for a few minutes, increased my*** anxiety. I knew now that both Daren and Karl were here. Although I didn't think either would cause her harm, I was still hoping she did not see them without me by her side.

Logan found me briefly before he was shepherded away, and I was once again left to my own devices. I spent the time scanning the room.

Daren had been easy to find. He and Gina were standing five tables away talking to another couple. There was no sign of Karl. If he was sitting down, however, I wouldn't have seen him. Too many people were up milling about now that the music was starting.

I glanced down at my watch. They had been gone for ten minutes. It wasn't long, but for some reason, my worry increased. I positioned myself so that I was constantly watching the entrance they would most likely use.

My back straightened as I saw Lily. I looked behind her for Brianna, but she wasn't there. Then I caught the look on Lily's face. Standing, I quickly closed the gap between us.

"Lily, what is it? Where's Brianna?" I demanded.

"She's . . . Stephan, you have to come. Karl . . ." It was all I let her say before I pushed her aside and almost ran out of the ballroom and into the lobby.

As soon as I arrived in the smaller room, I saw there had been a commotion. Everyone was trying to act normal, but I noticed their eyes continued to glance over to a short hallway to my right. Turning to look in that direction, I saw two figures obscured by a large plant. Only the end of Brianna's dress confirmed she was behind the greenery. I wasted no more time crossing the space separating us.

What I hadn't expected to find on the other side of the overshadowing foliage was Cal Ross. The man had been a thorn in my side ever since he'd taken over Ross Builders from his father over a year ago. I leveled a not-so-friendly look at him before turning to Brianna. Her hair had come down a little and there was a large, red mark on her neck. I knelt down next to her.

Hearing the raspy sound of her voice as she confirmed Karl had done this to her made me cringe. Two members of the hotel's security decided to pick that moment to check on things. They asked if I wanted the police called, but I declined. The last thing we needed were the police involved. I assured them that since Karl was my employee, I'd make sure the situation was handled. Thankfully, they accepted this, used to dealing with matters of discretion, and left us.

I pulled her to me and placed several kisses on the top of her head before turning slightly to face Cal. He was watching me closely. I didn't care.

As much as I didn't like Cal Ross, I knew that he must have been the one to come to Brianna's rescue. She wasn't acting scared of him, which she would have been if he'd just harmed her. He was acting extremely protective of her. That, I had to admit, I didn't like very much. Offering my thanks to him for coming to Brianna's aid, I bit my tongue at his curt reply and only nodded. Cal Ross was the least of my worries right now.

I stood and helped her up. My eyes roamed every inch of her. There were red marks on her arms, but they weren't bad. The main thing was her neck. It was worse than I'd originally thought. Not only was it red where Karl's hand had been, but there was a deeper, angrier red mark where he'd obviously pushed her collar into her flesh. I took my index finger and traced the line it had left and felt the anger boiling inside me. Karl would pay.

Lily was standing just behind me, and I asked her to retrieve Brianna's wrap from our seats. She'd been through more than enough tonight. I was taking her home.

Suddenly, Cal's hand gripped Brianna's wrist. He addressed her only. "You live with him, Anna?"

*Anna?*

A cold feeling ran down my spine. My arms tightened their hold on Brianna. She was mine. Mine until she told me she no longer wanted me. He would not have her.

I only half-heard her answer him as Lily came back with the wrap. All I wanted to do was get us out of there.

As I took the wrap from her hands, Lily told Brianna she'd call her tomorrow. As Lily walked away, my eyes stayed on Ross. No matter my feelings, he'd been there for Brianna tonight when I had not. He'd protected her. I placed the wrap around Brianna's shoulders and pulled her against my side. Extending my free hand, I offered it to Cal, thanking him again. This time, he reluctantly took my offering.

I moved us to the elevator. The business part of the evening was over and some other couples were leaving as well. Two stood with us waiting for the elevator to reach our floor.

When the light came on above the metal doors, I began to relax. Then someone called my name. Although I wanted to ignore it, I knew it would be impolite to do so. I turned us both around, and saw Daren walk toward us.

Brianna reacted. It was what I'd feared. We had not discussed Daren, or what had happened at the party where he'd seen her. I had no idea what, if anything, had happened between them. It was that unknown that had me wanting to keep them apart tonight. Unfortunately, short of me throwing Brianna over my shoulder and running down the stairs, we were going to have to face whatever demons were lurking there.

My arm tightened around her.

"Stephan, I'm so glad I caught you," Daren said as he came to a stop in front of us.

"Hello, Daren." I could feel Brianna's panic rising, and I wanted to get her out of there as quickly as possible.

My old friend smiled at me. "I'm glad to see you here." He turned to Brianna and his face fell.

I have no idea what happened concerning him after that. Brianna had all my attention. Her breathing was heavy and unsteady. I could feel her body trembling under my hands. "I'm sorry, Daren, but we'll have to do this another time."

Without waiting for his response, I lifted Brianna off her feet and moved us the few yards it took to reach the stairwell. It was the quickest exit, and the one with the least amount of people.

I set Brianna's feet back on the ground once the door had closed firmly behind us. She fell back against the wall, unable to support her own weight. I grasped her arms to steady her, but that was the least of my concerns. "What number, Brianna?"

She didn't answer.

Sure she wasn't going to fall, I let go of her arms and brought my hands up to her face, forcing her to look at me. "Number."

Still nothing.

Then I noticed that her lips had started to move. No sound was coming out, but I finally realized that she was trying to say 'red.' My heart broke for her. I knew that her seeing Daren would not be good, but I had hoped her reaction wouldn't be this bad.

With steady resolve, I took her into my arms and began whispering to her. Letting her know that she was safe. That he was gone. No one would hurt her. This was the first time she'd reached this level of panic since she'd been in my care, and so it took an unusually long amount of time to calm her. Finally, she began to settle down. Her breathing returned to normal and she was no longer trembling.

"He won't hurt you, Brianna. I promise."

She made no response other than to take hold of my jacket, pulling me closer. I held her for a few more minutes before telling her we were going to walk down the stairs. Still there was silence, but she stayed glued to my side as we walked slowly down the four flights it took to reach the lobby.

The main entrance to the hotel held a lot more people than the lobby area we'd just come from, and I felt her draw even closer, if that were possible. I tightened my grip on her waist and kissed the top of her head before crossing the short distance to the valet. Thankfully, the hotel had staffed extra valets for the evening so we didn't have to wait long for our car.

I felt a movement from Brianna, subtle though it was, and glanced down at her as I helped her into the passenger side of my car. She wasn't going into a panic attack as she had been upstairs, but she wasn't relaxed either. The look on her face was almost . . . blank.

The young man who'd brought our car came up to ask if something was wrong since I hadn't moved from my position. I quickly assured him that everything was fine and went to get into the car myself.

Brianna was quiet the entire ride home. She'd barely moved aside from blinking. Her lack of reaction was bothering me. I would rather have had her hysterical than as she was now.

I parked my car and walked around to help her from the vehicle. She took my offered hand almost as if she were a robot following programming. I held her close to my side and prayed that once we were in a familiar space she would come out of it.

Unfortunately, nothing changed once we walked through my door. If anything, she seemed to become more distant.

Taking her hand, I led her into her bedroom. A small light flickered in her eyes, but was just as quickly gone again.

I led her over beside her bed, and then went to get her something to change into. Reluctantly, I handed the clothes to her. Normally, I would have had no qualms about undressing her; however, given all of her trauma tonight, I felt it was best not to test her limits.

I lifted her chin with my index finger. Her eyes followed until they were looking into mine. Blank. Where had my Brianna gone?

"Go change and get ready for bed," I said, nodding toward her bathroom. "I'll wait here." As soon as I let go of her chin, she slowly walked toward the bathroom and disappeared behind the door.

No longer able to see her, I pulled out my phone and dialed my assistant, Jamie. I tried not to disturb her on weekends, but it couldn't be helped. She answered on the fourth ring and efficiently took down my instructions. Monday could not come soon enough.

**Brianna**

Numb. That was the only way to describe how I was feeling as I removed the purple gown from my body. I stood in front of the full-length mirror, but it almost felt like I wasn't even there.

Habit was what drove me as I put on my nightclothes, washed my face, and brushed my teeth. There was no feeling as I scrubbed the make-up from my face or spread the mint toothpaste along my teeth and gums. They were just things. Actions. Nothing had meaning beyond doing what I had been told to do.

I walked slowly back into the room and came to a stop directly in front of . . . him. *Him.* Who was he? I thought I knew but . . .

It was just better not to think.

He turned down the covers and told me to lie down. I obeyed.

I stared up at the ceiling. There were tiny patterns. I'd never noticed before.

He sat down beside me on the bed. His fingertips brushed the side of my face. I heard him speaking to me, but nothing registered. Nothing made sense.

The bed shifted and then I felt arms come around me. He had joined me in the bed. I knew I should be concerned. Should do something. Say something. But I couldn't.

He didn't try to talk to me again. The only noise in the room besides our breathing was the slight sound his lips made as they brushed against my hair. It was meant to be comforting. I knew that. Somehow, I knew that. I just felt . . . nothing.

At some point, I must have fallen asleep, but I couldn't remember the falling. The morning sunlight filtered in through the single window of my room. He was no longer there beside me. I listened closely, and could hear movement in the other room.

Where last night I had felt nothing, today I felt everything. I replayed Karl's attack and reached up to feel my collar still in place.

My collar. Cal.

And . . . Daren?

Stephan's . . . friend?

Before I could halt them, the tears were running down my face, and I couldn't get them to stop. He knew him!

A sense of betrayal ran through me. Lies. Lies!

Just then, Stephan walked through the door. His eyes were watching me closely. Apparently waiting, but for what I had no idea.

I sat up and told myself to stop crying. It didn't work. If anything, the tears came quicker and with more force.

He crossed the room, sat down on the bed, and reached out for me. I pulled away, huddling in the far corner of my bed. He looked hurt, and I felt a pain in my chest.

There was no sound, but my crying. He was watching me. I knew he wanted to touch me, but he didn't try again. We sat for a long time just watching each other. There were times when he looked like he wanted to cry, too. I was so confused.

Finally, he broke the silence. "Brianna, I want to tell you something. Will you listen?"

There was no need to think about it. I nodded.

"It appears we have a lot to talk about, but first I think I need to explain something—or should I say—someone." He paused as if he was gauging my reaction, but I didn't respond at all. "Do you remember my telling you that a friend had told me about you? That he'd seen you at a party? It was Daren. The one you saw last night. He is the one who told me about you being with Ian. If not for him, I would never have known you were there most likely against your will."

"Daren?" I said slowly. "He . . . told you about me?" They were the first words I'd spoken since last night.

"Yes." He shifted a little closer. "I have no idea what happened at that party, Brianna."

"He beat me," I whispered.

He paused. "Explain."

And I did. As memories of my time with Ian went, this was one of the least traumatic. At the time, I had no idea of the man's name. If he had spoken it, I had not heard.

Ian had bound me in ropes and suspended me from two hooks in the ceiling. I remembered him talking to the man as he was working and the man, Daren, telling him that Gina had not been able to come.

My old Master told the man that it had taken a lot of work to train me. That I had been a stubborn one, but now that I was trained, he wanted to show me off.

With every word, I was reliving that night. Stephan just sat, listening as I spoke through my tears.

"Ian offered to let Daren . . ." I choked. I couldn't finish what I'd been about to say.

"He offered to let Daren play with you," he said matter-of-factly.

I shook my head so hard that it started to hurt. "He took a stick and beat me!" I screamed.

Stephan closed his eyes. "A cane."

"You know what it was?"

His eyes opened again. He was regarding me as if I was about to bolt, which given the circumstances, was entirely possible. "Of course I do. I'm a Dominant. Canes are very common."

"Common!" I screamed.

"Yes," he said in a voice that was so calm it made me want to pull my hair out.

"Would you use it on me?"

He knew what I was asking. "Yes, if you would let me."

"Let . . . let . . . I couldn't . . ."

At that moment, my legs decided to work. I threw the covers from my body and ran for the door.

I only made it as far as the living room before his arms came around my waist, halting my progress. What had been a surge of energy only a moment ago died in my limbs, and the tears once again began to flow as I went limp.

Stephan bent down, scooping me up into his arms. He carried me over to the couch but kept me on his lap, all the while, whispering calming words in my ear.

Eventually, the tears ebbed and I stiffened. "Please," I begged.

He rubbed the tears from my cheeks with his thumbs and held them there. He looked into my eyes with so much emotion that I could not doubt his next words. "Brianna, I've told you repeatedly that I will not hurt you. I would never do anything to you that you told me you were not okay with. You were in a situation where things were done to you against your will, without you having a say one way or the other. That would not happen with us.

Communication is so important. I need to know what you feel, how you feel, and why. You will have fears," he said. "Especially given your past. But we can work through them." He brushed my hair back behind my ear and stopped talking as he let everything sink in.

I wanted to believe him. Oh, how I wanted to believe him. The tears returned.

"Shh," he whispered as he kissed the tears away this time. "Shh, love. I need you to trust me. Trust me enough to know that I will respect your limits." He pulled back enough to look into my eyes. "I told you I would push you, and I will. But, Brianna, I never want you to fear me or what I do to you."

I could tell he meant what he said, but I still felt afraid. "I don't . . . want to be afraid."

He smiled. "You have a lot to learn. Some things may be scary, but that will be because you do not understand them. What I want from you . . . to become my submissive . . . it's a learning process. For both of us."

I thought about what he had said. Ian had never talked to me as Stephan had. He'd never explained anything to me other than that I was now his, and that he could do whatever he pleased to me.

So many feelings were warring inside me. I still didn't want to leave. No matter how scared I was, that hadn't changed.

I looked up at him, searching. Could I trust this man? Should I?

There were things about him I didn't understand. Ian liked to hurt me. Loved it, even. Stephan seemed so different and yet he seemed to want to do some, if not all, of the same things.

No matter the logic of it, I knew what my answer would be. "I trust you."

He leaned in so that his lips hovered above mine. "That, my dear Brianna, is all I ask."

# Chapter 7

**Brianna**

*Stephan pulled me back into his arms and held me for the longest time. I* didn't understand why I felt so safe with him, but I did.

Slowly, my emotions settled down and I was able to remember all the things I'd said and done. I felt terrible. This man had done so much for me. He'd helped me through countless times when I'd panicked. He didn't deserve this from me.

"I'm sorry," I whispered into his neck.

"Brianna, you have nothing to be sorry for." I started to protest, but he stopped me. "No. You will not apologize for getting upset over something you clearly don't understand."

"But . . ."

The look on his face made the words die in my throat. He wasn't going to accept any type of 'sorry' no matter how I worded it.

We sat and watched each other for a few minutes. I kept trying to see some sign in his face as to what he was thinking, but I still had no idea when he moved me off his lap to sit beside him.

He turned to me. "Will you wait here? I have something I want to show you."

I nodded.

He stood, and walked into his bedroom.

While he was gone, I kept wondering what he could possibly have to show me. My question was answered the moment he stepped back in the room. In his right hand, he held a long stick. A cane.

On instinct, my feet came up onto the couch, my whole body crunching into a tight ball. I waited for the first strike to hit me.

It didn't.

I looked up slowly to find Stephan standing over me, waiting patiently.

When he saw that he had my attention, he said, "I'm not going to cane you, Brianna. Put your legs down, please, and hold out your hands."

My brain kept shouting at me not to, but I wouldn't forget what he'd told me again. He wouldn't lie to me, and he'd proven it more times than I could count. I could trust that when he told me something, it was true.

It took effort to uncoil my body, but I managed. One by one, my feet found their place on the floor in front of me. I put my hands out and opened them, hoping my trust in him was not misplaced. I watched as he took a seat on the coffee table directly in front of me, the cane lying across his lap.

"This is a rattan cane," he said, lifting it up with both hands. "There are many types of canes made out of a variety of materials. They come in all different thicknesses, but this is one of my favorites." When he was finished with his explanation, he offered the cane to me. I didn't know if I should take it. "Go on. It won't bite, I promise," he joked.

I tentatively reached across the small distance and touched the wood. It felt almost like a spindle on a chair.

He held perfectly still as my fingers examined the cane. It was as if he didn't want to spook me. When I retracted my hand, he sat back and shifted his weight a little.

"Close your eyes for me, Brianna." My eyes widened instead. What was he going to do? He seemed to know what I was thinking. "I want to show you something, but you need to close your eyes first."

Trust. With a deep breath, I clenched my eyes tight. It was the only way I could do this.

He took my hands, and helped me stand. He led me a few steps before stopping and asking me to hold perfectly still.

My breathing was starting to get out of control when I felt his breath graze my ear from behind me.

"Relax."

He ran his hand slowly down my arm, leaving heated warmth in its wake before heading back up the same path it had just traveled. I didn't know what to think. Or feel. My brain was battling with itself. Why did he make me feel this way?

Whether by choice or not, my body started to forget about everything except him touching me. His fingers were doing wonderful things to the most innocent places, while his lips were doing something amazing at the junction of my neck.

I felt a slight pressure against my right hip. It was just a tap of something. Then his hand and mouth suddenly left and I felt another pressure on the back of my left thigh. The weird thing was that it felt almost familiar.

My heart pounded as I waited to see what he would do next. I felt a tap on my breast and gasped. Our day in the woods, when he'd blindfolded me. That's why it felt familiar.

He didn't remove the pressure from the top of my breast. "Open your eyes." There, in front of me, resting on my left breast was the tip of his cane. "I improvised a little in the woods, but the basic principle is the same." He lowered the cane to his side. "The cane can cause pain because the person wielding it controls its use, but in and of itself, a cane is not something to be feared."

I knew what he was trying to tell me. It was the same thing he'd been telling me since I walked through the door of his home. He wanted me to trust him. "Do . . . ?"

"Go on," he prompted. "You can ask me anything."

"Do people . . . actually . . . like that?"

His lips turned into a smile I'd never seen before. "Yes. Some submissives enjoy being caned."

I swallowed. "Do you think . . . I mean . . . would I . . . ?" As much as the thought frightened me, some part of me wanted to know how anyone could enjoy being hit with a cane. It was probably a very stupid curiosity considering everything I'd been through, but with him, everything just seemed different. Better.

He cupped my cheek and stepped closer until I could feel his breath on my face. "We can find out," he whispered, and I felt a shiver, tinged with a hint of fear, run down my spine. "But not today. Today," he said, leaning down to place a kiss that was barely there on my lips. "Today, we have things we must discuss."

My eyes rolled back in my head as his lips covered mine. He wrapped his arms around me, and crushed me to him. All I could do was hold on.


**Stephan**

My kissing Brianna was purely impulse. I wasn't used to doing things this spontaneously, but with her, my control always seemed threatened. She made me crazy. There was not five minutes that passed in my day where I did not think of her.

As I forced myself to release her, I knew that once again, I'd be spending some quality time in my shower tonight. I wanted Brianna as I had wanted no other woman, and I couldn't have her. At least not yet. Soon though. I didn't know how much more of this I could take. Her slight pout as I put space between us did not help my trying to do the right thing. I smiled down at her. "We should get you fed."

She followed me into the kitchen where I had laid out some fresh fruit and granola. We set everything on the table, and she began to eat. I let her get a few bites in before I spoke again. "How is your neck feeling today?"

Her hand came up to cover the area in question before going back to her food. "It's better."

I reached out and brushed my index finger lightly against the still slightly red flesh. "Sore?"

"Yes," she whispered.

"I'll put some salve on it after you shower. It doesn't look like the bruising will be too bad."

She nodded.

"Are you hurting anywhere else?"

"No," she answered. Brianna didn't comment further on her injury as she finished eating. After all she'd experienced with Ian, I doubted a little bruising on her neck was something she'd consider a big deal.

She took her bowls into the kitchen when she had finished, and returned to where I sat. I opened my arms, and she took a seat in my lap. There was not as much room here as in the living room chair, but it would do for now. Her body leaned against mine. I wrapped my arms around her and tucked her head under my chin.

"Tell me what happened with Karl. How did this happen?" I said, once again touching the angry mark he'd left on her neck.

It seemed very innocent, she and Lily going to the bathroom. It would have been had it not been for Karl. As she told me what had happened, I still couldn't believe he had the nerve to try something like that with her at all, let alone in a very public setting. The man was either all about risk, or he was looking to be caught.

Brianna finished off the tale by saying how Cal pulled Karl off her, and then made sure she was all right.

"Cal Ross seems to have been in the right place at the right time." She shrugged. I could tell by the way she was reacting that she didn't wish me to pursue the line of conversation further, but we needed to talk about this. "Cal Ross knew you. You knew him."

Reluctantly, she nodded.

Her hesitancy made me more curious. "How do you know him, Brianna?"

She pressed her face into my shoulder, as she did when she wanted to hide herself for some reason. I wasn't letting this go.

Her voice filtered up through a mixture of skin and clothing. "His dad and . . . my dad . . ." I heard a sharp intake of breath. "They . . . used to be best friends."

I'd been right. They did know each other from her past. It wasn't what I'd wanted to hear, but it was better that I knew. "Used to be?"

Hands took hold of my shirt as if anchoring her to me. "Cal and his dad moved to St. Paul when I was ten."

"So you haven't seen him in years?"

"No," she answered, shaking her head. "Not since they moved."

"And he recognized you?"

She shook her head. "I told him my name."

As much as I didn't want to continue talking about Jonathan Reeves since I knew how much it upset her, I thought it would be best under the circumstances. The more I knew, the better I could protect her. "Do you think they are still in contact with your father?"

"I don't know," she answered honestly. "I . . . I asked him not to tell anyone he'd seen me. Not his dad. Not . . . John."

"Do you think he'll do as you asked?"

"I . . . think so?"

She wasn't sure. That didn't bode well. Then again, they'd not seen each other for eight years.

I leaned back and took her face in my hands, forcing her to look at me. Her blue eyes were full of worry. "Even if your father should find you somehow, Brianna, you don't have to go with him. You don't have to leave here if you don't want to. I won't let him take you against your will."

"Do you promise?" she asked. Her voice was almost childlike.

"I promise," I answered, and pressed a soft kiss to her nose. She released a small sigh at the contact, and I felt some of the tension within her release itself. "Better?" I asked.

"Yes."

"Good," I smiled, and gave her a pat on her thigh. "Why don't you go take a shower and get dressed? It will make you feel better." She arose from my lap, and disappeared into her bedroom.

I waited until I heard the water turn on in her bathroom before going upstairs. Just in case Brianna finished while I was still on the phone, I wanted to be far enough away that she didn't hear.

My first call was to Jamie. I wanted to make sure all my instructions had been followed, and that everything was in place for Monday morning. She was an efficient assistant, however, I had a *very* personal interest in this particular set of instructions.

The second was to my lawyer, Oscar. Unfortunately, his man was still looking into some leads on John Reeves and didn't have anything yet. He said he'd give me a call back as soon as he knew something. I also shared with him the new development that was Cal Ross. My lawyer didn't seem to like the new addition any more than I did.

Just as I began to hear movement downstairs, my cell phone rang. The caller ID said 'Cooper'. It was Sunday afternoon. No matter how upset I was with my uncle, I still missed Diane. "Hello?"

"Stephan! I was hoping you'd be here today."

"Jimmy?"

"Of course it's Jimmy. Who else would it be?"

"Well," I said, leaning back in my chair. Something told me this was not going to be a short conversation. "Considering you are calling from my aunt's house . . ."

He laughed. "Samantha and I are here having dinner. We thought you'd be here. I'd been hoping we could catch up."

I sighed. My reasons for not attending Sunday dinner were not something I wished to discuss with Jimmy. I might consider him a friend, but we'd not been close since high school, and even then, our friendship hadn't come close to what I'd shared with Logan. Jimmy didn't know half the stuff I'd gotten myself into in those days. "I'd love to catch up. Maybe we can meet for lunch sometime this week. What's your schedule look like?"

"Yeah, sure. Lunch is good."

We spoke for a few more minutes before I noticed Brianna at the top of the stairs. She was cautious, not certain if she should disturb me. I reached out, beckoning her to me.

Brianna crossed the room slowly but eagerly. I pulled her into my embrace and took in the scent of her still-damp hair, which now smelled of her coconut shampoo.

"How does Tuesday at noon work for you this week? We could meet at Gino's?" I asked Jimmy.

"Tuesday's good."

"I'll see you Tuesday then," I answered quickly, just wanting to get off the phone now that I had her in my lap. The call ended and I wrapped my other arm around her. "How are you feeling?"

"Better?" she answered as if it was a question instead of a statement.

"You don't sound sure of yourself. Did the shower not help?" She pressed her lips tightly together. "Brianna?" I said in a tone she knew well.

"I started thinking again. I mean, what if John finds me?"

I would not lie to her. "What if he does?" A shiver rippled through her body. I pulled her closer. "I promised you I would not let him take you away if you didn't want that. Do you not believe me?"

She seemed somewhere between shocked and hurt at my words. "I believe you," she insisted. "But he's the sheriff. What if he tries to take you away from me instead? I mean your uncle—"

"I don't care what my uncle said." Letting her speak to my uncle alone was becoming one of the worst decisions I'd ever made. "I'm not keeping you here against your will. You may leave at any time you so choose. Your father can't have me arrested for allowing you to stay here as my guest." I conveniently left out the fact that he could probably have me arrested for human trafficking since I'd bought her from Ian. Of course, he'd have to prove that, and no one knew what the money was for except for Ian, Brianna, Alex, and me.

She relaxed against me. "I'm glad."

I kissed her forehead. "So am I." She looked up at me with those sweet eyes that showed innocence I knew she shouldn't have given her experiences. "Let's go to your room so I can take care of your neck."

She followed me down the stairs to her room where I put some more salve on the bruises that were forming. They seemed to be mainly toward the back where the tips of his fingers had dug into her skin.

When that was done, I put everything away, sat back against her headboard, and pulled her against my side. There was so much to talk about and it had to start somewhere. The outside world kept throwing us curve balls, but it hadn't been detrimental to the overall progress we had made.

"Have you been writing in your journal?"

She nodded.

"May I?"

Again, she nodded.

I picked up the journal I'd given her, and opened it. I read the last few entries picking up from where I'd left off the last time. "I see you've written every day. That's good," I said, running a comforting hand up her arm. Even sitting here with her in my arms, it was not close enough.

I continued to read. Her entries caused a full feeling to settle in my chest. She wrote about everything from our make out session in the chair the other night when she'd felt my obvious need for her, to her workout with Brad a few days ago. It seemed he had taken to teasing her about her blushing every time he mentioned my name. I was amazed by her unusual reaction to the personal trainer. She didn't feel threatened by him in the slightest. Brad had a very easygoing demeanor even if he was a demanding trainer. It was the only explanation I had for her view of him.

She seemed confused by her feelings in regard to me, and I couldn't help but smile. She liked to feel my touch and when I wasn't near, she anxiously awaited our reunion. Her description of our kissing made me want to forget our talk and pick up where we'd left off the other night. I couldn't dismiss the other parts she'd written. The feelings she was having toward me frightened her in many ways, but she desired them at the same time. For the most part, her feelings mirrored my own. The only difference was that I understood what they were. I loved her.

There was also her mention of the fear she had of being my submissive. It was laced through almost every reference to me right alongside all the positive things she was feeling. I needed to find some way to alleviate that fear.

When I finished reading, I closed the journal and laid it to the side. "What is it that scares you the most regarding me?" I could see the wheels turning in her head as she considered the question. She really would make a very good submissive.

"I'm afraid I wouldn't be able to be what you want me to be."

"And what do you think that is?"

"You want to do stuff to me," she whispered. "What if I can't . . . ?" Her breathing was picking up its pace.

"Relax, Brianna," I said in a soothing voice. "Remember what I said about communication? If I don't know what you're feeling or why, then this isn't going to work. Lack of communication is really the only thing that will make this *not* work."

A few seconds passed before her body began to relax again.

"Good girl. Now, let me tell you some of the things I enjoy and you can tell me if it's completely distasteful to you." She didn't respond, but I knew she was listening. "When I used to come home and you'd be kneeling there waiting, ready to serve me, it would please me to see you there like that. How you smile when you serve me my dinner, or taking such pleasure in doing something for me. I enjoy you sitting in my lap while I pet your hair and caress you. Do those things sound distasteful to you so far?"

She shook her head. "No."

"Good," I said, taking the opportunity to act on one of the things I'd just mentioned and ran my fingers through her hair as if she were a pet or a small child.

"But you said . . ."

When she stopped in midsentence, I prompted her. She needed to learn to complete her sentences, but I was hoping that would come in time as her fear subsided. "Continue."

"What about the cane?"

"That's something we would work up to as you become more comfortable with me and what we do together." I brushed the hair away from her face as I spoke. "You seem very scared of sex in general, which given your history is understandable. I think that's what we need to work on first." I felt her tense. "Shhh. Relax. I'm not going to jump you." I chuckled.

Her muscles began to release their tension once again, but I needed to ask. "Is this something you want, Brianna? I can show you that sex can be very pleasurable, but it has to be something you want."

"I . . . want to know what everyone talks about." Again, it came out more as a question, but then she added, "I don't get it. Sex isn't fun. It doesn't feel good," she whispered.

"Oh, but it can be," I said, tilting her face up to mine. "You know how you feel when I kiss you? That feeling of energy building up inside of you? It feels good, doesn't it?" I didn't wait for her to answer. "Just imagine that feeling continuing to get bigger and bigger until it explodes, leaving every muscle in your body feeling as though you no longer have bones to support them," I whispered against her lips. "It's an amazing feeling, Brianna. I want to show you."

My lips brushed against hers. I'd been trying to bring all those pleasant feelings she'd written about in her journal to the surface. It looked as though I'd succeeded. Her lids were heavy. Her breathing was labored. Her body was unconsciously leaning into mine. *Perfect.*

"Have you ever had an orgasm, Brianna? Have you ever felt that *explosion*?"

It took her a moment. She swallowed. "No," she whispered. "I don't . . . think . . . so?" she squeaked.

"Well, we will just have to fix that, won't we?" I said, placing a hard kiss on her lips before pulling back and getting up from the bed. She looked at me in confusion. "I need to go out for a while. I'll be back in about an hour. If you need me before I return, call my cell. All right?"

"Okay," she answered, still plainly confused. And aroused. Just how I wanted her.

I turned on my heel and left Brianna sitting somewhat dazed on her bed. It would be very interesting to read what she wrote in her journal tonight.

# Chapter 8

**Brianna**

*I was so confused.*

One minute, I was lost in that feeling I got so often when his arms were around me. In the next, he was gone. I felt like something was missing.

I shook my head, trying to clear it. It was silly. Stupid, even. I didn't understand how or why he made me feel this way when he kissed me or held me.

He walked out of my room, and I listened as the front door opened and then closed behind him. I was alone. The vast amount of empty space that I now felt in his home was hard to believe. It just didn't feel the same without him in it.

After a few minutes, I got my body moving and walked into the kitchen. It was already close to four and I wanted to start dinner. Actually, I needed to start dinner. I had to have something that would help get my mind off the things running through my brain. When it came to Stephan, I always felt lost and then found at the same time. It didn't make sense.

I put the turkey breast in the oven and started working on the vegetables. Although it kept my hands busy, it couldn't completely keep me from thinking. The things he'd said . . . the things he liked . . . they were things I liked, too. I hadn't expected that.

When I was with Ian, I'd knelt a lot. But with him, it had always felt wrong. With Stephan, it was so different. He made me feel special. Like he cared about me. Like I was able to make him happy. I never felt that way with Ian. With him, it had always seemed like no matter what I tried to do, I was always wrong.

Once everything was cooking, I went back into my room and opened my journal. I needed to write my thoughts down. Maybe that would help me to make sense of them.

I had been writing for about twenty minutes when I heard the door open. He was home. Warmth spread through my chest as I tossed my journal aside and exited my bedroom.

He was standing in the kitchen when I walked into the main room. His back was toward me as I watched him survey what was cooking. I wanted to go to him, but I was stuck, rooted in my spot just outside my bedroom door.

He turned seconds later. A sly smile covered his lips as if somehow he'd known I'd been there the whole time. I gave him a shy smile in return.

*Talk*, I told myself. He said he wanted me to talk. I could do that. At least I was going to try.

"Hi," I said, still a little unsure.

"Hello, Brianna."

He didn't come toward me as I'd hoped. Instead, he leaned back casually against the kitchen counter and watched me.

"Um, dinner should be ready soon," I managed to squeak out.

He nodded, but didn't say anything.

Had I done something wrong? He had said he wanted me to talk to him. Had he changed his mind? My eyes lowered to the floor and my hands began to tremble. Did I mess up?

"Look at me."

He was no longer across the room, but standing directly in front of me. My eyes rose to meet his. They didn't look angry at all. I started to calm down.

"Tell me what you're thinking," he whispered, the back of his right hand caressing my face.

"I thought . . . I thought maybe I'd done something . . . wrong," I whispered.

"Why did you think you'd done something wrong?"

"You didn't . . . I just . . ." I took a breath, and looked down shyly. "You stayed in the kitchen. And you didn't say . . ." I shrugged. "I wanted . . ."

"What did you want?" he encouraged.

My brain was shouting at me not to be stupid. But somewhere in another part of my brain, my body was saying to answer him. "I wanted to . . . go to you. In the kitchen."

He surrounded my face with both his hands, lifting my face upward. "Why didn't you?"

His voice was gentle. It had my insides doing those funny things they sometimes did when he was near. "I was scared."

"You didn't think it would be what I wanted you to do."

I nodded.

"I never want you to be afraid to come to me. I will always be there for you. For as long as you want me." His voice was smooth, calm.

Our eyes held for what seemed like forever before he pulled me closer to him and wrapped his arms around me. I felt his breath against my hair, my skin. It was comforting.

After a few minutes, we broke apart and he followed me to the kitchen. He sat and talked to me while I put the finishing touches on dinner.

Our conversation probably wouldn't be viewed as anything special by most standards, but it was to me. He told me he'd talked to Jimmy, the man I'd met at dinner with his aunt and uncle, and that he was meeting with him for lunch Tuesday. He told me more about the foundation he ran. He asked me about my mom. I found that it was much easier to talk about my mother than I thought it would be. She and I had always had a good relationship. At least, I'd thought we had.

She'd taught second grade until she'd gotten sick. At the age of thirty-five, she was diagnosed with stage-four breast cancer. The chemo made her too sick to work. My mom had some great doctors, but in the end, they couldn't save her.

I hadn't realized that I'd started crying until he was there holding me. He rocked me in his arms while I remembered my mom and finally, truly said goodbye to her.

The food I'd made burned due to my meltdown and he decided to order out rather than having me make something else or trying to salvage our ruined dinner. For the rest of the night, we sat on the couch and watched a movie and then some television.

The few other times I'd remembered my mom since she'd died I had felt totally and utterly alone. John had never wanted to talk about her, and I knew that the few friends I'd managed to make at my new school didn't want to hear about it, so I kept it to myself. Stephan didn't make me feel that way. He acted as if he really wanted to know, and I found that I wanted to tell him. I didn't feel alone anymore.

**Stephan**

Even though I'd known Brianna's mother had died of cancer, hearing about it firsthand had taken its toll. I couldn't imagine a young girl going through that by herself. She'd been alone. That was never going to happen again if I could help it.

After her breakdown, we had a quiet evening sitting on the couch, watching television and eating Chinese food. It couldn't have gotten much better.

We talked a little, cuddled, and just relaxed. I'd never really had this with anyone else. Tami rarely came over to the house unless we were playing. Sarah, my first collared submissive, was very active. She always had to be moving, unless we were playing and I had ordered her not to. Even then, I could always tell it was taking an effort on her part to stay still. For her to sit and just cuddle with me on the couch would have driven her nuts.

I went to bed that night feeling more content than I could ever remember being. Brianna was tucked into bed next door, and I had real hope for us. She was opening up more with each passing day. Her trust in me was growing. I just had to be patient.

My alarm didn't even have the chance to go off the following morning; I was up with the dawn. You would have thought, given my peaceful intro into sleep that it would've continued throughout the night. It didn't. As if my body knew what was coming, it woke up alert and ready.

I dressed quickly, ate a simple breakfast, and went in to kiss Brianna goodbye. She was still sleeping since I was over an hour ahead of my usual schedule. Although I would have loved to have seen her beautiful eyes to start my day, I let her sleep. Instead, I left her a note and attached it to her alarm clock where she'd be sure to see it.

When I pulled into the parking garage attached to my office, I saw Jamie walking toward the elevators.

She saw me and straightened her posture. "Everything's in place, Mr. Coleman."

"Good," I replied with equal seriousness. Although I got a slight sense of satisfaction from what I was about to do, it was not a time for levity.

We rode up to our floor in silence. Two security guards were already waiting as soon as we stepped off the elevator. The sight made me smile.

I took a detour into Karl's office—or what used to be his office—to make sure everything was gone. Jamie had had everything stripped over the weekend. There was nothing left in the room except a few pieces of furniture and a single box with his personal belongings. After seeing it, I smiled.

All the department heads and executives, minus Karl, were waiting in my office when I arrived, including Lily. Our eyes met and I knew she was behind me one hundred percent. Not that I ever had any doubt about that.

Everyone was briefed on what had happened—although most had heard through the grapevine—and what was going to happen. Not surprisingly, there weren't any protests.

Karl's security codes had been deactivated, so he would be unable to use the staff elevator. At seven forty-five, the front desk called my office to inform me that a not-too-happy Karl had entered the front of the building. They'd been instructed to let him pass, but he was being monitored through the security cameras.

I heard the elevator doors open only seconds before Karl responded to the security guards that surrounded him. "I don't need an escort! What the—"

"We are to escort you, sir."

"Karl," I said as calmly as I could. "Why don't you come with me?" I turned, and walked toward his old office knowing he would follow.

"I should have known you'd be behind this, Coleman," he said as he followed me down the hall. "What's wrong? Upset that your girls like a little variety?" he taunted.

Karl could taunt all he wanted. I was the one who was going to have the last laugh.

I stepped into the now sparsely decorated room and motioned for him to join me. Max and Ben waited outside. It was obvious the minute Karl registered the changes in the room.

"You have no right, Coleman." He was about to launch into a rant that I didn't want to hear.

"Actually, I do." I removed several sheets of folded paper from my jacket. "These are statements from women in the finance department, women who work under you now or have in the past. Once people heard what you'd done over the weekend, it didn't take much for them to go on record on how you'd treated, and continue to treat, every female that works for you. I also have statements from witnesses and hotel staff documenting what happened Saturday night." I let that set in for a moment then added, "I have *every* right."

It was as if something snapped inside him. I saw the look in his eyes change only a moment before he launched himself at me. I managed to get out of the way for the most part, but he still knocked me off balance and sent me tumbling into the desk.

He was back up in record time, but I was ready for him. When he came at me, I stepped to the side and landed a punch to his gut. The punch slowed him down a little, but he was not giving up. When he came after me again, he took a swing at my face.

He missed.

I didn't.

My fist landed solidly on his jaw, and his head jerked back from the impact. This time, I didn't wait for him to get his feet back under him. I took him by his shirt collar and hit him once more for good measure before bringing his face to mine.

"I suggest you move to another city, Karl. You will never find a job in Minneapolis again unless it's flipping hamburgers. And if I *ever* hear of you 'imposing yourself' on a woman again, I will see that you spend a very long time behind bars."

With that, I shoved him toward the door where the two security guards were waiting. They'd been instructed to watch but not interfere unless I said otherwise. I wanted witnesses. There'd been a good chance Karl would become violent once confronted, and I was smart enough to cover my back. I had too many people this could affect not to.

Ben and Max escorted Karl down the elevator and to his car. Jamie followed with his box of belongings. I didn't trust Karl, so Ben and Max were also in charge of following him for the day. They would be calling me with follow-ups every hour.

I was ready for the end of the day by the time it finally arrived. Karl had attempted to come back once. We knew he was on his way, of course, and he was greeted with two additional security guards and a police officer, who very kindly let him know that if he was seen here again, he would be arrested. Officer Ballis was a friend of my assistant. It hadn't taken much convincing for him to stop in and put our former CFO in his place.

Last night, I'd told Brianna not to fix anything for dinner because we would be going out. It was the last thing I wanted to do; however, she needed to be among people as much as possible. The interaction, simple as it may be, would be good for her.

She was waiting for me when I got home. Her hair was pinned back on the sides just enough so I could see her ears. She wore a cute black and red dress that came to a stop precisely above her knees. It showed off her tiny waist and gave the slightest hint of her cleavage. I felt both my mind and body wondering on the possibilities.

As I walked toward her, her lips pressed together so tightly that her lower lip completely disappeared. She always did that when she was unsure of herself or nervous.

I stopped in front of her without touching. "Good evening, Brianna. Is there something you wanted to tell me?"

Her eyes opened wide, knowing she'd been pegged. "I was just . . . wondering?"

I gave her a sly smile. "And what were you wondering?" She started to look down. "No," I said in a firm, but soft voice. "I want you to look at me when you tell me."

She obeyed, but I could tell she didn't want to. "Should I be kneeling? I mean, now that I know you like it?"

I couldn't help the small chuckle that escaped as I embraced her. "Oh, Brianna, how I love you," I whispered into her hair. Pulling back, I looked down into her face. "I do love when you kneel for me, but maybe not every time I come home, hmm? Maybe soon we can discuss some specific times I'd like to have you kneeling for me," I said suggestively.

My eyes watched her closely, waiting for her reaction. It was subtle, but it was there. The pulse in her neck picked up its pace, as did her breathing. She even tensed for a few seconds before visibly forcing herself to relax again. It was as if her body and mind were arguing. I wanted tonight to be casual and relaxing for her, so I took her to Tony's again.

He greeted us at the door with his same excitement. "Stephan! Brianna!" He showed us to a table toward the back and asked us both how we were as he handed us menus.

After ordering two waters, I focused on Brianna. "Tony has a lot of great Italian dishes. I thought we'd try some tonight."

"Okay," she nodded and began reading the menu.

Tony's daughter, Maria, brought us our waters and said she'd be back shortly to take our orders. Brianna glanced up at Maria, but didn't say anything.

A minute later, I saw her put her menu down. "Have you decided?"

"Yes. I think I'll try the lasagna."

"That's a good choice. Tony makes all his own noodles. I think you'll like it."

"I used to like my mom's," she whispered.

I reached out and took her hand over the table. "Don't hesitate to talk to me about your mother. I know she was important to you, and I want to hear about her." She visibly relaxed.

I noticed Maria making her way to our table. "I want you to order for yourself, Brianna." I saw her tense once again. "You've done it before, and I'm right here with you."

She made it through ordering much better than she had at her first attempt. Brianna was still fighting her nerves, but she was winning. That was very good.

Dinner was pleasant. I even got her to laugh a little when I told her a story about Lily.

The food was wonderful, but I wouldn't have expected less. I offered her a bite of my cannelloni. It might not have been the right thing to do, as watching her lips wrap around my fork sent sensations to areas of my body that I was desperately trying to keep repressed.

I wasn't ready to go home after dinner, so I took a detour to a park a few blocks away. The night was warm, and it wasn't raining. There wasn't much more that you could ask of this time of year. It was still light out so there were people walking, kids playing. If it bothered Brianna, she didn't show it. I held her hand as we walked. There was nothing about this that felt wrong.

She talked a little more about her mom and about her dog, Rusty. It seemed as though she'd had a normal childhood until her mom had gotten sick. I wanted to know more about her father, but she seemed so relaxed by the time we headed back that I didn't want to bring it up.

It was after nine when we arrived at my condo. I followed her into her room. She walked over to her nightstand, picked up her journal, and handed it to me. I opened it, and flipped through the pages as she went to her dresser to get something for bed.

She'd written more both yesterday and today. After leaving her hanging yesterday, I could feel the tension in her writing. She wanted to get closer, but she was still so scared.

Today's entry was less emotional, but still filled with her feelings regarding me. Confusion again seemed to be the prevailing one; however, safe, warm, and fearful seemed to be following close behind.

Although I would probably never fully understand what she had gone through, I knew without a doubt that she didn't want to be that scared little girl anymore. Everything she was telling me, showing me, confirmed that.

I placed the journal back in its place and turned to find her sitting on the bed, the tank top and shorts still sitting folded beside her.

With deliberate steps, I walked to stand in front of her. My hand came up to cup her chin and raised it. There was such a mixture of emotion on her face, just like in her journal. I released her and took a step back.

"Stand up, Brianna." She did. "Turn around and face away from me." Again, she did as instructed.

I stepped closer and took the clips from her hair. The newly released locks tumbled down into their rightful places on her shoulders. I grazed my fingers along the soft skin where the hairs now touched before following the outside of her dress until I reached the zipper. Watching her closely, I made sure I wasn't going too fast for her. She was doing well, and appeared to be okay.

With a gentle tug, I began slowly lowering the zipper, making sure that the back of my knuckle brushed against her spine all the way down. A narrow V of flesh showed down her back with only a hint of bra halfway down and red panties visible at the bottom. Even with the scars marring her skin, there was no way for my body not to react to that sight.

The tips of my fingers ran up her sides, causing her to shudder a little. I wasn't sure if it was from excitement, nerves, or if she was just ticklish. I paused for an extra-long moment when I reached the top of her dress before pushing it off her shoulders. Material slid down her body and pooled at her feet, leaving her clad only in her underwear.

I leaned down and placed a soft kiss to the top of each shoulder, and then reached between us to unfasten her bra. With a little assistance the straps fell, giving me the amazing view of the tops of her naked breasts.

My hands went to her waist. Her panties were simple. They were red satin with just a little lace around the edges. My fingers slipped just under the edge of the lace at the top, lingering just enough to tease her.

She was responding very, very well. Not once had she tensed in fear, but I asked anyway. "Are you all right, Brianna?"

"Yes," she whispered, and it was huskier than normal.

I smiled against her shoulder. "Good."

Removing my fingers from inside the satin, I began doing the same along the outside of the lace. At first, I stayed at the top, just as I had on the inside. Then I started tracing the outside edges starting in the back.

This time, she tensed. "Shhh, Brianna. It will be good, I promise." I gave her a minute to register this. "Do you want me to stop?"

She shook her head and squeezed out a no.

"All right. Just relax. Remember you're safe with me."

All through the conversation, my fingers had not stopped brushing over the smooth round flesh of her backside. I kept them there until I felt her relax again. Then, I started to move them with a slightly more deliberate purpose.

I slid my fingers down to the junction of her legs still following the lace. I felt her tense momentarily before willing herself to relax. "Good girl," I whispered and placed another kiss on her shoulder. "Now spread your legs a little for me." She complied and I began the plan that had formed in my mind.

Ever so slowly, I began to draw small circles. For the most part, I stayed on the edges with the lace, but every now and then, I would divert from my path and place a circle farther in.

I continued this pattern as I watched her body start to respond. She was taking deeper breaths, and I began to feel the moisture under my fingertips. "Do you like this, Brianna? Does it feel good?"

"Yes," she breathed.

"One day, I will make you feel better than you've ever felt before," I promised as my finger moved forward and I placed a deliberate circle directly over her clit.

She gasped.

I pressed again a little firmer. "Is that something you want, Brianna?"

"Yes."

Brianna was leaning back against me now. I don't think she even knew she was doing it. She was totally lost in the sensations I was giving her.

"That's a good thing. I want you to think about that tonight when you're in your bed. I want you to think about how my fingers felt on you. And I want you to tell me if tomorrow night you would like for me to do the same thing except without the barrier of your panties," I whispered in her ear.

With that, I removed my hands and brought them back up to her waist. I pushed her panties down her legs to join her dress and turned her around. Her face was flushed, her chest moving up and down at a more rapid pace than was normal.

I took her face in my hands and gave her a long, slow kiss, enjoying the feel of her lips and tongue. Brianna kissed me back without hesitation. It was amazing to see how far we'd come.

I released her mouth and looked down at our bodies standing together; hers naked, mine completely clothed. She was beautiful, and I told her so. "I do hope you give me the honor of truly worshipping your body one day."

She didn't respond outside of her blush deepening. I wasn't sure if she would ever truly be able to take a compliment regarding her body, but it was something we were going to work on. Brianna was the most beautiful woman I'd ever seen, naked or clothed.

I helped her put her bedclothes on and tucked her in, reminding her of what I'd said. Then I headed to my own room.

It was after ten, and I was in desperate need of a shower.

Stripping out of the suit I still wore, I walked into my bathroom and turned on the spray. The water hit my naked body, but it didn't ease the tension. Only one thing could do that.

I reached for the soap and lathered up my hands before reaching down and taking a firm hold. It was only as I was coming down from my climax that I recalled what I'd said to her earlier in the day when I'd come home. I'd told Brianna I loved her, and she hadn't even noticed.

# Chapter 9

**Stephan**

*It was a restless night's sleep for me. Even though I'd gotten release in* the shower before going to bed, my mind had quickly floated back to Brianna and what had happened between us.

At just after two in the morning, I'd awoken from a fitful sleep thinking only of her. I'd walked next door to her room to check on her. She was beautiful with her hair lying tangled on her pillows. Her legs twisted in her sheets where she'd obviously been tossing and turning. From the looks of it, she was not having a completely peaceful night herself. Of course, I really hadn't planned for her to.

She hadn't woken while I was in her room, so eventually I went back to my own bed in hope of a good night's sleep. It wasn't easy. My mind kept replaying the evening in vivid detail, and my body liked the images just as much as it had the first time. I refused to give in, however. One session of self-pleasure a night was all I was allowing myself. I did manage to get a little sleep, but it was taken in short naps rather than one long, deep rest.

Brianna was in the kitchen making breakfast when I strolled into the main room of our home. She was still wearing the shorts and tank top she'd worn to bed. The shorts ended just a little too low for my taste, but were loose enough to provide easy access should it be needed.

It was difficult not to think of all the things I wanted to do to her when she was like this, and totally oblivious to my presence. She was beautiful and sexy standing there cooking, and she wasn't even trying.

Whenever I thought of her not being here with me, there was a sharp pain in my chest. That had never happened to me before. But then again, I'd never been in love with anyone. I could only hope that she felt the same way, or at least was beginning to.

We ate quietly before I picked up my briefcase and headed for the door.

She followed behind.

I set my case down on the table next to my keys, and turned to face her. Brianna looked up at me, her eyes so full of emotion. I wrapped my arms around her waist to pull her closer. She melted into me and I began to wonder if she'd been nervous about my reaction to her this morning. "Are you all right, Brianna?"

"Yes," she sighed.

"You have nothing to be nervous about. I'll take care of you. Every part of you."

I felt all the tension leave her as she buried her head against my chest. "I want . . . that," she whispered.

I smiled. "I'm very glad to hear that." I pulled back and placed a kiss on her forehead before tilting her head up. "You'll be okay today?"

"Yes."

"Good," I said, leaning closer. "Now, give me a kiss before I go."

Brianna's lips met mine. She wasn't hesitant. She was almost eager.

The kiss only lasted for a minute before I had to separate us. I was still worked up from last night, and as much as I loved her lips on mine, it was not helping my heightened state.

Jamie greeted me with her usual, cheerful smile when I arrived at the office. The morning was busier than usual since I had to oversee the finance department now that Karl was no longer in charge. I hoped that human resources would have some candidates for me to start interviewing next week.

Just before noon, Jamie knocked on my office door to let me know that Jimmy had arrived.

Gino's was packed with the lunch rush when we arrived. Being a regular meant that the hostess found us a table quickly despite the crowd. It wasn't private by any means, but as this was just a friendly lunch between old friends, I wasn't worried. Jimmy wasn't Daren. Just thinking of my Mentor made my anger surge. He should have told me he'd be attending the hospital dinner.

I forced myself to push my ire for Daren to the back of my mind as we took our seats. Our server came to our table almost immediately and took our drink orders. Leaning back in my seat, I enjoyed being out of the office.

Jimmy was quiet as we waited for our server to return. As was becoming normal for me, my thoughts drifted to Brianna. I wondered what she was doing with her day. Would she give me the green light to take things farther tonight, or say she wasn't ready? Although, I was trying to prepare myself for the possibility of her wanting to slow things down, I was hoping that wasn't the case.

My thoughts were interrupted when Jimmy asked, "What's going on with you and Dr. Cooper?"

"I don't know what you're talking about," I said as our server returned with the drinks.

It didn't take us long to order food, and we were on our own again. I barely managed to take a sip of my water before Jimmy returned to his inquiry. "Samantha thinks you're reliving your rebellious teenage years."

"I'm not rebelling, Jimmy. I also don't appreciate your wife trying to psychoanalyze me."

He chose to ignore my comment about his wife. "I was talking to your uncle. He seems concerned about you. I know we're not as close anymore, but if something's wrong—"

"Nothing's wrong," Before he could start again, I changed the subject. "How's your residency going so far?"

Jimmy gave me a long look, and then sighed. If he remembered nothing else from our high school years, how stubborn I could be should be burned into his brain. "Exhausting. I thought med school was grueling."

The conversation continued along those same lines throughout our lunch. It was good seeing Jimmy again, but I wasn't going to discuss my issues surrounding my uncle with him. He was right, we weren't that close anymore. Even if we'd continued our friendship during our college years, I doubted this would be something I would confide in him. Not only did I think he wouldn't understand my lifestyle, there was also Samantha. She'd never cared much for me, nor I her. The fact that she was now training to become a psychiatrist only added to the problem.

My history with psychiatrists was not good. Richard had insisted I see one about a year after my parents died. If I never met another one in my life, it would be too soon.

I walked back to the office alone and found it much like I'd left it, with only one exception. There was a bright pink note on my desk where I couldn't possibly miss it.

*Talk to your uncle. Please.*

There was no signature, but I would know that handwriting anywhere. Diane didn't like this rift in her family, and she wasn't above begging to get what she wanted.

With a sigh, I picked up the phone and dialed my uncle's office. His receptionist picked up the phone on the second ring. He was with a patient, of course, but I was told he only had patients scheduled until two o'clock today. After hanging up, I looked at my workload. I really shouldn't leave early, but Diane was right. Richard and I needed to come to some sort of understanding.

It took some doing, but with Jamie's help, I was able to delegate a couple of things to other executives. I was taking the rest home with me. Bringing my work home was not a habit I wished to start; however, it couldn't be helped in this case. I needed to talk to my uncle, and there was no time like the present. Besides, it would make Diane happy.

His car was still in the parking lot when I pulled into a space in front of his office. There were two other vehicles in the lot besides his. One, I knew, belonged to his receptionist. It was almost a quarter after two, so I was hoping my uncle would just be finishing up with his last patient.

Janice, his receptionist, greeted me with a smile as soon as she saw me walk through the door. "I wondered if we might see you today, Stephan."

"Hello, Janice. How have you been?"

"Good. Great, actually," she beamed. "Would you like to see the latest pictures I have of the grandkids?" Janice didn't wait for me to answer her. She took out two pictures from her wallet, showing them to me like any proud grandparent would.

Her daughter had married a military man, so they moved around a lot. Last I'd heard, he'd been stationed in Florida.

"They're growing up," I smiled.

"I know! I can't believe Jason will be starting school this fall. It seems like just yesterday I was with Amy and Andrew in the hospital waiting for him to be born."

Before I could comment, my uncle walked around the corner with a middle-aged man about the same height as me. They were talking, but it didn't appear to be serious as they were both smiling.

"Janice will get you set up for your next appointment." He turned to look up at Janice, but paused longer than was natural when he saw me standing there. After a few seconds, he seemed to get a hold of himself again. "Can you get Mr. Thompson scheduled to come back and see us in three weeks?"

Janice nodded. Then Richard patted his patient lightly on the shoulder and motioned with his head for me to follow him.

Nothing had changed since the last time I'd followed him down this hall over a month ago when I'd brought Brianna to see him. Just remembering that night brought with it all of those protective feelings. They were so much stronger with her than they had been with anyone in the past. I wanted to get this over with and get home to her.

My uncle took a seat behind his desk. He gestured that I should take the one opposite.

No matter how old I was, sitting there took me back to being a teenager. Whenever I'd done something serious, I'd always end up in his office. He'd say he'd brought me there so as not to upset my aunt. I'd believed him at the time. Now I thought it had more to do with the air of authority sitting behind that desk gave him.

I wasn't going to be intimidated today. "We need to talk."

"Yes." I waited to see if he was going to say anything else, but he remained silent.

As much as I wanted to keep him in the dark about what was happening —what had happened to Brianna—I'd come to the conclusion that he would have to know at least some of it, or else our relationship might possibly never repair itself.

"You don't think that I'm good for Brianna because of what I am." I let that hang in the air for a minute before continuing. "I know what Tami told you, but I'm going to tell you what I tried to tell you months ago.

Everything she and I did was consensual. We had an agreement. It's in writing if you'd like to see it. I didn't do anything to her that she was not on board with, and it was consensual in every aspect. Including the bruising she showed you."

"Stephan, I don't understand how a man of your upbringing . . ."

I laughed. I couldn't help it. "Uncle, it has nothing to do with my upbringing and everything to do with what I find sexually stimulating." Some of the color drained from his face. "You don't understand it. That's perfectly fine. I'm not asking you to. What I am asking you to do is trust me. Trust in the man you helped raise enough to know that I would never do anything to a woman that she would not allow me to do to her."

My words were met with silence. You could have heard a pin drop.

Eventually, he sat forward in his chair. "Okay, Stephan. If I believe that—and that's a big if—what about Brianna? She is my concern."

I sighed. "As much as I don't want you to know any of this, I see that keeping it from you is no longer an option."

"You should know that you can tell me anything," he said, a little offended.

Nodding, I continued. "I told you that Brianna was in a bad situation before, and that I got her out of it." It was his turn to nod. "It's a little more involved than that. She was actually being held against her will by a man, and I got her out of there by . . . well . . . by rather nonlegal means."

He shifted nervously. "What do you mean 'nonlegal means'?"

Again, I sighed. "I bought her."

He shot up from his chair as if the office was on fire, but then caught himself, and sat back down. "Stephan . . ."

"This is why I didn't want to tell you. And why it can't go any farther than this room."

"But the man who—"

"That's not your concern."

"But—"

"Richard," I said, making sure I had his attention. "It's not your concern."

The stare I leveled at him hopefully conveyed my meaning, but I couldn't be sure. I waited to see what his next reaction would be.

"So, all her injuries? Her fear?"

I knew what he was asking. "Yes."

"Then Stephan . . . I mean, I know how you feel, but she needs to talk to someone. Someone who knows . . ."

"No." I saw that he was about to jump in again, and cut him off. "I know you mean well. You meant well with me. But no, she's fine with me and is getting better every day."

He seemed to consider his next words carefully. "But you . . ." Then he reconsidered. "Will you do to her what you did to Tami?"

"That will depend on Brianna, and what she wants."

"Stephan, how could she?" He gasped. "I mean the girl has been through so much. How could she want something like that?"

"It's simple. You don't understand Dominance and submission. There is a level of trust and devotion between a submissive and their Dominant. Brianna has many fears thanks to her past, but I can help her face them."

"By beating her?" he asked, clearly outraged.

"Possibly," I said in a dismissive voice.

I could see he was gearing up for a rant, so I stopped him yet again. "You don't have to agree with my lifestyle or my methods. I'll tell you that when she first came to my home, she was scared to do anything beyond breathing without being told. Her only words were 'Yes, Master' and 'No, Master' and even the 'No, Master' was a challenge to get out of her. She can now carry on a pretty decent conversation once you get her going. She is getting better."

"I just . . ." For the first time, my uncle looked defeated. He really didn't know what to do.

"You're worried."

He nodded.

"When you talked to her, the worst thing you could have done was tell her that you didn't think she belonged with me. You proposed to take her from the only person she feels safe with right now. *Me.*" I paused. "You can't do that to her. I won't let you. I . . ." Once again, I was going to be putting something out there for the first time. "I love her, and I won't let you hurt her unnecessarily like that."

My uncle's jaw dropped open. It was the only indication that he had in fact heard me. After a few minutes, he recovered himself. "You . . . love . . . her?"

"Yes," I said with much more conviction this time. "I love her. I won't have her taken away from me. Not by you. Not by her father."

"Her father?"

"Yes. Her father seems to be looking for her, but from what she's told me, he may have been involved in how she ended up where she was."

Richard cocked his head to one side and gave me the first sign of a smile, albeit small, since he'd spotted me. "You really do love her?"

"I do."

My uncle tried to press more information out of me, but I refused. He attempted once again to plead with me to let her talk to a therapist, saying that he feared she was developing Stockholm Syndrome. In the end, he still wasn't happy I had no intention to seek out professional help for Brianna. However, he also didn't think I was going to do irreparable harm to her in the near future either. We parted ways in the parking lot and I drove home, anxious to see Brianna.

Just as I was pulling into my parking space, I received a call from Oscar. "I can't find any direct connection between Jonathan Reeves and this Ian Pierce."

"So we have nothing?" I asked.

"I didn't say we had nothing. What I did find was a mutual . . . friend."

"Who?"

"His name is Jean Dumas. He's well known in less than legal circles and has his hands in quite a few ventures."

"How exactly does he know Brianna's father?"

"Keep in mind that this is purely circumstantial. I can't prove the conclusions I'm drawing here."

"I trust your judgment."

"Jonathan Reeves appears to have gotten into some money trouble a few years back. From what I hear, he was in pretty deep from gambling debts to a not very nice character. Then suddenly, around the time his daughter came to live with him, all his debts, his money troubles, disappeared like magic. Word has it that the money came from Dumas."

Therefore, John borrowed money from one twisted man to pay another. Not a very smart thing to do. "And Ian Pierce?"

"Again this is just hearsay, but . . . apparently, Dumas has a taste for fine art work. Art work that isn't always available to the general public. Pierce has some connections that might make acquiring such art work possible for the right price."

"Brianna was payment for a painting?" I yelled, unable to contain my anger.

"It's just a guess, but yes, that's what I'm thinking." My fist hit the dashboard, leaving a small mark. "What was that?" Oscar asked.

"Nothing," I dismissed. "And Jonathan Reeves gave his daughter to Dumas to pay off his debt?" I seethed.

"That's the only thing that makes sense. Again, this is just conjecture. We have no proof."

"Keep looking. I want to know more about Reeves's debts and more about this art ring that Pierce is apparently involved in."

"I'll have my guy stay on it." He paused, and I could tell he wanted to say something else. I waited. "I noticed your picture in the paper. I'm not sure, given the circumstances, that it was a good idea for you and her to be seen out publicly together."

"I know it's a risk, but I'm not going to hide her. We'll just have to deal with whatever comes."

We hung up a minute later, and I headed up to my condo. I expected to find Brianna working in the kitchen. Instead, I was met with nothing.

I called out her name, but still nothing. I quickly tore through my home looking in every room. They were all empty.

There was no sign of a struggle, which was good. I'd noticed Brianna's car in the garage so I knew she'd not gone anywhere in it. Maybe she'd walked somewhere.

My heart was pounding as I picked up the phone and called downstairs to the security desk.

"Hello, sir."

"Tom," I breathed a small sigh of relief. He knew Brianna and would be able to tell me if he'd seen her recently. "Have you seen Brianna today? Has she been down?"

"Yes, sir. She's down here now. I do believe she is visiting with a friend."

She was downstairs. Safe. "Thank you, Tom. I'll be right down."

I nearly ran to the elevator. The doors opened to the lobby, and it only took me seconds to spot her. Instead of finding her talking with Lily as I had thought I would, I came face to face with Cal Ross.

## Brianna

After his goodbye kiss when he left for work this morning, I felt much better. I'd been nervous about how he'd react this morning given what he'd done to me last night, but he'd just been the same Stephan.

I spent most of the day reading, writing in my journal, and watching TV, just waiting for him to get home. For all my fears, I wanted to see what would happen if we did what he wanted tonight. Just the thought of it made me nervous. But it also made me feel something else. That . . . excitement? I think that's what it was. It was sort of like what I felt when I knew he'd be home soon, but stronger. *More.*

I'd just sat down on the couch with a book I'd found upstairs in his library when the phone rang. Not my cell phone, the main phone.

Reluctantly, I picked it up. "Hello?"

"Hello. Miss Reeves?"

"Yes?"

"I'm sorry to bother you, Miss, but there is a man here in the lobby who says he is here to see you. A Mr. Cal Ross. His name is not on Mr. Coleman's approved list. Do you know him?"

"Um." I didn't know what to say. "Yes."

"Should I send him up?"

As soon as he said the words, I felt the panic start. My eyes darted around the room as I tried to picture him up here. In the only place I felt safe. Alone with me. "No," I said a little louder than I'd intended, so I tried again softer this time. "Um, no. Can I . . . come down?"

"I'll have him wait."

"Thank you."

I ran to my room. The closet on the far right held my jeans. For some reason, it just didn't feel right to go down and see Cal in the skirt I was wearing.

Fifteen minutes later, I had changed into the most casual clothes I could find. I grabbed my cell phone, and rode the elevator downstairs to the lobby.

The doors opened, and I slowly stepped out. I'd never been down here without Stephan. It felt strange.

I saw Tom first. He smiled up at me from behind the desk.

Then I saw Cal. His eyes were watching me, and it made me somewhat uncomfortable. My brain was screaming at me to run. To get back into the elevator and go upstairs where it was safe.

No. I wasn't going to do that. Tom was here. Stephan trusted Tom. I'd be okay.

I had my cell phone. Stephan was only one call away, the first person on my speed dial.

I walked toward Cal, one step at a time. He kept watching me. It was as if he was looking for something.

When I came to a stop a few feet in front of him, he reached out toward me. I flinched away, and he dropped his hand.

Tom was watching us, but I couldn't help my reaction. I willed myself to do better, though.

"Hi, Cal."

"Are you all right?" he demanded.

I flinched again, but not as much as the first time. "I'm fine." He looked doubtful. I looked around and saw a couch across the room.

Cal followed my gaze. "Come on," he said and walked over to take a seat. I trailed behind him, and sat down on the opposite end of the couch.

He started to move closer, but then stopped himself.

Neither of us said anything for a long time. Cal seemed to be waiting for me to say something, but I didn't know what he wanted from me, so I kept quiet. He finally broke the silence.

"So it's true. You live with Coleman." His voice was accusing, and I shrank back into myself. Cal seemed to realize his mistake. "Sorry. I just . . . you're different, Anna. I mean . . ." He seemed mentally to shake himself. "You look . . . different."

"I'm sorry. Is what I'm wearing wrong?"

"What?" he asked, startled. "No. You're beautiful, Anna." He paused. "I meant that you . . . well . . . you seem . . . has he hurt you?"

"Who?" I asked, not understanding.

"Coleman. Has he hurt you? Brianna, if he has, you can tell me."

Then, I understood. "Stephan? No," I shook my head. He looked skeptical. "He's been great to me." Then I clarified. "He *is* great to me."

There was a look on Cal's face at my statement, but he dropped the subject. He asked how long I'd been in Minneapolis, and after that, he started telling me about the city.

After a while, I started to relax. I knew Cal. He'd always been nice to me. He wasn't going to hurt me.

I was telling him about Tony's when the elevator doors opened, causing me to look up.

*Stephan.*

I smiled. My body stood automatically, happy to see him.

But then I noticed the look on his face. It didn't mirror my own. He looked upset.

My eyes immediately lowered to the floor as he began to walk toward me. His arm came around me, pulling me to his side. However, it wasn't me he addressed. "What are you doing here, Ross? What do you want with Brianna?"

# Chapter 10

**Brianna**

***Stephan's arm stayed securely around me. I leaned into him, burying my*** face in his chest.

His body was tight, coiled as if ready for a fight. Something had made him upset, and I didn't know what. Was I not supposed to talk to Cal?

"What's it to you, Coleman?"

"You're here. Where *I* live. That makes it my business, Ross. Now answer the question."

There was silence for a long moment before Cal answered. "I came to see Brianna. I didn't realize I needed your permission," he sneered.

Stephan didn't answer right away, and when he did speak, it was to me. His hand came under my chin, making me look at him. "Do you wish to continue speaking to him, Brianna?"

I bit my lower lip. He was waiting. "Yes, please," I whispered, not knowing if that was the right answer, but wanting to be honest.

He nodded once and placed a kiss on my forehead before turning back to Cal. "You may come upstairs, and talk to her if you wish."

Stephan didn't wait for Cal to respond. He just turned the two of us, and we walked to the elevator. The doors opened and we stepped inside, followed by a not-too-happy-looking Cal.

For some reason, it felt small inside the elevator, much smaller than usual. Stephan didn't let go of me the entire ride up. Not that I wanted him to.

We all exited the elevator, and walked to the only door on the top floor. I heard Cal mutter something that sounded like, 'Penthouse. Figures,' but I couldn't be sure.

Once inside, Stephan told Cal to wait in the living room while he guided me toward his bedroom. I must have tensed up, because Stephan pulled me closer and told me to relax.

He released me once we were inside his room, and walked over beside his bed. I followed his every move with my eyes. He bent down and gathered the cords of his laptop before tucking them and his computer under his arm. He walked back to where he'd left me standing.

It was different here when it was just the two of us. The nerves I had felt just minutes before with Cal weren't present. And even here, in his bedroom, I was okay.

Stephan turned slightly to his right, and laid his computer down on top of his dresser. He took a final step toward me, placing him so close I could feel the heat radiating from his body.

He just watched me. It was similar to what Cal had done earlier, but different as well. Both stares made me uncomfortable, but in different ways. I really couldn't explain it. Maybe I should ask Lily.

His warm hand came up to rub lightly on my cheek. "Did you know Cal was coming over?" he asked, his voice soft.

"No. Tom called me from downstairs." I paused and asked the question that had been on my mind earlier. "Was that all right?"

A crooked smile crossed his face. He didn't look upset, but he didn't exactly look happy either. "Yes, it was all right. You made a good decision, and I'm proud of you."

Just hearing him say those words to me had me beaming. I so wanted him to be proud of me.

Suddenly, I was in his arms. One of his hands was around my waist. The other tangled in my hair. He held me close for several minutes before bringing his face to mine to kiss me. It was aggressive—more aggressive than I was used to from him. For a moment, panic crossed my mind, but then it was gone. This was Stephan.

I let myself return his kiss with everything I had. He seemed to like that as he walked me backward and pressed me up against the wall beside his door.

He pulled back after only a short while, and looked deep into my eyes. He was breathing harder than normal. "I don't mind if you talk with Cal, Brianna, but I don't want you to be alone with him. Do you understand? Will you do this?"

"Yes," I said, still a little breathless.

"Good girl," he said, and then placed another hard kiss against my lips.

He took a step backward to retrieve his laptop, and gave me a long look. A devilish smile that I didn't understand crossed his face. With his free hand, he grabbed one of mine and led me back out into the main room where Cal was waiting.

Cal looked like he'd been pacing when we reentered the room. His eyes locked first upon me, then Stephan, and then came back to me. Again, his stare made me uncomfortable. It was as if he was trying to find something wrong with me.

I supposed that made sense, really. There *was* something wrong with me. A lot of somethings, actually. I was still scared of my own shadow most of the time.

Stephan placed a kiss on my hair. "I'll be at the dining room table working. You'll be fine. You're perfectly safe."

I looked up and met his eyes for a brief moment. He smiled at me and walked across the room past Cal, who gave him what I thought was supposed to be a menacing glare.

My eyes followed Stephan as he sat down at the table and began working. When I turned back to Cal, he was watching me again. I could do this.

Forcing myself to move, I started walking toward Cal. His face softened just a little as I drew near.

We stood facing each other for an awkward amount of time before he suggested we sit. I nodded, and we both sat on the couch. Without thinking about it, I kept two feet between us.

Cal looked over his shoulder at where Stephan was sitting, then back at me. "Protective, isn't he?"

I looked up at Stephan. "Yes." Stephan was protective. But he made me feel safe. Cal snorted. "What's wrong?" I asked, not understanding.

"The pretty boy doesn't have enough? He has to own you, too?"

At his words, I curled in on myself. My legs came up onto the couch, and my arms wrapped around my knees. "He doesn't," I whispered.

I felt his hand on me, and I jumped. He pulled back. "I'm sorry, Anna. I just . . . I'm worried about you."

When I finally calmed myself down, I answered him. "Don't be." My voice was still shaky, and he didn't look convinced.

There was movement from behind Cal, and I glanced up to find Stephan looking straight at me. His eyes were guarded, as if he was trying to force himself not to react or something.

Cal began speaking again, and it brought my attention back to him. "Can I ask you something?"

He seemed more hesitant now. I nodded. His mouth opened and closed again. I watched, but didn't say anything.

Cal looked back over his shoulder at Stephan, who'd returned his focus to his computer. He turned back to me. "How long have you and Coleman been dating?"

Dating? Cal thought that I was Stephan's girlfriend. "I'm n—" I stopped myself. If I denied being his girlfriend, Cal would want to know why I was living with him. I wasn't ready for anyone to know that, especially not Cal. "We've been together for almost two months."

"Almost two months?" Cal's eyebrows rose high on his forehead. "Two months? What does the man have, magic or something?"

The last part he said almost under his breath, but I heard him anyway. "Be nice, Cal Ross," I snapped.

Cal looked at me again as if he didn't know what to say. Then he sighed.

"All right. I'll leave Coleman be for now."

"Thank you."

And I was thankful. I didn't like it when people said bad things about Stephan, or even hinted at them. He'd been better to me than anyone had. And he was helping me.

My eyes drifted back over to where he was working. I noticed the way his shoulders were slumped forward a little as he leaned into the computer screen. How his long fingers typed effortlessly on the keyboard. It brought back the memory of what those fingers had done to me last night. I felt the heat of a blush burning my cheeks.

Cal was talking again. He was telling me about his and his dad's business. I made myself focus on what he was saying.


## Stephan

When I'd first seen Cal there in the lobby with Brianna, I'd wanted to grab her and take her out of his reach as fast as possible. Ross was not on my list of favorite people. He fell into the category of individuals I had to tolerate given his family's support of the foundation.

That reaction had lasted only as long as it had taken me to realize that Brianna had gone down to see him. On her own. I still felt the need to protect her, but it was mixed with a feeling of pride as well.

The last thing I wanted was to have Ross in my home, but I wasn't about to leave her alone downstairs with him. He was from her past. He had connections to her father. And he'd been nothing but a thorn in my side since he'd taken over from his own father. I didn't trust him.

I left him in the living room, and brought Brianna into the bedroom with me while I retrieved my laptop. I would let them talk, but I would be watching. No reason I couldn't try to make some progress on the work I'd brought home at the same time.

Before we headed back out to where Ross was waiting, I pulled her into my arms and kissed her. Maybe it was stupid or immature, but I wanted to leave my mark on her. I wanted her to think of me while she was talking to him.

Her eager response to my kiss caused me to get a little carried away, and I pushed her back against the wall, wrapping my hands in her beautiful brown hair. By the time I released my hold on her, she looked properly disheveled. Let Ross think about that while he sat and talked to her.

He stayed longer than I would have liked. It was well after six by the time he walked out of my door, giving me a hard stare and her, a vow to return soon. I had to suppress the retort on the tip of my tongue.

As soon as the door closed, I had her in my arms.

She was stiff for about two seconds. I knew I'd caught her by surprise. Then she sighed, and slipped her arms around my waist.

Given the time, I decided we would once again go out for dinner. Tonight, I wanted something casual. Brianna was in jeans, and I wanted her to feel comfortable. Mitchell's American Bistro was perfect. When we walked in, it was clear I was overdressed in my suit and tie.

The hostess showed us to a booth and left us with our menus. Brianna had been quiet on the ride there. Not that she was usually overly talkative, but it was the kind of silence that seemed to speak volumes. I knew there was something on her mind so I waited until our server had taken our orders and disappeared into the kitchen before addressing it.

"What are you thinking, Brianna?"

She pressed her lips together and thought for a minute before answering me. "You don't like Cal." Instead of following that up with a question, she just left it hanging there.

I decided to answer her anyway. "No. I don't." Anxiety returned to her features with this confirmation. "Was there something else you wanted to know?" She glanced over at me, and then down. Before she could open her mouth I added, "And a question this time, please."

Again, her lower lip disappeared. I waited.

"Why don't you like him?" she whispered.

I took a drink of my water before I answered. "Last year, he took over running Ross Builders from his father," I explained, not knowing what she'd been told. "They contribute to The Coleman Foundation. Neil was very generous. Cal . . . has been less so."

She looked confused. "I don't understand," she finally said.

With a sigh, I turned to face her. This was not something I really wanted to discuss. In fact, I'd rather talk about anything else besides Cal Ross. "Neil Ross promised the foundation a certain amount of dollars this past year. Cal didn't see the need to donate such a large sum of money." At least, that was what he'd said. I had my doubts about his reasoning, but I'd keep that to myself. Cal had always given me the impression that it was his dislike of me—for whatever reason—behind the difference in his attitude.

"Cal doesn't like you," she whispered as our food arrived.

I waited until our server walked away again before addressing her statement. "No. He doesn't. Although, I'm not sure exactly why that is. I've never done anything to the man." She seemed to be contemplating this. "Eat your food, Brianna." She could think about it all she wanted while she was having her dinner.

After a few minutes, I tried to steer the conversation in a new direction and asked her about her day. It worked for a while, but eventually, as she worked herself toward telling me about the end of her day, Ross returned to the forefront.

Brianna lowered her head before looking back up at me through her eyelashes. "You aren't mad at me about Cal? Even though you don't like him?"

"No," I answered before laying my fork down on my now-empty plate.

She thought about it for a long minute, and then went back to eating, seeming to be satisfied with my answer.

Once Brianna was finished with her meal, I paid the check and we headed home. It was still early, which worked out perfectly. I wanted to go slow with my plans tonight. That was, if she was willing. There was also the added bonus of getting Ross off her mind. I was definitely up to the challenge.

Upon entering our condominium, I walked over to my chair, sat down, and waited to see what she would do. Her eyes followed my movement. Once I was settled and waiting, she walked over. I gestured to let her know that she could sit.

I wrapped my arms around her as soon as I felt her body sink against mine. This was comfortable. This was perfect. Her head rested against my shoulder as my hand ran up and down her arm. It'd been a few days since we'd been in my chair. I'd missed it. And from the contented sigh she'd just released, I'd have said she felt the same way.

I was happy to let us sit there for a while. We had hours before bedtime for me to push her more if she would allow it. So that's what we did for the next forty-five minutes.

When the clock on the mantle read eight thirty, I knew that if we were to accomplish anything tonight it would have to begin. I brushed her hair back from her face and placed a kiss on her forehead.

"Did you think about the question I asked you last night?"

She nodded.

"What did you decide?"

"I . . ." She paused. "I'd like to try."

I contained my excitement and just nodded. "If you need me to stop, say 'red', and I will stop. We'll end for the night, and you can think over whether you'd like to try again another time. If you just need a minute, or if I'm going too fast and you need to take a break before continuing . . . say 'yellow', and I'll stop until you are okay to start again. Do you understand?"

She nodded.

"I want to hear the words, Brianna."

"Yes." She visibly swallowed. "I understand."

"Good," I said and patted her thigh to let her know that I wanted her to stand.

Once on my feet, I took her hand, led her back to her bedroom, and brought her over beside her bed.

The fitted top she was wearing buttoned down the front. I reached out, and beginning at the top, began slowly undressing her. Every chance I got, I made sure my fingers or the back of my hand brushed against her skin. I pushed her shirt from her shoulders and let it fall to the floor, leaving her in only a beautiful cream-colored bra.

My fingers traced the outline of the straps and cups, but stayed clear of where I most wanted to touch. We would get to that later. Right now, she needed to be teased. She needed to feel the want of this.

As my hands reached the underside of her breasts, I trailed them down her torso to the clasp holding her jeans. It would have been easy just to release and remove them, but I wanted to play with her. Wanted her to know just how desirable I found her body.

My fingers were light along her stomach. It was soft and just slightly rounded. Perfect. I couldn't wait to have my mouth on every inch of her body.

I looked directly into her eyes as the button of her jeans gave under my hands. My lips touched hers in a soft, brief kiss as the zipper released its hold and I pushed the material from her hips.

Her panties were cream-colored to match her bra. They were just a few shades lighter than her skin.

With my assistance, she stepped out of her jeans, and they joined her top. I took a minute to drink in her stunning features. Although I'd seen her many times in varying stages of dress, her beauty never failed to amaze me. Was this why her father had sold her?

I closed my eyes, dispelling that thought from my brain. Later, I'd think about that when I was alone. Right now, there was only her.

Closing the distance between us, I pulled her into my arms and kissed her. She was more tense than usual. I pulled back just a little and whispered for her to relax before brushing my lips down her collarbone to the spot on her neck that I knew she liked so much. Just as I'd hoped, I felt her muscles begin to release that nervous tension.

I reached around to her back and unclasped her bra, revealing the angry red cigarette marks around her nipples. I made quick work removing her bra, leaving her bare breasts pressed against me. It was heavenly feeling their softness, their weight. The only thing that would've made it better would have been if I had been in the same state of undress as her. All in good time, I told myself.

Her panties were next. My lips left her skin as my fingers dipped inside her undergarments. The hair that had been waxed was growing with vigor now. I would have to talk to Lily and see if she could talk Brianna into being waxed again. If she decided to become my submissive, it would be a requirement, but right now, it was her choice.

The hairs brushed against my fingers as I stepped behind her. I wanted to ease her into this, so my first touch would be with her panties still on.

My touch was light and gentle as I continued to draw nearer to the junction between her legs. Her body was giving mixed signals. She was tense—not in a good way—but she was also leaning back against me. I knew this was due to her past, which was why we were going slowly.

I finally found her soft folds with the tips of my fingers. She was wet, but not as much as I would have liked. I knew it was because of her nerves.

I found her clit as I had last night and pressed down with a slow and constant force. Her body responded, and I smiled.

"That's it, Brianna. Just relax. Enjoy what my hands are doing to you."

She tried to relax, but for some reason she didn't seem as into it as she had last evening. I wondered if that was due to the knowledge that we would be going farther tonight, that it was an unknown, or maybe it was to do with her visit from Cal Ross. I was really hoping it was not the latter. Brianna didn't need more obstacles to overcome.

I circled my index finger around her clit several more times before I removed my hand completely. Her hips moved reflectively toward my hand as if she didn't want me to stop. That was a good sign.

I easily pushed her underwear down her legs, and she stepped out of them.

Last night we had done this standing up, but I wanted her in the bed tonight for several reasons.

"Lie down," I said, motioning toward the bed.

I saw the tension completely return to her body, but she did what I asked. The amount of trust she had in me was amazing.

Once she was lying on the bed, I climbed on, and lay down beside her. I didn't want to be fully clothed. I wanted to have my own naked body pressing against hers, but I knew that wasn't possible—*yet*.

I pulled her against me so that her back was to my front. I grazed my lips across her shoulder as I cupped her breast. "You are so beautiful," I whispered. "So, so beautiful."

While I continued to explore her neck liberally with my mouth, I massaged and played with her breast. Once I got her to relax, I found that she had the most remarkably responsive nipples. I couldn't wait to get my mouth on them in the future.

I played with her breasts until she began pressing her body back against mine. She really had no idea what her responses did to me. My body was primed and ready even though nothing would happen tonight, and every little sigh, moan, and movement just added to that.

I continued my assault on her neck and shoulder all the while. Now, as I moved my hand down her body once again, I scraped my teeth against the soft skin of her neck. I was going to leave a mark on her, and I didn't care. In fact, I wanted it. I wanted Ross and anyone else who saw her to know she was spoken for. That she . . . was mine.

As my hand reached its destination, her legs parted for me. "Good girl," I said as I picked up where I'd left off before.

She was more receptive this time, which was encouraging.

I alternated between a feather light touch and one with deliberate pressure. She was breathing heavily. And when I went with too little pressure for too long, she would move her hips forward just a little, looking for contact.

Brianna was doing so well. I was so proud of her.

Most of her neck was red from my attentions, but I wasn't willing to stop.

Her little moans when I'd reach a certain area were too valuable to ignore.

I dipped my fingers lower, headed toward her opening. I went slowly because I didn't know how she would react.

It was a good decision on my part. As soon as the tips of my fingers reached her entrance, her whole body went rigid. It was as if a switch flipped. I knew her well enough at this point to know that if I pushed, she'd be heading toward panic.

"Brianna?"

No answer.

I removed my hand completely and turned her toward me. Her face was blank, as if she was preparing herself for something.

I wrapped my arms around her, and tucked her head under my chin. "Shh. Relax."

Slowly, she did.

Then the tears began.

I held her until she cried herself to sleep in my arms, and then I tucked her into her bed.

It was well after eleven before I crawled into my own bed. We had a long way to go if just the feel of my fingers was going to cause her to panic.

# Chapter 11

**Stephan**

***Another long night. I continued to think over what had happened, and*** how best to help Brianna. I was worried about her. We'd reached her limit, but she had not used her safeword. Instead, she'd gone into that frozen panic again—something we had to get past.

I woke a little early, got ready for work, and went to check on Brianna. She was still sleeping, so I left her a note saying I'd call her later and kissed her forehead before leaving for the office.

The ride to work was uneventful. I wished I could have said the same thing for my arrival at the office. The moment the elevator doors opened to my floor, standing there in pressed khakis and a polo shirt was Cal Ross.

With a mental sigh, I walked forward. Jamie, already at her desk, had glanced up at my entrance. She was watching the two of us intently. "Good morning, Mr. Coleman."

"Morning, Jamie. Any messages?"

She looked over my shoulder at Ross, then back at me. "Nothing urgent."

I nodded to my assistant, turned my head slightly to look at Ross, and motioned for him to follow me into my office. If we were going to discuss Brianna—and I was certain that was why he was here—then I would not do it as an open forum for passersby to hear. It was bad enough he was at my office to begin with.

He followed me inside and closed the door behind him. At least he appeared to want privacy as well; a point in his favor.

I took a seat behind my desk, and motioned to the chair opposite me. He shook his head and stood with his arms folded.

The staring contest continued for several minutes before I finally leaned back in my chair and said, "You can stand there all day, Ross, or you can just say what you've come here to say. I, for one, have a business to run."

Ross's eyes narrowed at my statement. He shifted his weight, leaning forward with his arms on the back of the chair in front of him. "What's wrong with Anna?" he demanded.

I was careful to keep my expression neutral and emphasize the first word. "*Nothing* is wrong with Brianna."

He threw his arms abruptly off the back of the chair in exasperation. "Nothing is wrong with her? *Nothing?*" His voice rose in agitation. "She looks like a scared mouse."

He looked like he was just getting started; I kept quiet and let him continue. I was in luck. He started pacing.

"If I move too quickly, I see her flinch. And if I try to touch her—" I bristled a little at his words; the thought of Ross touching her did not sit well with me. No man was ever coming that close to her again. "—you'd think I'd tried to burn her or something. Then you . . . you hover around her as if she's going to break or something. Something has to be wrong with her, and don't think that I have ruled you out as the cause, Coleman."

His posturing was aggressive, but I wasn't going to give him the satisfaction. "What has she told you?"

"She hasn't told me anything," he said, clearly frustrated.

I leaned forward, rested my forearms on my desk, and folded my hands. "I'm not going to tell you anything either."

If Brianna wanted him to know about Ian, or about her father, then she was going to have to tell him herself.

Ross just stood there dumbfounded and clearly frustrated. Good . . . so was I.

He stared at me with a blank look on his face before turning around and leaving without another word. I'd known from the start that Cal Ross wasn't going to stay out of Brianna's life. It didn't mean I had to like it.

I took a few minutes to settle myself before turning on my computer and calling Jamie to get my messages. There was only one. Lily wanted to see me.

My feelings toward my friend were mixed at the moment. I'd spoken to Logan to see if he'd given her instructions that would have kept her in the bathroom for longer than normal. He'd assured me that he hadn't since he'd known that she would most likely be escorting Brianna. That, of course, left normal human reasons for her to have taken so long, leaving my girl alone. I knew I couldn't fault her for that, even if I wanted to. She couldn't have known that simply having Brianna wait for her outside the ladies' room would get her accosted. No one had thought Karl would go that far, although I should have.

I checked my e-mails. Most of them were routine; however, there was one from Daren.

*Stephan,*

*I debated sending this a hundred times. But in the end, I thought it best.*

*I wanted to apologize. My presence disturbed your girl, and that was never my intention. By this point, I'm assuming you've discovered that I played with her. It was at the party I told you about. If you would like details, you know how to reach me.*

*Your friend,*

*Daren.*

The fact that Daren had contacted me wasn't what surprised me; it was that he'd chosen e-mail as his method. I'd been expecting a phone call, or even for him to show up at my office. E-mail was definitely unexpected. It made me wonder why.

Before I could think too much about it, I called his cell. He picked up on the second ring.

"Stephan, I'm glad you called."

"I got your e-mail."

He sighed. "I figured as much."

"I have to say I'm a little surprised you e-mailed me. Why didn't you just call?"

"Maybe I should have. No—I should have. But I wanted to give you time with your girl. It was obvious she reacted very badly to seeing me again. Is she all right?"

"Yes. She's better now. Seeing you was obviously a shock. I didn't know you were going to be there. She had no warning, which didn't help."

"I know. I'm sorry about that, too. It was a last-minute decision. Someone couldn't go, so I stepped in. Otherwise, I would have said something."

This caused me to feel mortified. He could have done something, made an effort, but he didn't. "You could have just stayed away from her. *That* would have been best."

He was silent for a long time.

"You're right. My apologies. I shouldn't have tried to make contact knowing what I did." He paused again. "How is she now?"

"Better."

"I'm glad she's better," he said with remorse. "Your girl told you what happened?"

"She didn't go into details," I acknowledged, making it clear I wanted more from him. "What happened?"

"Ian and I struck up a conversation. He was bragging about his new slave. I was talking about Gina. Very normal. Brianna knelt at his feet with his Alpha the whole time. I had no reason to suspect that something wasn't right. The conversation turned to the new cane he'd gotten, and he offered to let me try it out on her. It wasn't until I'd been caning her for a few minutes that I realized something wasn't right. She was so still, like she wasn't there. It wasn't a normal submissive reaction at all. She wasn't in subspace. She wasn't enjoying it. I began watching her mannerisms, and saw how she was trying to escape her discomfort.

"I decided to test my theory and asked Ian what her safeword was. He told me she didn't have one. At that point, I asked if there was a room where I could play with her privately. He was happy to oblige my use of his slave. Once I got her alone, I began again and saw how scared she was not only of me, but afterward she was even more so of going back to her Master. Before, in Ian's presence, she'd been almost void of emotion entirely. By then I knew for sure. After that, I decided to keep an eye on the situation."

I knew from first-hand experience what Brianna was like when she became deathly still.

Shortly after that, I ended the call. I needed to check on Brianna, it was almost ten o'clock. Instead of hearing her beautiful voice, I heard mine as the answering machine picked up. I quickly left a message, hung up, and tried her cell next. Again, I got voicemail. I was beginning to worry. Why wasn't she picking up?

I left another brief message telling her to call me on my cell, and then hung up. Closing my eyes, I tried to calm myself. Maybe she was still sleeping. I was doubtful, but I would give her some time and try again.

A knock sounded on my door. I saw Lily peek her head in as she opened it a few inches. "May I come in?" I gave her a terse nod, and she stepped into the room. "I wanted to apologize and make sure that Brianna was okay. I shouldn't have left her, and I'm sorry."

"No. You should *not* have," I snapped.

"I know," she responded, lowering her head. "I'm sorry."

"I trusted you. As a friend, you should have known what I expected when I had you escort Brianna. I'm disappointed."

Her head lowered further. "I know."

"You aren't to leave her alone like that again, Lily."

She didn't speak, but I knew she'd heard me.

"She's recovered from Saturday for the most part," I answered, somewhat forcefully, continuing to remind myself that it wasn't really Lily's fault.

"I'm glad." Lily was still walking on eggshells, which was good. She should feel bad. "Let me help?"

Considering that I couldn't reach Brianna this morning, I had an idea. "Brianna isn't answering the house phone or her cell. She may still be sleeping, but you could go spend the day with her. I have a meeting this afternoon."

"I can go now."

"If she is still sleeping, then let her rest. If she's up, have her call me."

She nodded.

"I'll be home early. You can help her make dinner, and have it ready by four o'clock."

"Anything else?"

"That should be it," I said. She turned to go and I added, "She had a rough night, Lily. Don't let her out of your sight for long, please."

Again, she nodded, and then she was gone. I felt a little better having Lily with her, but this day could not be over soon enough.

**Brianna**

It took all of thirty seconds after my eyes had opened for me to start crying.
I remembered everything. He'd been wonderful last night. It felt so good
having him touch me like that. And then . . .

The tears fell harder. Why did I have to be such a mess?

His note hadn't helped. Well, it did, but it made me feel worse.

After a long cry, I'd finally gotten myself out of bed, taken a shower, and
made myself breakfast. Most of my food went uneaten, however. I just
didn't have an appetite, and every few minutes I had to fight another wave
of tears.

The clock read nine thirty when I decided to start cleaning the house. I
needed something to keep myself busy, and it was the best idea I could
think of. Why couldn't Brad be coming over today? He would have been
able to keep my mind off things. Instead, I was left to my own methods.
Dusting seemed like the perfect distraction until a spot on the kitchen floor
caught my eye. For some reason it bugged me, and I had to remove it
before I did anything else.

With a bucket of soapy water and a sponge, I lowered myself to the floor
and started scrubbing. It took some effort, but eventually there was no sign
of the spot I'd seen.

I leaned back on my heels just staring at the floor. My mind once again
filled with the pain I'd been trying to push away. It wasn't working, and I
didn't know how to fix it.

I wanted to call him. He told me I could call him anytime, but I didn't
know what to say. I didn't know where to start.

Just then, the main phone rang, causing me to jump. The sudden
movement landed both the bucket of soapy water and me on the floor. I was
now a wet mess.

Without thinking, I tried to get up and ended up slipping on the sponge
I'd also dropped on the floor. I went flying forward and landed face first in
front of the stove. My cheek hit the marble tile with force. Tears were now
stinging my eyes for an entirely different reason.

Stephan's recorded voice came on, picking up the call, as I began slowly
sitting up. I touched the part of my face that had hit the floor, and I winced
as the machine beeped and the caller began speaking. My head rose as I
once again heard Stephan's voice coming through the answering machine,
only this time he was the caller.

"Brianna?" There was a long pause. "Call me, please. I'd like to speak
with you this morning."

I heard the click as he hung up the phone, leaving me not knowing what
to do. Should I call him back now? Later? I wanted to talk to him, but what
would I say? Plus, I couldn't talk to him this way.

While I was debating what to do, the cell phone in my pocket began to vibrate, making me jump again. This time I managed not to fall or bang into anything.

The name across the caller ID was just as I knew it would be.

*Stephan.*

I held the phone to my chest, but didn't answer it. No matter how much I wanted to talk to him, I couldn't. I needed . . .

I didn't know what I needed, but I knew I wanted to be composed to talk to him. Not like I was now.

I had no idea how long I sat there before I heard keys in the door. Panic started to set in before I saw that it was Lily, not Stephan. She took one look at me, walked over, and helped me up. She wrapped her arms around me, and just when I thought the tears had dried up, more came.

Finally, I calmed down, and Lily helped me into my room. She ushered me into the shower, and told me she'd be back in a few minutes. I tried to enjoy the way the water felt against my skin, but I couldn't. The only thing I wanted was Stephan.

Lily found me sitting in the shower, the water cascading down my head and back. She turned the water off and helped me to dry off. We went back into my room and I changed into clean clothes.

She guided me back out into the main room and walked toward the couch. We sat down, and she held my hand. It was nice. But it wasn't Stephan. It wasn't the same.

"Do you want to talk about it?" she asked.

Did I?

She was the only friend I had, and I needed a friend. I needed someone to tell me if I was going insane or not, so I started talking. "Cal came over yesterday." I looked up and made sure she knew whom I was talking about.

She just nodded, so I went on.

"It was strange. I liked seeing him again, but it wasn't the same as when we were little." I added in a whisper, "I'm not the same." She squeezed my hand tighter, but she didn't speak. It was as if she knew I just needed to get it all out. "I was nervous the whole time he was here. Afraid he'd figure out that I'm . . . damaged. He tried to touch me last night and I . . . I . . . why can't I just be good for him?"

I crumbled forward and she held me for a while, rocking me. She let me cry it out and then helped me clean myself up again with some tissues.

"Stephan tried to touch you last night?" she asked.

I nodded. How she'd managed to follow my random train of thought I had no idea, but I was grateful that I hadn't needed to explain what I'd meant.

"Can you tell me exactly what happened?"

I tried very hard to keep the tears inside. "We were on my bed. He was kissing me and touching me. I liked it. Sometimes, when he touches me, I can forget."

She smiled at me and wiped some more tears away from my face. I hadn't realized I'd started crying again. "So you were enjoying it, and then what happened?"

"I don't know! I mean . . . one minute he was touching me and then . . ."

When I didn't finish, she said, "Then what?"

"It wasn't him."

"What do you mean it wasn't him?"

"It was this other man. I don't know his name, but he was a friend . . . of Ian's. He would come by sometimes. He liked me."

"Oh, sweetie. I'm sorry."

"How do I make it stop, Lily? I want it to stop. Everything was going so good and then I messed it up."

She brushed the hair back from my face. It reminded me of Stephan and made me miss him even more. I wanted him here more than anything. Nothing made me feel better than when he held me.

"You didn't mess up. It sounds like you had a flashback. I think that's normal."

"But I want to be good for him."

"Have you told Stephan what happened?"

"No," I said, shaking my head. "I fell asleep last night, and then he was gone this morning. He called me earlier, but I . . . I didn't know what to say and didn't answer the phone." I lowered my head. "I was bad. He isn't going to be happy with me."

"He's worried about you."

My head snapped up. "You talked to him?"

"I spoke to him before I left."

She encouraged me to call him. I wanted to, but I was nervous. In the end, though, it was the fact that I had done something wrong and needed to make it right that won out.

He answered on the first ring. "Brianna?"

"Hello, Sir."

I heard him sigh. "Are you all right?"

"Yes. I'm all right. Lily's here."

"Good. Why didn't you answer the phone when I called?"

"I don't know," I whispered.

"You can do better than that, Brianna."

"I . . . I was afraid that you were mad at me."

"And you thought not answering my phone call would help the situation if I was?" he asked in a voice that clearly showed his displeasure in me.

"I'm sorry, Sir. I'll not do it again."

"You're right. You won't," he said. I didn't like the sound of that. "I have a meeting this afternoon, but I'll be home after that. Have food finished by four. We will talk about this tonight."

"Yes, Sir," I said.

"Put Lily on the phone, Brianna."

*Need*

I handed the phone to her and stepped away. I'd been so afraid I'd messed up that I really had. If he hadn't been upset with me before, then he certainly was now. He was most likely going to punish me when he got home, but it was the least I deserved. He'd been very clear that he had given me a cell phone so we could get in touch with each other at all times. I'd intentionally ignored him.

Lily walked into the kitchen as she talked. She looked like she was trying to calm him down. I knew I was going to be punished tonight. I just didn't know how badly.

When she was finished, she hung up the phone and put it back in its cradle. "I'm staying with you until he gets home. He doesn't want you left alone."

I nodded and mumbled, "He doesn't trust me."

"He doesn't want you left on your own today."

I didn't argue. It didn't matter anyway. I liked having her here.

We didn't talk about Stephan for the rest of the afternoon. Lily made us some lunch, and we watched television. She told me about Logan's job, and how she missed him when he was out of town, like he was now. The way she talked about him, the way she felt, was almost how I felt about Stephan. He was everything to me. All I wanted was to make him happy.

When it was time to start making dinner, Lily came into the kitchen and helped me. It was nice having her there.

As we cooked, I remembered something I'd wanted to ask her. "Lily?"

"Hmm?" she asked as she chopped up some carrots for the salad.

"Can I ask you something?"

That got her attention. "You can ask me anything," she said sincerely.

"Yesterday . . .Cal, well . . . he looked at me. Stared at me, I mean. And . . ." It still felt odd saying his name. "Stephan stared at me, too, but . . ."

"But . . ." she encouraged.

"But it was different. I mean, it didn't feel the same when Cal did it."

"I see," she said. "And how did it feel when Cal was staring at you?"

I thought about it for a minute. It was hard to put into words. "Like . . . like he was trying to find something wrong with me."

"And Stephan?"

"It made me feel uncomfortable, too, but not like with Cal. And I felt . . . warm? I don't know how else to describe it."

"So did you not *like* Stephan staring at you?"

"I don't know. It's . . . I feel like he's looking at me without clothes on even if I'm fully dressed," I whispered.

She laughed. "And do you ever look at him that way?"

I blushed. "I've only seen him without his clothes once."

She smiled, obviously happy with that news for some reason. "I guess that would mean that you do," she replied with a wink.

I hid my face and blushed again, only deeper this time. I could feel the heat in my cheeks. "Maybe, sometimes."

At four o'clock, the food was ready and the table was set. All we were waiting on was Stephan. I took my apron off and went to wait by the door.

The lock turned and the door opened. I kept my head down as he walked straight past me to Lily. I knew she wouldn't interfere with any punishment he gave me.

My heart sank when he didn't greet me. He really was mad.

"Lily," he greeted. "How is everything?"

"Good," she answered. "Did you need me to do anything else? I need to get home and call Logan."

"No. I think we're fine here. Oh, and I called Logan to let him know what was going on. Thank you, Lily."

"Anytime," she replied as she began moving toward me. She hugged me, but I didn't respond. I was too nervous. "I'll see you later." I heard her heels click across the floor and the door close. I knew that the time had come to face my fate.

He was moving around behind me, but he didn't speak. I stayed where I was. There was more movement, then a chair scraping across the floor. "Come eat, Brianna." Stephan's voice was sharp and crisp, but still even and calm at the same time.

I made my way over to my chair and slowly sat down, keeping my head lowered. He put food on his plate and began eating before I served myself.

Dinner was tense. We didn't always speak during meal times, but this was different. I knew I'd done wrong, and I just wanted him to punish me and get it over with, but that wasn't my decision. I knew that.

When he was finished, he got up and went to his chair, leaving his dishes for me. I tried to finish, but without him there beside me, the food seemed tasteless. After a few more bites, I was done. As quietly as I could, I cleared the table and put the food away. The door to the dishwasher clicked shut, and I set the timer.

"Bring your phone when you come."

His voice came out of nowhere and I jumped a little, startled. Quickly, I grabbed my phone from the counter where I'd left it earlier and went to his side.

Instead of opening his arms to me as he usually did, he motioned to the floor. "On your knees, Brianna." I complied and put my head down. "Give me your phone." I did as he requested, and sat there waiting. He flipped the phone over in his hands a couple of times before hitting a few buttons. He set it down on his leg. "It appears to be working properly. I see no reason why you couldn't return my phone call today in a timely manner."

"No, Sir."

"What do you have to say for yourself?"

"There is no excuse, Sir. I should have picked up the phone when you called, or called you right back."

He sighed. "I've told you more than once that communication is the most important thing between us. If you don't tell me what is going on in that mind of yours, there is nothing I can do to help you. I'm not a mind reader, Brianna."

I felt the weight of his disappointment in me.

His gaze burned through me even though I couldn't see it. I just wanted to be in his arms again.

Stephan handed me back my phone. "Starting tomorrow, for the next week, you will text me at the top of every hour while I'm at the office. It will be no more than five minutes early and no more than five minutes late. Do you understand?"

"Yes, Sir."

"If you miss one, Brianna, there will be consequences," he said pointedly.

"I understand."

"Good. Now go put your phone on the charger and come back."

I did what he said and returned to his side. This time he indicated that I was to sit in his lap. It felt so good to be there. I didn't ever want to upset him again, although I knew I would.

"Now, you said on the phone that you were afraid I'd be upset with you. Why?" Stephen asked.

"Because of last night. I . . . I messed up."

He sighed. "You didn't mess up, Brianna. Have I ever been upset with you before when you've had a bad reaction to something?"

"No," I whispered.

"No," he confirmed. "Then why would you think that my view would suddenly change?"

I was quiet for a long while before I answered him. "I wanted to make you happy. I failed."

His hands surrounded my face, brushing the moisture from my cheeks. "You didn't fail. This is a process. We set the pace. If we need to go slower, we'll go slower."

I nodded.

"Can you tell me what happened? You seemed to be enjoying my touching you, and then everything changed."

The next half hour was difficult for me. He'd not been satisfied with my skimming over details of my flashback. He wanted to know everything, from how often Ian's friend had used me to how he found pleasure in shoving as many different objects inside me as he could find. It had become a challenge for him to see what strange and unusual item would fit inside me. Ian hadn't cared, and even encouraged his friend's game.

Stephan listened in silence for the most part, comforting and encouraging me when I arrived at a difficult bit. I didn't want to relive this, but I'd do it for him. I'd do *anything* for him.

At nine thirty, he motioned for me to get up, get ready for bed, and meet him in his bedroom. The entire time I was in my room getting ready I was trying to figure out what he was going to do. I'd thought it was over, but obviously, it wasn't.

When I walked into his room with one minute to spare, he was sitting on his bed wearing nothing but his boxers, waiting for me. He indicated that he wanted me to kneel in front of him. I was visibly shaking.

"Now to correct your behavior, Brianna." His voice was calm. "For the next seven nights you will sleep on the floor, on that spot next to my bed." I followed his gaze down to where he was looking on the floor. "It seems that I can't trust you to tell me when you're in distress. You will also be in the same room as I am at all times when I'm home, unless I say otherwise." He paused. "Go to the dresser and bring back that blanket and pillow lying on top."

I moved quickly to retrieve the items and came back to kneel in front of him. He took the pillow from my hands and tossed it to the floor.

"Do you understand why this is happening?"

"Yes, Sir," I said, not wanting to meet his eyes.

Then he surprised me by pulling my face to his and kissing me. It was deep and passionate, and left me breathing hard by the time he let me go. "Good girl. Goodnight, Brianna," he said with a smile as he climbed into his bed.

I didn't know if I should speak, but I decided to chance it. "Goodnight, Sir."

As I lay down on the floor beside his bed, I realized how stupid I had been in not wanting to tell him. He was always there for me. I shouldn't have doubted him.

# Chapter 12

**Stephan**

*I rolled over the next morning and looked down. To my surprise, Brianna* was gazing up at me with wide eyes. The blanket I'd given her was pulled up to her chin, and I could see the apprehension in her eyes. "Good morning, Brianna."

"Good morning, Sir."

Although I'd not missed the 'Sir' she'd tacked on at the end of her sentence, I let it slide. I wanted to see if she continued to use it once she realized I was no longer upset with her. Her correction was still in effect, but I wasn't going to chastise her again as long as she followed through.

Flipping the covers back and sitting up, I saw her swallow nervously. Her eyes were no longer looking at my face. They were now focused on my lap where my morning erection stood proud.

I chose to ignore her reaction and stood, stretching. "I'm going to shower. Fold your blanket and place it and your pillow back on the dresser, then go to your own room and get ready for the day. You have thirty minutes, and then you are to meet me in the kitchen." Without waiting for her to respond, I walked over to my dresser, pulled out a fresh pair of boxers, and walked into my bathroom.

Contrary to my normal evening showers, the one this morning was quick. I addressed the throbbing between my legs by turning on the cold water. My focus had to be on Brianna today, and not in a sexual way. She needed me.

Before I walked out into the main room, I glanced at the clock beside my bed. I'd taken my time getting ready to give her the full thirty minutes. Six twenty-five. *Perfect.*

I tossed my suit jacket over my arm, and strolled out of my bedroom. My eye immediately went to the kitchen, but I didn't see Brianna. Stopping to listen, I didn't hear her moving around in her bedroom either. Glancing inside the open door, I noticed that both her bedroom and bathroom lights were off. She had to be here somewhere. Throwing my jacket over the back of the couch, I crossed to the kitchen and nearly stumbled over her. Brianna was kneeling, waiting for me, beside the island.

Instead of saying anything, I reached out my hand hoping she'd take it. It took a few minutes, but eventually she lifted her hand and fitted it into mine.

Once she was on her feet, I guided her over to the couch. "Why were you kneeling?

"You told me to wait for you, Sir."

"Brianna, do we have to go through the conversation about you ending every sentence with my title again?" I raised one eyebrow in question, waiting for her answer.

She shook her head. "No."

"Good girl. Now, explain to me how my telling you to wait for me in the kitchen translated into you kneeling."

"I thought . . . I thought that was what you . . . wanted."

She'd been looking down at her lap, but I wanted her eyes on my face when I spoke, so I lifted her chin up. Her gaze followed. "I promise you that I will be more than clear when I wish for you to kneel for me. You seem to be under the impression that I am angry with you. I'm not. Am I disappointed? Yes. Very much so. I thought we'd come far enough that you would tell me if something was wrong. Apparently, I was wrong."

"I'm—"

The last thing I wanted was to hear she was sorry. "If you're truly sorry, fix it."

She pressed her lips together. I knew there was something she wanted to say, so I waited. "How do I fix it?"

"By not making the same mistake again. You need to tell me when something is bothering you. I can't read your mind."

She nodded.

"How did you sleep last night?"

"All right," she said.

I waited for her to continue, but she didn't. "You need to give me more than that, Brianna. Did you have any trouble falling asleep? Did you have any dreams? Nightmares? How did you feel about being made to sleep on the floor next to my bed?"

She glanced back down at her lap before she answered me. "A little," she shrugged. "I don't remember any dreams or nightmares." She pressed her lips together before she continued. "I . . . I don't know how I feel about sleeping by your bed. It . . . wasn't what I was expecting."

I chose to ignore the fact that she'd had some trouble falling asleep for now. That could be due to the stressful evening. Instead, I directed the conversation to her last few sentences. Those seemed to be weighing the most on her mind. "What were you expecting?"

She shook her head quickly.

Taking hold again of her chin, I stopped her motion. Her eyes were wide as she looked at me, but I waited.

"I know you said . . . that you wouldn't . . . but . . ." She closed her eyes. "Whenever I slept on the floor beside a man's bed it was so he could . . . use me."

"And your fears wouldn't go away."

"No," she said. "They wouldn't."

I scooted closer, closing the distance separating us, and pulled her into my arms. "Thank you for telling me. I know it was hard, but I promise you if you keep trying it will get easier." Instead of answering, her fingers tangled in my shirt, and I heard the sound of muffled sobs. "Shh. There is nothing to cry over. You did well." Even though she nodded, it took a few minutes for her to calm down.

The rest of the morning was spent making breakfast and going over—once again—what I expected from her throughout the day. When she asked me what she was supposed to text, I smiled and kissed her temple before getting up and taking my plate to the sink. "I want you to tell me what you are doing, whatever it is."

She looked pensive, but nodded.

I walked to the couch to retrieve my jacket, and she followed me as she always did. Gathering her in my arms, I gave her a lingering kiss on the lips while trailing my fingers over the hickey I'd left on her neck two nights ago. She'd not said anything about it and neither had I, but I couldn't deny how much I enjoyed seeing it there just inches below my collar.

Her gaze followed my hand, and she blushed. I smiled and skimmed my fingers down her arm before stepping back toward the door. "I'll see you tonight."


**Brianna**

I couldn't believe how fast my day went. It was hard to get involved in anything for too long because I had to stop and text him. A few times he texted me back and asked me a question, like when I said I was fixing lunch he asked what I was making. Every time I sent a text, I could feel the weight of what I'd done. Or not done.

He'd said he was disappointed in me, and if I was being honest, I was disappointed in myself as well. I had to do better. Talking wasn't easy, but I'd do it. He'd done so much for me. I could do this for him.

As I cooked dinner for us, I finally let my mind drift back to last night and how it felt sleeping on the floor beside his bed. I couldn't make the fear completely go away, so I'd woken up several times during the night. I'd wake, eyes wide, waiting, then my brain would kick in, I realized where I was and that it was Stephan in the bed, not Ian or one of his friends.

I couldn't help my reaction when I saw his erection pressing against his boxers. I wonder if that added to his disappointment. He'd told me repeatedly he wouldn't do anything unless I asked him to. Why was that so hard to accept?

As soon as I asked myself that question, I knew why. Stephan was very different from the men I'd met over the last year. Whenever I saw their physical excitement, I knew what was coming. With Stephan, he never did what I expected. He always kept me guessing.

When he walked in the door, I was still in the kitchen putting the final additions on the food I was making. I was happy he was home. Even though I was sometimes confused about my life with him, I always felt better when he was near.

He smiled when he spotted me, and walked to where I was standing. Without any words, he pulled me against him, and buried his face in my hair. "Good evening, Brianna."

I hugged him back. He felt good, warm. I tried to remember what he'd said to me this morning . . . *he wasn't angry*. He wasn't angry. I needed to keep reminding myself. "Good evening," I said, although it was muffled since my face was partially covered by his jacket.

He held onto me a few more minutes before tilting my head back and kissing me. It was soft, and I wanted it to last longer, but before I knew it, he pulled away. "Is dinner ready?"

"Yes. I just have to bring it to the table."

"Nothing will burn for the next few minutes?"

"No."

"Good," he said. "I want to get this jacket and tie off before we eat."

He turned and walked toward his bedroom. Halfway there, he paused to glance back at me expectantly, and I remembered I was supposed to stay with him at all times now that he was home.

I left the kitchen, and rushed to his side. He didn't say anything, but I thought I might have seen a small smile tug at his lips. I liked when he smiled.

Just as he'd said, he walked into his room and removed his jacket and his tie, placing them both on a hanger. I stood by the door trying to stay out of his way since I didn't know what exactly I was supposed to do.

He walked to the bathroom, and I debated whether or not I should follow. He stopped at the door, but didn't turn. "Wait here," he said, pointing to a spot just outside his bathroom door.

He left the door open, but I didn't look. I could hear everything, though, and it brought back memories I'd rather not remember, making me shiver. Would I ever be able to see and hear simple things without panic?

Closing my eyes, I recited my mantra. Stephan. Not Ian. Stephan. Not Ian.

Slowly it began to work. I could feel the panic lessening. When he walked out of the bathroom a few minutes later, my breathing was only slightly labored, but my eyes were squeezed firmly shut and my head tilted toward the floor.

I felt him beside me, his hand cupping my face, raising my chin. I still didn't open my eyes.

"Number?"

I thought about it before I answered. Two minutes ago, the number would have been higher. "Four."

"Tell me why."

Slowly, I opened my eyes and looked at him. His face was full of concern. "I was . . . remembering. Things."

His head tilted slightly to one side. "What triggered your memory?"

"I could hear you," I whispered. "In the bathroom."

His brow furrowed. He seemed confused for a moment, then his eyes softened in understanding and he wrapped his arms around me, holding me tight. "I wish I could take all those unpleasant memories from you, love."

I clung to him. He had no idea how much his words meant to me. I wished he could take them all away, too, but just having him with me helped so much.

His lips lingered in my hair. "What's for dinner tonight?"

"Fish."

"Fish?"

I nodded against his lapel.

Taking a step back, he laced his fingers with mine and we walked back out to the kitchen.

After we finished dinner, he went to his chair as he always did. I cleaned up, and walked over to him. He opened his arms for me, and I sat down on his lap.

This was my happy place. If I had to pick one spot in the world I'd rather be than any other, it would be here, sitting in his lap.

As the evening wore on, I began to feel a little disappointed. We talked as we always did, only now, every time I made a face he made me tell him why and what it meant, but never once did he mention or lead me to believe we would be ending the night any differently than we had last night. Yes, I'd panicked when he'd touched me the other night, but before that, it had actually felt really good. I liked when he touched me, and I badly wanted to try again.

When nine thirty came, he patted me on my leg letting me know he wanted me to stand. Other than the gentle caresses and kisses he always gave me whenever we were close, he didn't try to touch me.

I followed his instructions to go change into my nightclothes, get one of my books, and meet him in his bedroom.

Walking back into his bedroom, I paused at the door when I saw him standing by his bed in nothing but his boxers. Maybe this was it. We'd never done anything in his bedroom before, but now that I was sleeping in here—*maybe*. Unfortunately, my hopes were dashed when he saw me.

He grabbed something off the bed before walking toward the bathroom. "Sit here outside the door and read while I shower."

Again, he disappeared into the bathroom, but didn't close the door. I sat on the floor obediently, opened my book, and waited.

# Chapter 13

**Brianna**

*The next day was much the same. He kissed me goodbye before leaving* for work, and again when he came home, but there was nothing beyond that. I wanted to say something, but I didn't know how. He caught me frowning once, and asked me what was wrong. I just said that I'd missed him. It was true. I did miss him. I missed him touching me like he had been. Friday night, I fell asleep lying on the floor beside his bed just as I had for the last two nights.

Instead of waking up naturally on Saturday morning as I usually did, the phone rang pulling us both from sleep.

"Hello," he answered groggily. Suddenly, he was on his feet and swiftly walking out of the room.

It took me a moment to register what had just happened, but then I remembered I was supposed to stay with him. I jumped to my feet, anxious, and scrambled after him.

He was in the kitchen, the phone pressed hard against his ear. There was a scowl on his face as he continued to talk to whoever was on the other end of the line. Standing still was difficult, and I didn't know what I was supposed to do.

After a few more minutes, he hung up and tossed the phone on the counter. He ran his fingers roughly through his hair, and took a deep breath before looking up and seeing me standing there, my lips pressed tight together.

His face softened a little as he walked toward me. He still didn't look happy, and I wanted to try and make it better. He'd said I could always go to him, but was this the same thing? I decided to take the chance. Before he could take the last steps separating us, I went to him.

Immediately he wrapped his arms around me, holding me close. "Are you all right?" he asked. I could hear the concern in his voice.

"Yes." I nodded against the warmth of his bare chest.

His arms squeezed me, and I smiled. I'd made a good choice.

All too soon, however, he released me with a sigh. "You have a visitor coming."

"Someone is coming to see me?" The only person I could think of was Cal. Lily said she was Logan's submissive on the weekends. Surely he wouldn't let her come visit me this early on a Saturday morning, but what would Cal be doing here this early either?

He must have seen the confusion on my face. "My uncle is downstairs. I told him we'd still been asleep, so he's giving us ten minutes to get presentable."

I tensed. I didn't want to see his uncle. He didn't like me, and was trying to take me away from Stephan.

Without thinking, I reached for him again, pressing my hands firmly against his skin. "I don't want to leave you," I whispered. I could hear the note of panic in my voice.

He brushed his lips against my temple before cupping my face, making me look up at him. "I'm glad to hear that," he smiled. "Relax. What did I tell you? No one is going to take you away if you don't want to go."

"Okay." I knew it was shaky, but it was the best I could do. His uncle made me nervous.

"Now, we only have about five minutes left. Run to your bathroom and do what you need to." He let go of me and began walking into his room. "Five minutes, Brianna," he called over his shoulder.

I ran into my room.

Five minutes later, I cautiously walked back into the main room to find Stephan standing in a pair of dark jeans and a T-shirt, talking to his uncle. Stephan glanced up at my entrance, and held out his hand to me.

I crossed the space quickly, never taking my eyes off Dr. Cooper. He smiled at me, but all I could think about when I saw him was what Stephan had told me. How could his uncle believe that woman and not him?

When I reached Stephan's side, he pulled me close, wrapping his arm around me.

Neither said anything at first. Then Dr. Cooper cleared his throat. "I brought a peace offering," he said, holding up a brown paper bag. There was a logo on the side, but I couldn't read it.

I didn't respond.

"My uncle has come by at this early hour to apologize to you, Brianna."

My gaze shot up to Stephan's, eyes wide. He wanted to apologize? To me?

"Yes," his uncle said, clearing his throat again. "I thought we could have breakfast and talk. Do you like bagels?"

I wasn't looking at him until Stephan motioned with his eyes for me to respond. "Um . . . yes?" Stephan's hold tightened briefly around my waist, and I knew he was trying to encourage me. "Yes," I said, firmer this time. "I . . . I like bagels."

"Good," Dr. Cooper said. It was then I noticed how tense he'd been as his shoulders relaxed at my positive response.

"Brianna." My head whipped back around at the sound of Stephan's voice. "Why don't you get the milk and juice, and bring it to the table."

I nodded, and left his side to complete my task.

Stephan and his uncle sat opposite each other as I placed the drinks on the table. I stood, unsure what to do. Normally, I would join him for breakfast. My gaze met Stephan's, and he nodded toward the chair. I breathed a sigh of relief and sat down.

Dr. Cooper had brought all different kinds of bagels. He said he wasn't sure which kind I'd like, and insisted I be the first to pick the one I wanted. I wasn't sure about that. I mean, I never went before Stephan. It just didn't feel right.

"It's okay, Brianna. Pick the one you want."

I looked at his face, making sure it was really okay, before reaching out and picking one with blueberries and placing it on the napkin in front of me.

Stephan and his uncle each chose a bagel for themselves, and then Dr. Cooper pushed a tub of cream cheese toward me. Hesitantly, I opened it and put some on my bagel. Then I offered it to Stephan.

He smiled and took it from me, spreading some of the white cheese on his own bagel. When he was finished, he handed the container to his uncle before taking a bite. As soon as he'd begun eating, I did as well.

I was trying to relax like he'd said. He was right here with me, and I trusted that he wouldn't let anything bad happen to me, but I knew his uncle was watching. I could feel his eyes on me.

Halfway through my bagel, Dr. Cooper cleared his throat again. "As I said earlier, Brianna, I wanted to come by this morning to apologize to you. I won't pretend that I completely agree with Stephan on this matter, but I can see for myself that you've improved over your time here. I can't dispute that."

He pushed back from the table a little, and I tensed. I felt Stephan's comforting hand on my leg.

My gaze met his uncle's. It was difficult for me to continue to look at him, but I tried. "Stephan has informed me that in my worry for you I've caused you distress, and for that, I am truly sorry."

I swallowed. He seemed to be waiting on me to say something. "Okay."

Dr. Cooper stayed for another half an hour. He calmly ate another bagel, and talked casually with Stephan. I heard some discussion about the two of us going to Sunday dinner again, but Stephan responded that he'd think about it.

When he got up to leave, he asked Stephan to walk him down to the lobby.

Stephan hugged me and gave me a brief kiss before leaving with his uncle, telling me to go get dressed. I was nervous the entire time he was gone. Dr. Cooper must have wanted to talk about something he didn't want me to hear. I only hoped he wasn't trying to convince Stephan that I should leave.

## Stephan

As soon as I'd realized it was my uncle calling, I assumed the worst. It didn't take a genius to realize that by showing up unannounced, he was hoping to get a better glimpse of our lives. I wasn't sure if he was hoping he'd catch us in the middle of something or just wanted to catch us off guard. Either way, I wasn't thrilled, but he was my uncle, so I gave him more leeway than most.

Thankfully, he behaved himself. Brianna was nervous—she had every right to be after their last encounter—but she'd done well. Her fear had not gripped her to the point she was unable to react or respond.

I knew Richard's gaze kept drifting toward Brianna throughout our meal. He was watching our interaction closely.

When he asked me to walk him downstairs, I wasn't surprised. I was sure he'd have an opinion on this morning.

He didn't disappoint. As soon as the elevator doors closed, he began. "Don't you think you're a little old to be leaving love bites?"

I couldn't help but laugh. Here I was thinking he was going to comment on Brianna's reluctance to select a bagel or her waiting to begin eating until I had started, but no. *No.* He zeroed in on the now-barely-there hickey I'd left on her. "You're going to lecture me about giving a girl a hickey? I'm not sixteen anymore, Richard."

"No," he said. "You're nearly twenty-five years old with a young woman in there who trusts you to take care of her. And against my better judgment, I'm trying to accept that neither you nor she is willing to seek professional help. But Stephan, do you really think that acting this way is the best thing for her? I've done some research into your . . . lifestyle. It still seems . . . barbaric to me, but I do see where the rules and structure could be good for her. I just don't think sexual—"

"Enough," I said. I kept my voice even, but firm. "What I do or don't do with Brianna, sexually or otherwise, is not your business. I wouldn't do anything to her that she doesn't wish for me to do. You're just going to have to accept that, whether you like it or not."

"Surely, you're not thinking . . . ?"

"Let me ask you this. How many years do you think it would take a therapist to get her to the point she is now? You saw her in the beginning. You know how bad she was. Can you honestly tell me that a professional could do better?"

He was shaking his head. I knew he didn't like what I was saying. "The speed of the recovery is not the point. It is the overall health of the patient that—"

"She is *not* a patient!"

His face paled. I couldn't remember the last time I'd raised my voice to my uncle.

The elevator doors opened, and he stepped forward, turning his back against one of the doors to hold it open. "I'm sorry I upset you. It wasn't my intention. I *am* trying here, but I won't pretend that I'm not concerned for her well-being, or what you're doing with her. She's vulnerable right now. I won't say anything else in front of her because, you're right, it will only upset her. I will not, however, censor my thoughts or feelings from you on the matter." He took a deep breath and turned to look out into the parking garage. "Your aunt would like for you to come to dinner again. Both of you. I understand if that doesn't mean tomorrow, but it would mean a lot to her if it was soon."

He didn't wait for my answer before stepping out and allowing the doors to close behind him.

The ride back up to my condo seemed to take forever. I knew we couldn't avoid my family long term, but I wasn't ready to face dinner with them again. Jimmy and Samantha had been there last week, and chances were they'd be regular guests for the foreseeable future. I was pretty sure Jimmy would leave us alone unless his wife put pressure on him again.

Diane wasn't a problem. The concern there was more of her smothering Brianna with affection than anything else. Just the thought of my aunt doting over Brianna made me smile. I was hoping Brianna would be in my life for a long time, and it was good that at least one of my family members loved her.

No. Richard was the big hurdle, but I had to admit today's visit had gone better than expected, even with *the talk*. I'd asked him not to upset Brianna, and he'd followed my instructions. I had to pick my battles.

Walking through the door of my condo, I scanned the room for Brianna. I'd told her to get dressed while I was gone, but that shouldn't have taken long.

I headed to her room to see if she was perhaps still getting ready. What I found caused a deep ache in my chest. Brianna was dressed and sitting on her bed, her knees pulled up to her chest. I couldn't see her face, but by her posture, I could tell she was upset.

The bed shifted as I climbed onto it to sit beside her. I reached for her. At the feel of my touch, Brianna turned and clung to me as if her life depended on it. She was crying.

"Shh. You're okay," I said, running my fingers through her hair. She climbed onto my lap, and I held her. As she calmed down, I brushed the hair away from her face. "Tell me why you're so upset."

"I don't know."

With my index finger, I lifted her chin so she was looking at me. "Yes, you do. What are you feeling?"

She started to look down, but I adjusted my grip on her chin. "I'm not . . . good enough and . . ."

"And?"

"How could Dr. Cooper believe that horrible woman? How could he . . . ?"

The words died in her throat as more tears fell. I wiped them away with my thumbs.

"First of all, you *are* good enough, Brianna. I'm not sure why you think you're not. As for my uncle believing Tami . . . I think it was more shock than anything. My uncle, as many parents, continues to see the children they raised—or helped raise, in this case—as kids. It's hard enough for them to acknowledge their children have sex lives, let alone ones that include things that are outside of the norm."

"You're not a bad person," she said in a firm, determined voice.

"Thank you." I smiled, kissing her forehead.

With that, she smiled and snuggled back into my chest.

I'd had plans for us this morning that included working out and then a walk in the park, but I was content to sit with her on her bed for now. There was always tomorrow.

# Chapter 14

**Stephan**

*We both ended up falling asleep on her bed.*

The only woman I'd ever woken up in bed with was my first submissive, Sarah, and it had never felt like this. With Sarah, I'd been indifferent about it. The few times it had happened were more accident than anything else, much as this had been. But with Sarah, there hadn't been this warm feeling that waking up next to her was where I most wanted to be. I began working on excuses to get Brianna into my bed.

What struck me the most, however, was that this feeling wasn't only sexual. That desire was still there, but if all I could do was hold her, then I would take it.

The phone rang, causing Brianna to shift on my lap. I answered it before it could wake her. "Hello."

"Good afternoon, Mr. Coleman." I glanced at the clock beside her bed and saw that it was in fact after noon. I'd need to wake her soon, whether I wanted to or not. "There is a Mr. Cal Ross here to see Miss Reeves."

I glanced down at her sleeping form. Even if she had been awake, she'd had a stressful morning and, if I was being honest with myself, I needed some time with her today that was just us. "Let me talk to him."

"Yes, sir."

A few seconds passed before I heard Cal's voice come on the line. "Anna?"

"No."

"Where's Anna, Coleman?" he barked.

"Brianna is unavailable at the moment."

"Why?"

I took a deep breath, trying to calm myself. It wouldn't do any good losing my temper with him. "She's taking a nap."

"Oh," he said, as if not expecting such a simple answer. It didn't take him long to recover, however. "Will you tell her I came by to see her?"

"Yes. However, might I suggest that you call first before you show up on my doorstep?"

"Why?"

"Because it's rude to show up unannounced." Did his parents not teach him any manners?

Silence.

"I don't have your number."

"That can be easily fixed if you ask for it. *Politely*."

I heard him exhale loudly. "May I please have your phone number so I may call Brianna?"

I played with Brianna's hair as I rattled off the number to him. Seconds later, the line went dead. I guessed it was too much to ask him to say thank you.

Closing my eyes, I let all thoughts of Cal Ross disappear and concentrated on the feel of Brianna's hair between my fingers. It was long and soft. I couldn't help but think of all the things I could do with her beautiful hair.

I let her sleep another twenty minutes before gently waking her.

Groggily, she turned to look up at me. "Hi," she said, looking embarrassed to find her head in my lap.

"Hi," I smiled. "How did you sleep?"

"Good," she blushed, glancing down.

I knew I hadn't been unaffected by her presence, but I was also trying very hard to ignore it. Her staring at my rapidly growing anatomy wasn't helping. Her mouth was so close. I could feel her warm breath through my jeans. I tightened my grip on her hair, and her eyes locked with mine. It would be so very easy to tell her to unzip my jeans and take me into her mouth. I still hadn't forgotten the last time. I wasn't sure I ever would. Her gaze held mine, and I knew without a doubt that all I had to do was give the word.

But I couldn't. She wasn't ready. It had been less than a week since she'd panicked from me touching her.

Reluctantly, I removed my hand from her hair and let it fall to the bed.

"Are you hungry?" I needed a distraction, and food seemed like the perfect choice.

"Yes, a little."

"Go clean yourself up. I'll wait here, and then we'll go get something."

She nodded, and walked into her bathroom.

I spent the time she was gone trying to calm myself down. That was too close, and I didn't want to do anything that either of us would regret.

**Brianna**

I splashed water on my face, trying to get the sleep out of my eyes. My reflection looked back at me with uncertain eyes. Why had he stopped? I could see—feel—that he wanted it.

But even as I asked the question, I knew that it was me. I had messed up. It was my fault he wasn't touching me anymore. I just didn't know how to fix it.

Maybe Lily would know. He told me that I could ask her anything, so I could ask her this, right?

The tips of my fingers grazed over my lips and then down to my breasts. I wanted to feel that warmth again, the tingly feeling his hands left on my skin.

I took a deep breath and closed my eyes. *Lily.* She'd know what to do.

For the rest of the weekend, I wasn't out of Stephan's sight for long. We worked out together, took a walk in the park, and he even helped me make dinner Sunday. But what he didn't do was push anything physical.

Monday came and went as I debated whether I could really call Lily and ask her such a question. By Tuesday morning, I was no closer to the answer. So instead of spending another day arguing with myself, I called Lily as soon as I hit send on my eight o'clock text to Stephan.

"Brianna!" Lily said with excitement.

"Hi, Lily."

"Is everything okay? I mean, not that I'm not glad you called, but I'm usually the one calling you."

"I . . ." Maybe this wasn't the best idea.

"You can ask me anything, you know. Even if it's about Stephan."

I closed my eyes and mentally crossed my fingers.

"How do I get him to touch me again?" I said, as quickly as I could get it out. I just hoped she understood what I'd said and I didn't have to repeat myself.

"What do you mean by *get him to touch you again*? What's he not doing that he was?"

"He hasn't . . . since last week. I panicked . . ."

"Ah," she said. "He's stopped the sexual stuff."

"Yes," I said, breathing a sigh of relief that she understood.

"Have you asked him? Talked to him about why he stopped?"

I pressed my lips together. There it was again. Talking. Communication.

"No," I admitted.

"Maybe that's what he's waiting for."

I continued to think about what Lily had said long after I hung up the phone. And the more I thought about it, the more I believed she could be right. I was sleeping on the floor beside his bed, texting him, following him around because I hadn't talked to him about something that was bothering me. Now this was bothering me, and I still wasn't talking. What was wrong with me?

When he came through the door that evening, I had talked myself into talking to him a dozen times. I'd also talked myself *out* of talking to him a dozen times.

He walked over to me, and pulled me into his arms.

Dinner was quiet as usual. I knew I was allowed to talk whenever, but it just didn't feel right unless he was holding me. It also helped if we were sitting in his chair.

I cleaned up before going to sit with him. Since I'd been texting him what I was doing throughout the day, our evening conversations had changed a little. Instead of asking me *what* I did, he'd ask me questions about what I'd told him I'd done.

Because I'd called Lily right after I'd texted him that morning, and the call ended well before the next text, I'd not mentioned talking to her. I knew it was time. I needed to do this. Lily was right. He was probably waiting for me to say something.

"I called Lily."

"Did you?" I couldn't see his face since I was in my favorite position with my head on his shoulder, but he sounded surprised.

"Yes." I pressed my lips together, nervous. "Was that okay?"

"Of course," he said, running his fingers gently down my arm. "It's just that you've never called her before on your own. I'm proud of you."

I breathed a sigh of relief and smiled.

When I didn't say anything else, he asked, "You know you can talk to Lily about anything you wish. Is there a reason you brought her up?"

"Yes. I . . . I called to ask her something."

"Oh?"

"She said I should talk to you."

To my surprise, he chuckled. I didn't know how I felt about that. Why was he laughing?

"And what are you to talk to me about, Brianna?" When I didn't answer right away, he shifted me in his lap and lifted my chin so I was looking at him. "Talk to me," he said, seriously.

"You . . . you haven't . . . touched me . . . since I . . . since I . . ." I could feel the moisture pooling in my eyes.

"Deep breaths. You can do this."

"Don't you want me anymore?" I whispered.

"Do you still want that?"

"Yes," I nodded. "I'll do better. I promise. I'll . . ."

He pressed his index finger against my lips, stopping my anxious words. "Thank you," he said. "I've been waiting to see if you'd approach me. I'm very glad you did, even if you spoke to Lily first. She gave you good advice. You need to be able to come to me with these things, Brianna. With everything. Good or bad."

I nodded, and when he released my face, I lay my head on his shoulder once again.

We sat there for a long time watching a movie on television. I only watched parts of it. I was too lost in my thoughts.

Did this mean that we'd be starting again? I thought it did.

I played with the buttons on the front of his shirt as I tried to think of ways I could make sure what happened the last time didn't happen again. But as much as I didn't want to panic or have a flashback, I wasn't sure I could stop it from happening no matter how much I wanted to.

Talk to him. I just had to remember to talk to him. It wasn't my panic that got me into trouble the last time, it was my *not* talking.

I closed my eyes and took slow even breaths, enjoying the feel of his hands as they rubbed gently on my back.

Suddenly, I realized the television wasn't on anymore. The room was quiet except for our breathing. I looked up at him, wondering if something was wrong.

"Time for bed, Brianna."

Nodding, I stood reluctantly. I couldn't believe it was time already. I didn't want him to let me go yet.

He cupped my face. "Go get your nightclothes and bring them into my bedroom with you. Do not change. You have five minutes, Brianna." Then he disappeared into his room.

# Chapter 15

**Brianna**

*I was nervous. And excited. He had something planned. As quickly as I* could, I brushed my teeth, gathered up my nightclothes, and made a dash into the bathroom before going to his room.

When I entered, he was still fully dressed, minus his shoes. My brow wrinkled in confusion. Every other night, he'd been waiting for me in his boxers. He smiled and walked toward me. I pressed my lips together, and I could feel my teeth biting into my lip.

"Relax, Brianna. Trust me."

I nodded, and tried to take some deep breaths. His right hand came down to tangle with mine as he walked backward, leading me into his bathroom.

This bathroom was so much bigger than mine. I'd been in it once before, but its size still amazed me. There was a large counter with two sinks lining half of one wall. Each sink had tall mirrors topped with bright lights. On the other side of the room was a large bathtub that looked as if it could fit more than one person. It was deep, wide, and very different from the bathtub in my house in Dallas, or even the one at John's.

I quickly closed my eyes and blocked that out. I didn't want to think about my father. Instead, I continued to follow him farther into the bathroom. We came to a stop in the back corner beside a large glass door.

He released my hand, took my nightclothes from me, and placed them on a bench I hadn't noticed to my left. "I want your eyes on me at all times," he said before he reached for the hem of my shirt and lifted it smoothly over my head.

I tried my best to obey him as he removed each article of my clothing. He didn't go slow as he had in the past. It was quick and efficient, and soon I was standing naked before him, feeling more exposed and bare than I had in two months.

He brushed his fingers across my cheek and trailed them down the side of my neck following the curve of my breast down to my waist. I closed my eyes automatically at feeling his touch again.

"Eyes open," he reminded me, and I quickly raised my gaze to look at him.

There was always something so intense about his eyes. The mixture of green and brown was unlike anything I'd ever seen before as he stared back at me.

"Now, I want you to undress me."

I froze. He wanted me to *what*?

As if sensing my hesitation, he took my hand and placed it against his chest, right over the buttons of his shirt, the same ones I'd been playing with earlier. I gazed up at him, questions in my eyes that I was too afraid to voice.

"Go on," he said. "I can't very well take my shower fully dressed, now can I?" He gave me a little smile.

Okay. I can do this. With shaky hands, I unbuttoned his shirt, fumbling the entire way. I kept glancing up at him to see if he was getting upset with me since I wasn't able to get him undressed as quickly as he'd been able to undress me, but there was no sign of anger or impatience in his face. He just stood there, waiting.

Finally, his shirt was unbuttoned, and he helped me push it off his arms so it fell to the floor. He'd taken my clothes and placed them in a hamper beside the bench, so I did the same with his shirt.

When I reached for the button on his pants, my hands were shaking. This was so much harder than what I'd thought it would be. I'd never undressed a man before. I could see the fabric straining against what lay beneath. He was aroused, and although I knew I wanted this, it didn't calm my fears.

He cupped my face, bringing my gaze back to his. Instead of speaking, however, he leaned down and kissed me. It was soft and gentle, but it made me feel tingly and warm just the same. "Slow, deep breaths," he reminded me when he ended the kiss.

Right. Slow, deep breaths. I'd seen naked men before. I could do this.

I released the button on the dark blue suit pants he wore, and with a deep breath I lowered the zipper and let the pants fall from his hips.

I stood staring with my hands hanging in midair. He was still wearing his boxers, but unlike the other times I'd seen him in this state, I knew that in moments the thin fabric hiding him from my view would no longer be there. He wasn't going to shower with his boxers on.

It moved under my scrutiny. Had that ever happened before? My mind couldn't help but think back to all the men who had used me over the last year, and when it did, I felt the panic rise within my chest. Breathing became more difficult. I couldn't get enough air in my lungs. Pinching my eyes closed, I tried to make the images stop.

I felt hands on my arms, my face. Who . . . ?

"Brianna," a voice said through what sounded like a tunnel. "Brianna," it said again, louder this time, closer. "Open your eyes. Look . . . at . . . me."

I didn't want to open my eyes. I knew what I'd find.

But the voice was persistent. Repeatedly, it called my name.

Slowly, I opened my eyes, bracing for whatever horror I would find waiting for me this time. Instead, I was greeted with Stephan's eyes, full of concern and something else I wasn't sure what to name.

Once I realized it was him—and what I'd done—I dropped my head in shame. How could I spoil this? I'd asked him if we could start again, and before he'd even really touched me I panicked.

I felt arms come around me, pulling against his bare chest, and all I wanted to do was get as close to him as I could. Why was this so hard?

"Tell me what happened," he asked after I'd calmed down.

"I saw . . . it move."

He chuckled. "My penis, you mean?" I nodded, and he laughed again. "Well, he does tend to do that when a beautiful woman is staring at him."

I peeked up from my spot against his chest to find him staring down at me. "He . . . moves?"

Leaning down, his lips grazed mine. "Yes. He has a very hard time staying still when you're nearby, Brianna."

I didn't know how I felt about that. There was fear, sure, but I loved when he called me beautiful, and he reacted like that because he found me beautiful, right? Everything I felt when it came to him was so confusing.

"What did you think when you saw him move? You seemed to go somewhere in your head. Did you have another flashback?"

I didn't know if it was a flashback. It was different from what had happened before. "I couldn't remember if I'd seen that happen before. Then, I started to remember times when . . . the other men would . . . but I don't remember," I cried in frustration.

His arms tightened around me. "Shh. You're safe. They can't hurt you now."

I held tight to him, my fingers digging into the skin on his back. I couldn't get close enough.

I have no idea how long we stood there, but eventually, he held me slightly away from him and said, "I'm going to give you a choice. We can get dressed and go to bed, or we can continue with what I planned for tonight."

There really was no choice. For almost a week, I'd wanted him to touch me again. "I want to continue, Sir."

He smiled, and kissed me. "Okay." Then he took my hands, and placed my fingers on the elastic waistband of his boxers. "Finish undressing me so we can have our shower."

**Stephan**

Seeing Brianna panic sent a pain through my chest every time. And even though I knew it was a necessary evil, given what she'd been through, it didn't make it any easier.

Her throat moved as she swallowed nervously. I knew it might take a moment or two, but she'd do what I'd requested. It took a very long two-and-a-half minutes, but her fingers dipped inside my boxers and pulled them down, releasing my erection into full view.

The boxers pooled at my feet, and I kicked them off and away from us. I could see how nervous she was, but she was trying to be brave. I was proud of her. Slipping my hand in hers, I backed us up into the large shower enclosure.

I loved my shower. Pink and cream marble covered every inch, and there were showerheads in both the ceiling and the walls, and a marble bench along the back wall where I kept all my shower supplies sitting in a neat line. Making sure Brianna was out of the spray, I turned on the water, letting it warm before pulling us farther into the shower.

The water felt glorious against my skin as it always did, hard enough to work out the tension in my muscles, yet soothing enough to relax. Brianna had dutifully followed me into the cascade of water, but still looked hesitant. I pulled her now-slick body against mine. It was the first time I'd felt her skin to skin like this, and I sucked in a deep breath. The contact felt amazing.

I ran my hand up her arm, her neck, before cupping the back of her head and bringing her lips to mine. She opened beneath my prompting quickly, but her hands remained firmly at her sides. "Touch me," I urged. There'd be a time in the future when I'd want her arms bound and out of my way for my pleasure, but that time was not now. Now, I needed to feel her hands on me. She needed to explore my body, to become comfortable with it.

Tentatively, her fingers made contact with my chest, and I hummed in approval as I enjoyed the sweet flavors of her mouth. She tasted of the mint from her toothpaste, but as always, there was the hint of something that was just her.

Gradually, she gained courage and her hands increased their movements, but I could still feel her tension. Breaking our kiss, I looked down into her eyes. They were dilated, darker than usual, and I was pleased. Beyond our first two weeks together, she seemed to enjoy our kissing. It was nice to know the lack of clothing hadn't changed that.

Stepping back slightly, I reached for the shower gel. "Give me your hand." She did, and I squirted a large amount of the gel into her palm. Lifting her chin, I forced her eyes upward and her gaze met mine. "I want you to wash me, Brianna." I could see the question in her eyes. "All of me. I don't care where you start, or where you end, but I want you to wash every inch of my skin." Once the words left my mouth, I took a step back, giving her room, and waited.

At first, she didn't move. Her gaze dropped down to the gel in her hand

and back to me. It was slightly amusing to watch, although I wished it wasn't so difficult for her. If she could gain some confidence, that would help her. I never wanted her to fear touching me.

Instead of prompting her again, I waited.

She started to move twice but stopped herself, before finally taking the step that would bring her close enough to my body where she could touch me again. She pressed her lips together as she rubbed her hands to create lather.

In many ways, it was fascinating watching her work through things. Sometimes her mind worked in the most simplistic of ways. Other times, the detail she put into things amazed me. I knew that most of that came from her having to overthink everything when she was with Ian, making sure it was the right choice because if she chose wrong the punishments would be severe. Nevertheless, her strength to push through her fear and not be a mindless robot made me love her more. I wanted to give her everything, including taking her to heights of pleasure she couldn't even imagine, if she'd allow me.

She pressed her small palms gently against my shoulders in tiny circles before moving lower to my chest. She glanced up at me, and I smiled encouragingly, letting her know I was pleased. This seemed to give her the boost she needed, and with a deep breath, she soldiered on. She took extra care washing my torso, back, and legs before standing back up and washing my face. There was only one area of my body left to wash and we both knew it.

Brianna's hands shook slightly as they began on my hips and moved inward. It was a painstakingly slow process, but eventually she made it to my penis. Then she stopped.

I waited, but she still didn't move. "What's wrong?" I asked.

"How do I . . . wash . . . it?"

I smiled. "Just be gentle. Other than that, you can wash him anyway you want to."

She seemed to think on that for a moment before reaching out one finger and touching. My penis bobbed in response, and she jerked her hand back. I chuckled.

Hesitantly, she reached out again. She was more prepared this time, and didn't react when he moved.

I watched as she softly used only the tips of her fingers to massage the soap into my penis, and then lower between my legs. The desire to have her use a firmer touch was there, but I didn't voice it. As with so many things when it came to Brianna, I assumed this was the first time she'd touched a man this way. From what she'd told me of her encounters with men, there hadn't been a lot of touching on her part. She was mostly just used and tossed away. I wouldn't treat an animal that way, much less a person.

Once she appeared satisfied that she'd washed all of me, she let her arm fall back down to her side, and her gaze dropped to the floor. Her lips pressed together again, and I could only imagine what was racing through her mind.

Turning to the side, I rinsed the remaining soap from my body before turning back to her. She looked so small when she was like this, although she was average size for a woman. Over the two months she'd been with me, she'd put on some much-needed weight. I could no longer see the outline of her hip bones beneath her flesh. Now her body was nicely rounded in all the areas it should be.

I took a deep breath. It would do me no good to get distracted, no matter how tempting seeing her like this was.

Closing the distance between us, I leaned in and brushed her damp hair away from her ear. She stood ramrod straight, waiting. "I do believe you forgot something," I said, allowing my lips to skim over her ear and down to her throat before stepping back.

She looked up at me with wide eyes, and I could practically see the wheels turning in her head as she tried to figure it out.

Deciding to help her out just a little, I leaned back into the spray again, this time wetting my hair. When I righted myself again, she was dutifully standing there with the shampoo bottle. I lifted my hand to her cheek, and caressed her soft skin to let her know I was pleased. Her gaze dropped to the floor, and I saw the hint of a smile tugging at her lips.

Dropping my hand, I leaned forward, presenting my hair to her. She wasted no time opening the bottle and lathering the shampoo into my hair. Her fingers grazed over my scalp much as she did when we were kissing in my chair, and I watched my body react to her innocent ministrations.

Eventually, her fingers left my scalp, and I rinsed the soapy residue from my hair. After repeating much of the same process again with conditioner, I picked the body wash back up and squeezed more of the gel into my own hand. "I'm going to wash you now, Brianna, and I want you to keep your eyes on me while I do, do you understand?"

She nodded. I just hoped that having me in her line of sight would help ward off any major panic or flashbacks.

I began slowly, starting at her shoulders, just as she'd done to me. Although I didn't think washing her back would cause a reaction, I stayed in front of her just the same, reaching around. It brought us chest to chest, and I could feel her nipples pressing against me. They weren't completely soft; however, it was no more than what a chill would do, and I wondered if her body was reacting to mine, or if it was *just* a chill.

"Are you cold?"

"N . . . no."

So maybe it was me. I smiled as I continued to wash her, bringing my hands back to her front. I glided my hands over her breasts, massaging each one carefully to ensure cleanliness, and watched as each nipple became harder under my palms. Her breasts felt good in my hands, and I had to resist the urge to pinch the tips. She wasn't ready for that.

Moving lower, I rubbed soap over her stomach before moving down to her legs. Her gaze followed me as I kneeled before her, working soap over her calves and thighs. She was doing well. Although she was breathing heavily, there was no note of panic in her expression.

I stood up, and added some more gel to my hands. "I'm going to wash between your legs now, Brianna. Remember to keep your eyes open and on me at all times."

She took a deep breath and pressed her lips together as if bracing herself.

Making sure my eyes never left her face, I placed my hands on her ass. My fingers lingered, enjoying the feel of her in my palms before slipping into the crack separating her cheeks. She tensed as I neared her rectum, but I could see she was trying to stay calm.

"Good girl," I whispered.

Keeping one hand behind her, I brought the other to her front and slipped it between her legs. I could feel the moisture from the water and some of her own as well, but it was minimal. As much as I would have liked to have dipped my fingers inside her, that would have taken a lot more preparation. Tonight was about getting to know each other's bodies better.

With great restraint, I kept my fingers outside her warmth and finished cleaning her. Her eyes never left mine the entire time, and while her breathing had halted briefly when I'd lingered near her entrance, she'd not panicked.

I stepped back, instructing her to rinse. I took the shampoo and washed her hair for her. This time, I turned her back to me, and let my fingers massage and relax her. She leaned back against me, and I thought I heard a soft moan of pleasure escape her. I smiled and delighted in the moment.

After having her rinse the shampoo and conditioner from her hair, I shut the water off and led her out of the shower. She took the towel I gave her, and watching me start to dry myself off, followed my example.

By the time we were both dressed and under the covers—me in my bed and her on the floor beside me—I was smiling. She'd done well tonight. I couldn't wait for tomorrow.

# Chapter 16

**Brianna**

*I woke up Wednesday morning on the floor beside his bed as I had for the* last week. It was early. He was still asleep.

Last night had been . . . I couldn't quite put it into words. I'd been so afraid that he'd call everything off when I'd started to panic, but he didn't. He'd helped me just as he always did.

The shower was not what I'd expected. I'd assumed he'd touch me, but I'd not expected him to have me wash him first. His body felt so different, and yet so familiar, under my hands. I liked feeling his chest and back. Even his legs were nice. It was the rest of it that made me unsure. After the way my life had been for the last year, I'd not even considered being able to touch a man like that so freely, and yet, Stephan had allowed me to do so.

Washing him like that—feeling him in my hands—was different. I'd seen many different sizes and shapes of the male anatomy over the last year, but I'd never taken the time and actually looked. He was hard and yet soft at the same time, and every time I touched him, his penis would move.

I had to admit, I was nervous about washing him like that. Stephan had told me repeatedly he wouldn't have sex with me until I asked him to, but what if I did something and he couldn't control himself? That happened, right? But he'd just stood there while I cleaned him. I knew I shouldn't have doubted him after everything, but I'd breathed a sigh of relief when I was finished.

The beeping of the alarm brought me back to the present, and I heard Stephan stir above me. Instead of waiting as I usually did for him to get out of bed, I dug my way out from under my blanket and knelt before the bed. He said he liked it when I knelt like this for him, and I wanted to give something back to him after last night. He was so good to me.

His legs came into view as he sat up on the side of the bed, but for a long moment he didn't do anything else. I waited, a little anxious. It had been a while since I'd knelt for him like this, and I had no idea how he'd react. I hoped he'd like it. Then I felt his hands. I sighed, happy, as his fingers tangled in my hair. I'd missed this.

"Good morning, Brianna."

"Good morning."

"And to what do I owe this lovely sight of you kneeling before my bed this morning?"

"I wanted to say thank you for last night."

"Is that all?" he asked as his fingers dug deeper into my scalp, making my body feel as if I was going to melt into his hands.

"No, Sir. I . . . I missed kneeling for you."

"Hmm. Well, we will have to change that, then, won't we?"

He slid his hands down to the base of my neck and tilted my head up. Our eyes met for a brief moment before he leaned down and placed a lingering kiss on my lips.

When our mouths parted, he smiled at me while running his thumb over my lower lip. "You're getting much better at thank you's," he said.

Before I could respond, he stood and walked to his bathroom, leaving me where I was. I scrambled after him. He left the door open as he usually did, but unlike what he'd done for the past week, he'd not given me any instructions on whether I should wait outside or follow him inside.

It was then I realized that my week was over. I was no longer required to stay with him all the time. Standing outside his bathroom door, I felt a little lost.

I was still standing there when he walked out of his bathroom.

"Are you all right, Brianna?"

"Yes. I just . . . I forgot that . . . I was waiting for your instructions, but then realized . . ."

"And you're feeling unsure?"

I nodded.

He took me by the hand and led me over to sit on the edge of his bed. "That's understandable. You've had me there giving you instructions on almost everything for the last week. But the point of this past week's exercise was not to take your freedom away from you, Brianna. It was to force you to communicate your thoughts and your feelings to me. Just because you'll no longer be following me around now doesn't mean that's changed."

"I know. I just . . ." I tried to find the right words to describe what I was feeling, "missed it."

He smiled, but it wasn't a completely happy smile. "I understand that as well. You had someone dictate your every move for ten months. You may not have enjoyed it, given what Ian likes, but it is what you became used to. I gave you that back to some extent, but Brianna, I don't want you to be a mindless robot that just does everything I tell her to do because I demand it.

There will be times, yes, when I will expect my word to be taken as law, and I will expect full and immediate compliance from you, but even then, I never want it to be mindless. You are still you, and I happen to like you." He smirked.

"So I don't have to text you anymore?"

"No, you don't have to text me every hour anymore. However, I do hope that if there is something bothering you, even a little, that you will text or call me."

"Okay."

"Now, do you want to freshen up before we have breakfast?" he asked.

"Yes, please."

He placed a chaste kiss on my lips before standing. "I'll be in the kitchen. Join me when you're finished."

Brad came by around ten to adjust my exercise routine. Apparently, they were getting too easy for me and he was afraid my muscles would get memory or something. He went on and on about it. He lost me after a few minutes, and I just did the new things he showed me.

I liked Brad. He was nice, and he never made me feel like he was going to hurt me.

After showering, I made myself some lunch, and sat down on the couch with a book. I was just starting a book called *Thread of Grace* that I'd found upstairs in the library. It was about the Italian resistance during World War II, and looked interesting.

Lost in my reading, I almost didn't hear the phone ring. Quickly shutting my book, not bothering to mark the place, I ran across the room to answer it. "Hello?"

"Anna?"

I didn't answer right away. "Wh . . . Who is this?"

"It is you," he sighed. "It's Cal. I thought maybe I'd be more likely to reach you during the day, but I wasn't sure."

Unsure of what I should say, I answered with a simple, "Yes."

"That's what I thought. He's at work, right?"

"Yes."

"Good. I'm glad. I was hoping I could come see you. Maybe we could get coffee or something."

"Um." Stephan had made me promise not to be alone with him, so I didn't know what to do. "Can you . . . can you hold on, please?"

"Sure. Is something wrong, Anna?"

"No. I just . . . give me a minute?"

"I'll be here."

Before I could think about it any farther, I grabbed my cell phone, ran to my bedroom, and dialed Stephan's number.

He answered on the second ring. "Hello, Brianna."

"Hi."

"Is everything all right? You sound nervous about something?"

"Cal called."

"I see."

"He's on the main phone, and he wants to come see me. He said something about going for coffee, but I promised you I wouldn't be alone with him, and I don't know what to do." I knew my words were rushed, but I couldn't help it.

"Do you want to see him?" he asked.

"Yes. I think so."

"I still don't want you to be alone with him, but if you'd like to meet with him, there is a coffee shop a block from the building. I'll call Tom downstairs and have him escort you. He can get one of the security guards to watch the desk while he's gone. Go into my bedroom, and in the drawer beside my bed is some money. Take whatever's there. You can put back what you don't use later. And when you're ready to leave, call me. I'll come pick you up and bring you home. I don't want him walking you, do you understand?"

"Yes, Sir. I understand."

"Please be safe. And if at any time you feel uncomfortable, or need me, you call."

"I will. I promise."

Holding the cell phone firmly against my chest, I walked back into the main room and picked up the phone.

"Cal?"

"I thought you'd gotten lost. I was about to send out a search party."

That made me smile, but feel a little bad at the same time. Had I really been gone that long? "No," I said. "I'm here. There's a coffee shop about a block from here. I can meet you there."

"You don't need to do that, Anna. I can come get you."

"No," I said a little too sharply. "No. I'll . . . I'll meet you there."

"Okay," he said. "Fifteen minutes?"

"Okay."

When I stepped off the elevator into the lobby, Tom was waiting for me. "Good afternoon, Miss Reeves. Mr. Coleman said you needed an escort."

I blushed. "Yes, please."

The walk was quiet. Other than the polite interaction of him opening doors for me, Tom just walked silently beside me to the coffee shop appropriately named *Cup of Joe*.

Tom came inside with me. I wasn't expecting that. When I turned around to ask him, I spotted Cal already sitting at a booth in the back. Tom must have noticed him, too, because he turned to me and said, "Have a good day, Miss Reeves. I'll let Mr. Coleman know you arrived safely."

"Thanks," I swallowed nervously. This was the first time I had really been out on my own, and I reached into my pocket to reassure myself that my cell phone was still there. I could do this.

Cal stood as I got closer to where he sat. "You came," he smiled. I just smiled back and sat down. "What do you want to drink? My treat."

Since I'd never been here, I had no idea what they had. The menu looked daunting, to say the least. "I'll have whatever you're having," I finally said.

"You want a caramel latte? You hate caramel."

Did I? I tried to think back, but I honestly couldn't remember. "What you're having is fine," I repeated. I was too nervous to concentrate on the menu to find something else.

Thankfully, he didn't argue with me anymore, and walked up to the counter to place our order. The place wasn't packed, but there had to be at least twenty other customers there, and it made me want to run back to my room and hide. Instead, I pressed myself as far as I could into the corner and waited.

"Here you go," Cal said, startling me. "Are you sure you're all right?" he asked, sliding in the booth opposite me.

"Y . . . yes. I'm fine."

He frowned. "Are you ever going to tell me what happened to you?"

Without answering him, I took a drink of my caramel latte. It wasn't bad. He was probably right that I didn't like caramel, but I'd had a lot worse things during my time living with Ian. After that, most things, if not my favorite, were more than tolerable.

Cal reached out, and I pulled back. "Anna, please. I'm trying to understand here. Really, I am. You're living with one of the most eligible bachelors in Minneapolis, you act as if you're scared of your own shadow, I'm actually amazed you agreed to have coffee with me, and you don't want me to tell your father where you are. What am I missing?"

"It's complicated."

"So spell it out for me, Anna. I'm here. I'm listening. I'm trying to be your friend, but you've got to help me out here."

Could I do it? Could I tell Cal what had happened to me? I didn't think so. Even when I was in Stephan's arms, I usually panicked when I started talking. Stephan wasn't here right now, and I wasn't going to chance it. What if I lost it and they called the police? John would be notified for sure. I couldn't take that chance.

"I can't talk about it, Cal. I'm sorry. Not here."

"Where, then? I'm not going to hurt you. I hope you know that."

"It's not that."

"Then what is it?"

"I have . . . I panic when I talk about . . . it. I can't . . . not here."

Cal looked around at all the people, and just nodded. "I came by to see you last weekend. Did Coleman tell you?"

"Yes."

"Well, that's something, I suppose," he sighed, seeming almost disappointed. Did he think Stephan wouldn't tell me? "He said he would, but I didn't know."

I asked what I'd been wondering for a while. "Why do you hate him so much?"

"I don't." At my skeptical look, he continued. "Okay, okay. It's just that the man has everything, and it was handed to him on a silver platter. He's what, twenty-four, twenty-five? He runs one of the largest foundations in the Midwest and lives in a penthouse in one of the most expensive parts of downtown. And what did he do to earn it? *Nothing.* It was all given to him dressed up in a nice fancy bow."

"So you don't like him because he has money?"

"It's not that he has money," he said hesitantly. "It's that he didn't work for it."

I didn't like the way he was talking about Stephan, and I shook my head disagreeing with him. "You don't know anything about him. He's helped lots of people. He's helped *me* so much. You shouldn't think bad things about him."

"How has he helped you, Anna? Tell me. Why is it that I should get on the Stephan Coleman bandwagon?"

I felt a mixture of anger at Cal for being so unfair and an ache in my chest I didn't understand. I needed to defend Stephan. It wasn't a want, it was a need, growing deep inside me that overrode everything else. "Because he saved me! He got me out of that horrible place."

It wasn't until the words left my mouth and I realized what I'd just said that the panic seemed to fill me. I knew I had to get away. Looking up, I saw a sign for the restroom. Without thinking, I got up and ran toward it, not stopping until I was safely locked inside the stall. I needed Stephan.

# Chapter 17

**Stephan**

*My day was going well until I received the call from Brianna telling me* Ross wanted to have coffee with her. There was no way I was allowing him into our home with her, without me there. I wasn't thrilled about her having coffee with him at all, but she wanted to see him, and I wasn't going to hold her hostage. She was allowed to have friends, even if I didn't care for them. Since the call, I'd been distracted. I tried to reply to e-mails, but kept having to reread them three and four times because my mind would wander.

Calling Tom to walk her to the coffee shop only eased my mind fractionally. I trusted Tom. He'd been working the front desk for years before I bought my condo, and had always shown the highest professionalism. He'd even called me once he returned to the building, letting me know Brianna had arrived safely and met with her friend. It did nothing to calm me.

I was anxious and knew something could easily happen to trigger one of her panic attacks. She was still fragile. The littlest things set her off.

I tried to refocus on work, but it was useless. Shutting my computer down, I grabbed my jacket and went to tell Jamie I was going home for the day. At the very least, I would be closer to her. Maybe that would make me feel better.

Just as I reached my car, my phone buzzed in my pocket. Brianna's name lit up the screen. I answered the called, but before I could get anything out, I heard her sobbing.

"I . . . I need you. I . . . I . . ."

"Shh. It's okay Brianna," I said, not wasting any time getting into my car. "Where are you?"

"C . . . coffee . . . shop." She hiccupped.

"Are you safe?"

"Yes," she said, seeming to have calmed down a little.

"Stay where you are, and keep talking to me. I'm on my way."

"Okay," she whispered.

"Tell me what you did this morning. Did you read any more of your book?" I was trying to distract her. Even breaking every speed law, it was going to take me at least five minutes to make the normal ten minute drive, and that was if too many red lights didn't stop me. It was downtown Minneapolis, after all.

"Yes. Only a chapter."

"What do you think so far?"

"I . . . I like the history."

"Yes, I liked that about it, too. You don't see that many books written about the Italian side of things during World War II."

Pulling up to the curb outside my building, I jumped out and walked as quickly as I could to the coffee shop.

"I'm here, Brianna. Where are you?"

"In the bathroom."

It wouldn't have taken me long to find it even if I'd not already known where it was located. Several people were crowded around the door leading to the women's bathroom. There with them, standing as close to the door as humanly possible, was Ross.

Pushing my way through the group of people, I reached out to open the door. Ross's hand landed on my arm for a brief second before my glare caused him to pull it away. I walked inside leaving him, and the others, behind.

"Brianna?"

The door to the back stall flew open and Brianna appeared. Her eyes were red-rimmed from crying, and her hair was a mess.

I opened my arms and she ran into them, starting to sob again. "Shh. You're fine now. I'm right here." She held on tighter as I rubbed her back trying to soothe her.

I had no idea how long we stood there. It took a while for her to completely calm down, although her sobs did lessen quickly. With some paper towels, I cleaned the tearstains from her face. It would also have been nice to get her some water to drink, but short of drinking directly from the faucet that wasn't going to happen.

"We are going to go home now."

She nodded.

I wrapped my left arm around her, and opened the door.

There were still a few people lingering, but most had thankfully moved on. Ross, however, was one of the few remaining. He looked at me with an unsure expression before dropping his gaze to Brianna. A frown pulled at his lips, but he didn't say anything. For that, I was grateful. I wasn't in the mood for his attitude.

Without saying a word, I guided Brianna through the coffee shop and out onto the sidewalk. Although the day was warm, her arms stayed wrapped around my middle as she huddled close. I felt Ross behind us, but chose to ignore him. With no idea what happened, I was trying to be rational and not lash out at him, as difficult as that was.

We walked inside my building, and Tom was there waiting for us. "Good afternoon, Mr. Coleman. I put some money in the meter for you. Did you wish for me to have your car taken to the garage?"

I paused. Putting money into the parking meter hadn't even crossed my mind. "Yes please, Tom. That would be most helpful, and thank you for putting money in the meter for me."

"You're welcome, Mr. Coleman," he said as I continued to move toward the elevator. "I hope you feel better, Miss Reeves."

Brianna didn't respond, but I didn't expect her to. The elevator doors opened, and we stepped inside. Ross followed.

The ride up the elevator was quiet, as was the walk to our condominium. Ross was practically breathing down my neck as I opened the door, led Brianna inside and over to my chair, but thankfully he remained silent. Once she was situated on my lap, her head resting on my shoulder, I spared him a glance. He was watching us with what appeared to be curiosity, rather than the contempt I'd seen on his face in the past.

I didn't offer him a seat, but he eventually sat down on the couch a few feet away. Brianna was still clinging to me, although she was now picking at the buttons on the front of my shirt, so I knew she was better.

Sending her into another panic was the last thing I wanted to do, so I worked to control the tone of my voice.

"What happened?" I didn't care which one of them answered me as long as one of them did.

**Brianna**

"It was my fault," I whispered.

"No. It was mine." Cal's voice echoed through the room, cutting off anything else I was going to say. The force behind it made me curl farther into Stephan, and his arms tightened around me.

"Explain," Stephan demanded, and I knew he wasn't talking to me. He'd never spoken to me like that, even when I'd messed up and ignored his calls.

"I was trying to get her to tell me what happened to her, but she wouldn't. Then you came up. It was a short conversation that ended with her yelling that you saved her and got her out of some horrible place. I knew she was protective of you, I just didn't think she'd react like that." I wasn't looking at Cal, but I heard movement, and the next time he spoke, I could tell he was standing. "You won't tell me what's happened to her. *She* won't tell me . . . I'm supposed to be keeping her whereabouts from her father, who I might point out, has contacted me looking for her. Someone needs to give me a reason why I'm lying to an old family friend who, to my knowledge, is desperate to find his missing daughter!"

I cringed. From what Stephan had told me, I'd been pretty sure John was looking for me. Hearing Cal confirm it—that he'd been in touch with him —sent shivers down my spine.

"If Brianna wants you to know what happened to her, she will tell you when she's ready. Is it too much to ask for you to respect her wishes?" Stephan asked.

"When it puts me in the middle of a situation where I'm clearly missing a huge piece of information, yes, it is too much to ask."

I didn't have to look up to know they were both sneering at each other. Cal had never been one to back down when he thought he was right. I couldn't see Stephan backing down either.

"Sir?" I whispered. Stephan's eyes left Cal's and focused on me. "Will you tell him? Please? I don't think . . . I don't think I can without . . ."

"Are you sure?"

I nodded.

"Okay," he said, kissing my forehead before turning back to Cal. "I'm going to give you the short version. It will tell you what you need to know. Anything else and you are going to have to wait for her to be ready to tell you. I will warn you now, if you push her again and she's not ready, you *will* be answering to me. Are we clear?"

Cal was silent for a long moment. At first, I didn't think he was going to answer, but finally he said, "All right."

I felt Stephan nod once before he started talking. "Up until two months ago, Brianna was held captive as a slave by a wealthy man outside of the city. She had many things done to her, and she has a very difficult time trusting anyone, let alone men. And from everything I've been able to find so far, it looks as if Jonathan Reeves is involved."

"You think Sheriff Reeves sold his own daughter into slavery?" Cal asked. I could hear his disbelief.

"Yes, but more importantly, Brianna believes it. He told her a car was coming to pick her up. That same car took her to her new Master."

Silence filled the room, and my curiosity won out. I glanced up to see Cal standing there with his mouth opening and shutting, but no sound was coming out.

Stephan noticed my change in focus, and brought his lips to my ear. "You okay?"

"Yes." I nodded. "Is Cal . . . ?"

As if hearing his name broke him out of the trance he'd been in, he found his voice again. "Is that true, Anna? You think your dad . . . ?"

"Yes," I croaked out. It was still so hard talking about this.

"I don't believe it," Cal said, but his words didn't seem to be directed at anyone.

"Believe it," Stephan said. "As long as Brianna feels he's a danger, Jonathan Reeves cannot know where his daughter is."

Cal's gaze lingered on mine for a long time before he spoke again. "All right. I won't say anything, but you have to know he's not going to give up. He's going to find her eventually."

Stephan's chest rose and fell harshly beneath me. "I know."

Cal left a short while later, after promising not to mention anything to my father. For the rest of the evening, Stephan stayed close to me. He rarely let me out of his arms, let alone his sight.

We ate Chinese food curled up on the couch watching a movie. I didn't watch much, and I don't think he did either.

When the movie finished, he pulled me onto his lap. "I want to talk to you about what happened with Ross today."

I nodded. I'd known this was coming.

"Do you know what triggered your panic?"

Yes, I knew. And looking back at it now, it seemed rather silly. "I was embarrassed," I mumbled, ducking my face into his shoulder.

"What were you embarrassed about?" he asked, tucking my hair behind my ear.

"I got upset with Cal for continuing to think bad things about you, and I yelled at him. When I looked up, everyone was staring at me, and . . ."

"And you panicked."

I nodded. "I didn't know what to do. I just wanted to get away, to hide. The first thing I saw was the restroom, so I ran in there as fast as I could and locked myself in the back stall."

His lips grazed my ear. "Thank you for calling me."

"I didn't know what to do. I just . . . I needed you."

Stephan lifted my head so he could look into my eyes. "There is nothing wrong with you needing me."

He caressed my jaw and lips with his thumb. Slowly that warm feeling I felt so often when he was near began to spread through my body, and the skin under his thumb tingled. There was no movement besides the slow and steady rhythm of his hand and our breathing. Time seemed to stop altogether.

My gaze dropped to his lips. He hadn't kissed me since this morning. Cal's being here had disrupted our routine, and I'd missed his welcome-home kiss.

He tightened his arms around me, and he slid the hand that had been on my face behind my neck, angling it up. My lips parted as his mouth made contact with mine. The kiss was slow, and he took his time as his tongue probed and explored. Heat from his body seeped into mine where we were connected, and his hand gripped the back of my head, pulling at my hair, bringing back the memory of my head in his lap.

He pulled away, breathing hard. His eyes had a warm glow to them as a smile spread across his face. I smiled back, even though my own breath wasn't close to being back to normal yet.

"Are you ready for our shower?" he asked. His voice was abnormally low and husky.

"Yes," I whispered.

He cupped my face and placed a kiss on my forehead before releasing me. "Go get your things and meet me in my room."

I stood, and turned toward my room. As I did so, I felt his hand swat my butt. It wasn't hard—more of a tap than anything—but it got my attention. I paused, stiff and waiting.

"Hurry."

I wasn't sure what had just happened, but I did as he said, and ran to my room.

# Chapter 18

**Brianna**

*Sun streamed through my window, waking me up. I stretched in my bed,* enjoying the feel of my muscles pulling. It was Saturday morning. I was going to get to spend the whole day with Stephan, and I couldn't keep the smile off my face.

It had been four nights now since we'd started showering together. He'd been very patient with me. That first night, and even the second after such an emotional day, he'd pampered me with kisses and his gentle touch.

Last night had been different. As the water streamed around us, he'd backed me up against the tile wall and kissed me like he had only a few times before. I could still feel the pressure of his lips against my mouth, his body pressing hard against me. He'd then placed my hand on him, and told me to stroke him.

I'd been unsure, but he'd wrapped his hand around mine for a while and showed me how he wanted to be touched. After a few seconds, I got into a rhythm, and he let go, allowing me to move on my own accord. His eyes closed and his head fell to my shoulder as I continued to stroke him. The grip of his hands on my hips felt good, solid. He was there, and everything was okay.

He kissed my neck and whispered to me how good it felt for him. I was happy I could please him like this, and I was okay. After touching him for the last three days, it didn't scare me as it had before. He was still him. Even if he was hard and aroused, it was still Stephan in my hand.

It hadn't taken that long for his breathing to become erratic and staggered. I'd paused for the briefest second, but he pulled me closer and in a slightly hoarse voice told me not to stop. Then he pulled back, making me look at him.

"I'm going to come. Look at me. Only me," he panted, taking my face

Sherri Hayes

firmly in his hands. His face tightened and then released as I felt warmth squirt out onto my hip.

After that, there was more kissing and touching. I could tell I'd made him happy, and I was proud of myself. He'd washed us up and put me to bed before going back to his own bedroom.

As I lay there basking in the morning sun, I felt my nerves returning, but there was a slightly different edge to them now. Sex was coming. I knew that. With every day, it got closer. Now that I'd seen how happy I could make him—how much pleasure I was capable of giving him—I wanted it. But wanting it and being ready for it were two different things. I was still scared—terrified, really—of sex.

Sure, he could touch me, but I still tensed up when his fingers got too close. It was frustrating, but I couldn't help my reactions. I'd had things put inside me, things I'd had no control over, by more men than most women had sexual contact with in their entire lives, over the ten months I spent with Ian. In that time, not one of those men had talked to me or taken even a shred of the care and patience Stephan did with me.

Thinking about all my shortcomings wiped the smile from my face. I wanted to be with Stephan, to give him everything. I just didn't know if I could. He seemed to be content to go at the pace I set, for now, but would that always be the case? What if I wasn't able to have sex with him? What if I tensed up and panicked? What if I froze?

I felt the moisture fill my eyes, and spill over onto my cheeks. No. I wouldn't think like that. A month ago, just the thought of any man, including Stephan, touching me in a sexual way had me trembling in fear, shutting down, and retreating inside myself. Now Stephan could touch me anywhere on my body and I was fine. I enjoyed it.

The next obstacle would be penetration, and I wasn't exactly looking forward to that. Most of the men I'd been with took me hard and fast, and many times, it had been painful. Nothing like the anal sex had been, but it still hurt. I was hoping it wouldn't be like that with Stephan. Nothing else he'd done had been like my other experiences. I was hoping the same would be true when he finally took me.

Movement pulled me from my thoughts, and I smiled as I saw Stephan leaning against the wall looking at me. "Hi."

"Good morning," he smiled, walking toward me. He was dressed in his workout clothes, so I knew we'd be going up to his gym. "How did you sleep?" he asked, brushing hair away from my face.

"Good," I said. I took a chance. "How did you sleep?"

He smiled, and I knew that once again I'd made a good choice. "I slept very well," he said before leaning down and kissing me. The kiss was soft, chaste, and completely innocent. There was none of the heat behind it that he'd shown last night, and I didn't see any evidence of his arousal behind his shorts. "Get dressed," he whispered against my mouth. "We're going to work out before we start our day."

Ten minutes later, we were upstairs in his gym. We stood side by side as we stretched, and I noticed he would glance over at me sometimes with a look I didn't quite understand. He almost looked like he was in pain, but that didn't make sense to me since we were only stretching our muscles. To my knowledge, he'd not done anything to overexert himself yesterday. I wanted to ask him if he was okay, but I didn't know if I should, so I kept quiet. Soon we were finished, and he told me to start on the bike.

Although I was now able to walk on the treadmill without falling, Stephan rarely allowed me on it unless he was standing there beside me. He'd even given Brad instructions that I was not to be on it unsupervised. It still felt strange to be looked after like I was.

My mom had been too sick that last year to look after me. The hospice nurses had shown concern, but my mom wasn't their only patient. They couldn't be there every waking minute. One of them had talked to Mom about sending me to live with John or even putting me in foster care when she started getting sick, but Mom had said no. I'd had to do things not many fifteen-year-olds would do for their mothers, especially toward the end. I'd do it again in a heartbeat, though. My mom was everything to me for most of my life. She deserved everything I could give her and more.

Gentle hands brushed tears from my cheeks, and I opened my eyes to find Stephan staring down at me. "What were you thinking about?" he asked.

I closed my eyes and swallowed hard. "My mom."

He pulled me against his chest, hugging me. "Tell me." He petted my hair, comforting me.

"I was just remembering when she was sick, and how I used to take care of her. One of the nurses tried to get mom to send me to live with . . . my dad . . . or a foster family. They didn't think I should be taking care of my mom like that, but Mom refused. She said that I needed to be with her. She was right." The tears started again, and he held me tighter. "I miss her so much."

"I know. And it's okay to miss her." He paused, and I could feel his breath in my hair as his lips brushed along the top of my head. "I miss my mom, too," he whispered.

He'd never mentioned his mom before, other than telling me his parents had died when he was fourteen. I was suddenly curious. She had to have been an amazing woman to have raised a wonderful man like Stephan. "Will you . . . tell me about her?"

A long silence filled the room. I didn't think he was going to answer me, but then he said, "She was one of a kind."

**Stephan**

My parents weren't something I talked about often. Thinking about them brought up feelings so full of anger, sadness, and frustration. Brianna wasn't asking about their deaths. She was asking about their lives. Something I hadn't concentrated on in a while.

Brianna glanced up at me with tear-filled eyes, and I knew I wanted to tell her more. She, maybe more than anyone else, could understand.

"She was a lady. Beautiful, elegant, but you didn't ever want to get on her bad side," I chuckled. "My backside became well acquainted with the palm of her hand on more than one occasion." That made me think of a question I'd been meaning to ask her. "Did your parents ever spank you?"

Her nose scrunched up as she thought. "Only once . . . I think." When she didn't continue, I prompted her. "I was young. Four? Five? I don't remember. But my babysitter had a daughter around my age, maybe a little older. A friend of hers had shown her how to make herself throw up, and so she showed me. Mom caught me the next day trying it in our bathroom. She was so mad. I couldn't sit down for a while after that." She smiled.

"What about the babysitter?"

"Mom called her and told her. I never went back there, though."

"I think your mom made a good decision with that one. That was very dangerous."

"I know."

After her sharing, I thought back to one of the times my mother had disciplined me. "The worst I can remember was when I stole a bracelet from our gardener. He'd taken it off while he was working around the pool. I knew it was his, but it was shining in the sunlight and I thought it was pretty, so I took it. Dad was out of town, but that didn't matter. Once my mother figured out I'd been the one to take it, she not only made me give it back and apologize, she also gave me a spanking I have yet to forget. My bottom was still sore when Dad came home the next day."

"How old were you?"

"Seven, I think. And the worst part was that everyone knew. For weeks after it happened, the housekeeper, the gardener . . . they all smirked whenever they saw me. It was humiliating. I never stole anything again."

Brianna smiled, and I hugged her to me. It felt good to talk to her about this. "She sounds like a good mom."

"She was." As much as I wanted to continue to hold her like this, I knew we needed to finish with our workouts. I helped her from the bike, and guided us both over to the weights.

Working out with her was a sweet torture. Her body had filled out since she'd come to live with me, and with the workouts, her muscles were tight and toned in all the right places. It was an exercise in control to be with her like this and keep my hands to myself. Instinct had me wanting to press her to the floor and ravish her. And although she would probably have welcomed my kisses—my touch—my body was aching for more each and every day. The closer we came, the more my body wanted it.

Last night had been amazing. Her touch did things to me that no other woman's ever had.

Before I'd entered the lifestyle, I'd tended to go for older women. It was the experience factor, more than anything else, and they were open to experimenting more than girls my age. My first kinky experience had been at seventeen with a woman twice my age. She'd let me spank her and tie her up. I'd loved it, and so had she. Back then, I'd had little understanding of what my enjoyment in that type of sexual play meant.

Things with Brianna were different. I wanted to share all those kinky sex things I loved, but I also wanted her to allow me to love her and take care of her the way she deserved. Feeling her hand around me, rubbing and squeezing my erection in her hand, brought me pleasure beyond the sexual release.

I realized the other night that Brianna was like a virgin in many ways. Yes, she'd had sex many times over, but the natural exploration and comfort level that usually occurred with sexual experience wasn't there. She'd been used and abused. She'd been a thing, a body, and nothing more. I was opening up a completely new world for her, and so far, even though she was still fearful, she was also enjoying it.

My biggest hurdle was penetration. She was now comfortable with me touching her body. But every time my fingers neared her entrance, she tensed to the point where I knew if I pushed things, it would be emotionally —and possibly physically—painful for her. I didn't want it to be painful in any way, physical or emotional.

After our workout, I guided her to my shower and we slowly washed each other as we had for the last few nights. She was more at ease with my body now, even when it was in an aroused state. This morning, I wanted it to be about her.

As I had last night, I pressed her up against the tiles of the shower. Water beat down all around us and pebbled on her pale skin.

Her mouth opened eagerly to me as I kissed her and pressed my body against her, letting her feel just how excited she'd made me. I was glad this didn't scare her anymore. Her trust in me was beyond my comprehension at times. She moaned into my mouth as my hands palmed her breasts and began lifting and tugging on them. The tips of her nipples hardened and she gasped as I took them between my thumb and forefinger and twisted. "How does that feel, Brianna?"

"I don't . . . I don't know," she said, her breathing heavy.

I did it again, slightly harder this time. "Does it feel good? Bad? Do you feel anything between your legs or in your lower belly when I do it?"

"In my belly. It . . . it feels . . . heavy?"

I smiled and went back to kissing her and playing with her breasts. She was soon panting and grasping at my shoulders. Good. That was just where I wanted her.

Slowly, I drifted my right hand down her front, over her stomach, and slid between her legs. The moment my fingers touched her swollen flesh, I felt her tense and whimper.

I pulled back slightly, resting my forehead against hers. "Focus on me. I'm not going to hurt you. I want to make you feel good." Her lips were pressed together, causing her nostrils to flare with her exaggerated breathing. "Trust me," I whispered.

She didn't move for ten very long seconds before taking a deep breath and nodding.

I gave her a quick kiss, thanking her, before continuing to massage her breast with my left hand, molding it, kneading it, and every so often tugging at its hardened tip. I wanted to kiss her again, but I needed to see her eyes. She seemed to do much better with new things if she was consciously aware it was me and no one else.

When she was back to breathing heavily again, I began moving my right hand in tiny circles on the inside of her thigh. In small increments, I edged closer to her center, gauging her reaction. She tensed once again when I reached her moist flesh, but after gazing into my eyes for a moment, relaxed slightly. I knew it was taking effort on her part, and I wanted to reward her for her trust.

Unlike some of the previous times when I'd touched her, she was moist today with more than just water. I could feel her juices coating my hand. Imagining pushing my fingers inside her and feeling that moisture covering them made my penis bob against her thigh, and I had to take a deep breath to calm myself.

With her lubrication on my fingertips, I searched out her clit and began my mission. It was still hidden behind its hood, probably from her tensing up, but it didn't take much coaxing for it to come out to play.

"Oh," she said, in surprise, her eyes wide as they stared into mine.

"Does that feel good?" I asked as I continued to rub little circles.

"Yes." Her voice was faint and her blue eyes were nearly glowing with the sensations she was feeling.

I could tell by her reactions that this was another first for her, and that filled me with a completely different kind of pride.

"Hold on to my arms and relax. Just *feel*. I promise you it will be good." She nodded, and her fingers dug into my biceps as I continued to pleasure her.

It didn't take long before her legs started to quiver and she began gasping for air. Her face flushed a lovely shade of pink, and it spread down her neck to her chest and over her breasts. It was stunning.

One of the most beautiful sounds in the world started low in her chest, building until it ripped from her throat and she screamed through her orgasm. I had never seen anything like it, and I knew I wanted to see it again and again. I never wanted to stop giving this woman pleasure.

When she came down from her high, I turned off the shower, carried her out, and dried her off before taking her to my bed, where I held onto her until she fell asleep.

# Chapter 19

**Brianna**

*My head was foggy as I started to wake up. The first thing I noticed was* that I had tucked my head into Stephan's shoulder, and his arms wrapped loosely around me. I blinked several times before finally opening my eyes to the bright sunlight that filled his room. His clock was on his nightstand behind me, but based on the harsh light streaming into his room and the growling in my stomach, it had to be afternoon.

Stephan's breathing was deep and even in his sleep, and I liked feeling the solidness of his chest moving beneath my cheek. We were still in the towels from our shower. Mine was wrapped around my torso, covering my breasts. Well, mostly covering. The part nearest the mattress was pulled taut, exposing the top half. My nipple was starting to show. His towel only covered his waist, leaving his chest bare. My hand rested over the steady beat of his heart.

I closed my eyes and smiled. Today had to be the best day I could ever remember. My legs still felt heavy, and I'd never felt so relaxed. Was this why people were always talking about how great sex was?

My eyes drifted down to Stephan's towel. I knew what lay underneath and it terrified me, but I could now honestly add curiosity to the mix. Sure, I'd been curious before, but that was more hypothetical; what was the big deal about sex? This felt different. I wasn't so much curious about *sex* anymore, more like I was curious about sex with Stephan. Everything with him was different. Wouldn't sex be, too?

I felt the uncertainty rise again, and I shivered. Arms tighten around me, and Stephan's breathing changed. He was awake.

"Hello, my love."

I looked up to see him smiling down at me. "Hello." I smiled back.

"How are you feeling?" he asked, brushing the hair away from my face.

I felt heat rise to my cheeks. "My legs feel heavy."

"Anything else?"

"I'm hungry."

He chuckled. "I could eat as well." His gaze drifted over my head. "It's already one o'clock. Why don't we make some salads to tide us over? Logan's in town this weekend, and we're meeting him and Lily for dinner at six."

"We're having dinner with Lily?"

"And Logan," he added.

I pressed my lips together before I took a deep breath and nodded. It wasn't that I didn't like Logan, but he was a man, and Stephan was the only man I trusted.

"It'll be fine. I won't leave you alone with him if you aren't comfortable, but I think it would be good for you to get to know him better. I told you how he and Lily met. He learned to be a Dom for her, and I thought you might have some questions that he could answer."

I thought about that for a moment. "Because you want me to be your submissive."

"Yes," he said, kissing my forehead.

"Okay. I'll try."

"Thank you."

Then he was kissing me in a way that had my body feeling warm all over again. My towel lost its last remaining hold on my breasts when he rolled over, pressing me into the mattress.

"I could kiss you all day, Brianna," he said, as his lips released my mouth and trailed down my neck. I loved when he kissed me, so I couldn't disagree.

"We need to get up, though," he said, reluctantly pulling away.

I saw his eyes travel down my body, leaving me feeling exposed. I held my breath, waiting.

Instead of touching me or kissing me again, he pushed himself up off the bed and stood, leaving his towel behind. His nakedness didn't seem to bother him. It never did.

This time, as he walked away from me over to his closet, I thought about something Lily had asked me. She'd asked if I'd ever looked at Stephan as a man. I mean, I always *knew* he was a man—that was hard to miss—but seeing him now, her question took on another meaning. She was asking me if I was attracted to him. *Physically.*

"Go get dressed, Brianna. I'll meet you in the kitchen, and we'll get those salads."

I jumped up from the bed and raced to my room, clutching my towel to my chest. I didn't know the answers to so many things. I didn't understand all these new feelings. Maybe it was good we were having dinner with Lily tonight. She'd be able to help me. She seemed to know everything I didn't.

Five hours later, we sat at a table in a nice restaurant. It wasn't as fancy as the one he'd taken me to where he'd ordered the duck, but it was still nice. I wasn't sure how I felt about the table. Whenever he'd taken me out in the past, we'd usually sat in a booth. He was right beside me. Of course, he was beside me now, too, but there was space between us.

The table was in the back so there were fewer around us, but it was still busy. My gaze kept darting around every time someone moved or their silverware made a loud noise. I was jumpy and I didn't know why. It wasn't as if I hadn't been out with him before.

I nearly fell out of my seat when his hand covered mine.

"What's wrong?"

My eyes met his as I held onto his hand. I took a deep breath and tried to figure out why I was having this reaction. The only thing that made sense was that he'd been too far away. As he held my hand, I felt myself calming.

"This is the first time we've been at a table." At his confused look, I knew I had to try to explain better. "Before we've always been in a booth. You were close. I could touch you."

He squeezed my hand gently. "I'm right here, even if I'm not always touching you."

"I know," I said, lowering my head.

"Eyes up," he ordered. When I was looking at him again, his voice softened. "I know this is hard, Brianna, but you are going to have to learn how to be around people. I don't know if it will ever be something you'll be comfortable with, but it is something you have to learn to tolerate. That's one of the reasons we're having dinner out and not at home." He released my hand, and brushed his knuckles against my collar. "Have you forgotten that I'm always with you?"

I shook my head. "No, Sir."

He smiled, and ran the back of his hand along my cheek before returning it to his lap. I felt the loss of his touch immediately, but I felt better than I had before. He was right. I always had his collar. He was always with me. I closed my eyes and took a deep breath.

When I opened my eyes, Logan and Lily were walking toward us. Logan arrived first with Lily standing just behind him to the right. Her head was bowed, but she was looking at me from beneath her lashes and smiling. It was then I realized it was the weekend and that she and Logan were *playing*. I hoped she'd be able to talk tonight.

"There you are," Stephan said as Logan pulled out the chair beside me for Lily. I was glad we'd at least get to sit beside each other. I wasn't sure how I would have done if I'd had to sit beside Logan. "I thought you'd gotten lost or something."

Logan smiled. "No. Lily just had some trouble deciding what she was going to wear. Finally, I made the decision for her."

"I'm glad you made it, then. I know how Lily is with her clothes." Stephan winked at her and I saw her glare at him quickly before looking down again.

I wasn't sure how I felt about the exchange. Knowing they'd *played* together in the past still gave me a funny feeling I didn't like. They seemed to have a connection I didn't understand, and it frustrated me.

"Yes," Logan said. "I see you and Brianna made it on time." He looked at me, and I glanced down.

"Brianna isn't obsessed with clothing, are you, Brianna?"

"No," I said, shaking my head.

"Well, maybe you can share that philosophy with Lily. I like her to look nice, but she tends to go overboard at times. Isn't that right, Lily?" Logan asked.

"Yes, Sir."

Then I saw him nod his head in my direction before turning back to Stephan. I didn't hear what he said, though, because Lily edged her chair a little closer to me and whispered, "I'm glad I didn't get myself into too much trouble tonight. I was hoping we could talk during dinner."

"Do you . . . do you get in trouble a lot?"

"Sometimes." She frowned. "Most of the time it's about running late because I can't find the right thing to wear. You'd think I'd be better at time management given what I do for a living, but there is always one more thing that needs to be done before I leave. Only seems to happen when he's home, though. I guess I get distracted." She giggled.

I thought about that, and I guessed it made sense. She was an event planner, so she was used to details.

"But enough about me," she said, waving her hand dismissively. "How are things going with you and Stephan?" I felt my cheeks heating again. She laughed. "That good, huh?"

"Yes, and . . . and I wanted to ask . . . ." I took a deep breath and closed my eyes. "Is it normal?"

"Is what normal?" she asked when I didn't continue.

"To feel warm. And . . . jittery?"

She looked confused. I hated when I wasn't explaining things well enough. "When do you feel warm and jittery?"

"When he holds me. When he kisses me. And . . . and when he . . . touches me," I whispered the last part.

Lily smiled and took hold of my hand. "That's great," she gushed.

I jerked from the sudden movement, and saw Stephan look in my direction. "Is it?"

"Of course it is. Don't you like the feeling?"

"Yes." I smiled shyly. "It's nice. I like when he kisses me." Then I asked the question that had been burning in my mind this afternoon. "Does that mean I'm . . . attracted . . . to him?"

She laughed. "It does."

I smiled back at her and felt a weight lift off my chest. It felt good to understand what I was feeling and relate it to what I'd read in books. My gaze drifted over to where Stephan was in deep conversation with Logan.

He'd angled his chair in a way that I knew he was still paying close attention to me and my well-being.

"So have you seen him naked yet?" Her abrupt question had me staring wide-eyed at her. When I didn't answer, she prompted me again. "Well?"

"I . . ." I felt another blush spread across my cheeks.

"I'll take that as a yes," she said. "What did you think? See anything you liked?"

It felt weird to be talking about this, even with Lily. Thankfully, I was saved when Stephan asked, "What are you ladies over there giggling about?"

"Just girl talk," Lily said.

"Hmm," Stephan said.

As if on cue, the waiter came with our drinks. I'd somehow missed him coming to the table the first time.


**Stephan**

I loved watching Brianna relaxed and enjoying herself. It was rare, especially when we were out in public. She'd been nervous at first, which was understandable, but it seemed that whatever girl talk Lily had engaged her in significantly distracted her from her nerves.

The waiter set our drinks down in front of us, and I informed him we would need another minute.

"Do you know what you'd like, Brianna?" I asked, motioning toward her menu.

"No," she said, quickly picking it up.

Turning my attention to my own menu, I looked over their steak selection. Logan loved his steak, which was the sole reason we were at this restaurant. Apparently, they had the best steaks in town. They had a decent selection, from prime rib to a chopped sirloin. I decided, however, to go with a nice rib eye since I'd never eaten here before.

Having made my selection, I looked over at Brianna. "Did you decide?"

Her menu was closed once again, and her hands were folded in her lap. "Yes."

"Good," I smiled. "You'll order for yourself when the waiter returns." I saw her tense and swallow, but she nodded. *Good girl.*

We didn't have to wait long for the waiter to appear again to take our orders. I prompted Brianna to go first. She stumbled over a few words, but overall she did well. I squeezed her hand under the table to show my pride in her accomplishment.

After placing my order, Logan ordered for both him and Lily. I noticed she scrunched up her nose when he ordered broccoli for her side dish. She hated broccoli, but she didn't get any say in what she ate on the weekends. That was part of their arrangement.

When we were left alone again, the conversation turned to Logan's most recent trip to New York. He loved to travel, which was good since he did a lot of it with his job. I, on the other hand, hated it—plane travel, at least. If I could avoid it, which I normally could, I did. Most of the foundation's business could be conducted over the phone or through teleconferencing. It was rare that I even had to leave town, let alone fly across the country. The two times it had happened, I had hired a private jet and interviewed the pilots myself.

Logan's line of work, however, was not only about fundraising for the hospital, it also involved lecturing at colleges around the country. His job was to promote the hospital in any and every way he could. He took Lily with him whenever possible, but given her own job at the foundation, it didn't happen very often. I had no idea how they could stand being apart so much, but they made it work.

Brianna didn't contribute to the conversation unless someone asked her a direct question. So when our meals arrived and we all began eating, I decided to change the subject. "Logan, I was telling Brianna how you and Lily became a couple. I thought it might be good for you to share with her why you chose to live the lifestyle with Lily when you'd not had any previous inclination."

Logan glanced over at Lily and smiled before going back to his steak. "Lily is one of a kind. The moment I met her, I knew there was something about her. There was this connection. I knew I wanted to get to know her better, but to be honest, when she told me what she wanted I was bewildered. I couldn't understand it. Why anyone would want that. Then . . ." he paused, taking a bite of his steak. "She dropped the other shoe and told me that my best friend—Stephan here—lived that way, too, and I'd never known."

I chuckled, remembering the night Logan had showed up at my condo wide-eyed and nearly incoherent. All he kept saying was, "Is it true?"

"Once I calmed down, things started making more sense. I'd rarely seen Stephan out with other girls since he'd been home from college, and the few times I had, he'd always taken the lead. They'd always wait for him to speak first and introduce them, always stayed one step behind him when walking." Logan took a few more bites of his meal before continuing.

Brianna was intently listening to every word he said. So much so, I had to nudge her to continue to eat.

"In the end, it came down to one thing. I liked her. A lot. I was clueless about it all, but I was willing to give it a try if it meant being with her."

After Logan's little speech, no one spoke. We all sat in silence, and I was hoping Brianna would speak up, ask a question, but she didn't.

"Do you have anything you'd like to ask Logan, Brianna?" She looked up at me, and I could see the panic building. I leaned over, took her hand, and whispered in her ear. "I'm right here. You can ask him anything you want. No one is going to get upset."

Her gaze met mine and she nodded. She tightened her hold on my hand and without looking at Logan asked, "Was it . . . hard?"

"To be what she needed me to be, you mean?"

"Yes," she squeaked.

"At first it was. It still is at times, but I also see the benefits for both of us. There is strength there, a bond that I've never had before with another person. The hardest part is when I have to punish her. I love her. Causing her pain, mentally or physically, isn't my favorite pastime. But I've also learned that it's something she needs. If I slack on handing out discipline, she gets worse until I do something about it. It was a learning curve, but we've figured it out," he said, smiling at Lily. She smiled back. "Is there anything else you wanted to know?"

Brianna shook her head before dropping her head again.

"If you do, you know where to find me," he said.

We finished our meal with dessert. I decided to order a large slice of chocolate cake for Brianna and me to share. She was timid at first, not wanting to take some for herself, so I took the first piece and fed it to her. "Now eat," I ordered. She smiled shyly and picked up her fork.

Later on that night, after another memorable shower where I helped her to her second orgasm, I reluctantly sent her to her own bed. As much as I wanted Brianna sleeping beside me, I wasn't sure I could handle it. I wanted to be able to make love to her, hold her, and touch her the way I wanted. We weren't there yet, and the last thing she needed was for me to do something in my sleep that I wasn't aware of until it was too late. How I'd stopped myself the last two times we'd fallen asleep together was beyond me. It had taken all the willpower I had to stop. She was becoming harder and harder to resist.

# Chapter 20

**Stephan**

***Sunday morning, Logan called to say Lily was asking to go to the mall—***
there was a big sale apparently—and he wanted to know if we'd like to
come along. He thought it might help Brianna, and I had to agree. I knew
we still had three months before school started, but she had a lot of ground
to cover in that time if she was going to be able to not only drive herself to
school, but deal with her teachers and classmates as well.

When I told Brianna we were going to meet Logan and Lily again today,
her excitement was obvious. It lessened slightly when she learned we
would be meeting them at the mall. As I opened the car door for her, I saw
her reach up and touch my metal collar that was still securely around her
neck before taking my offered hand and exiting the vehicle.

The mall was busy. Lily hadn't been exaggerating on there being a big
sale. Everywhere I looked there were banners touting anywhere from
twenty to fifty percent off. Retailers were doing their best to drive business
to their stores, and from what I could see, it was working. Over half the
people we passed were carrying a bag of some sort.

Brianna held tight to my hand as we weaved through the crowd to the
food court where I'd agreed to meet Logan and Lily. Every time someone
would get too close, Brianna would use her other hand to grab onto my
upper arm and pull herself closer.

Halfway there, I stepped off to the side, and turned her to face me.
"Number?"

"Five." She kept moving her eyes back and forth, trying to monitor all the
people passing us.

"Eyes on me." Her gaze returned to the front, and she gave me her full
attention. "Thank you. Now explain to me why you're at five."

"All the people," she whispered.

"What about them?"

"They're so close. I can't keep track of them. They keep moving."

"Yes, they do. In places like this, no one ever stays in one place for too long. And if you're never comfortable coming to a place like this by yourself that's okay. It can be overwhelming. But today, right now, I'm here. I won't let anything happen to you."

"I know. I just . . . I get scared."

I hated seeing her like this. All I wanted was to make it better for her. "Is there anything I can do that will make you less scared?"

She didn't answer right away, taking her time to think about the question. This was one of the things that made her a lovely submissive partner. Too often, a submissive was quick to answer with whatever they thought their Dom wanted to hear. Once Brianna understood that I wanted real answers from her when I asked, she took the time to think the answer through instead of spouting out nonsense that meant nothing at the end of the day.

I saw something change in her face, and before I knew what hit me, she was hugging me. She wrapped her arms around my waist, and her face nestled in against my chest. Before I could ask her anything, however, she started to talk. "When I was . . . was with . . . Ian, sometimes . . . sometimes, he'd attach a chain to my collar. I didn't like it," she said, shaking her head so hard it caused her entire body to twist in my arms. "It meant that I couldn't get away from him, not even for a minute. And if I tried, he'd just pull the chain." She fell silent.

I was sure I understood what she wanted and why after that explanation, and to be honest, the thought of having her on a leash was very appealing. However, I needed to be sure. This would be a bigger step into Dominance and submission play, one I needed to make sure she was ready to embark upon. The last thing I wanted was for it to trigger another one of her flashbacks. I rested my hands on either side of her cheeks, forcing her to look at me.

"You want me to put you on a leash? That would make you feel more comfortable?"

She pressed her lips tight together and nodded. "I . . . I think so?"

"You don't sound sure."

"I didn't like it . . . before, because it meant he had even more control over what I was doing and where I was. It meant he had better access to hurt me." Her words were getting softer and more distant the longer she spoke. "I feel safe with you."

A smile tugged at the corner of my mouth. She was amazing. Pressing a quick kiss to her lips, I took her hand and laced our fingers. "Stay close," I said, as I continued walking toward the food court.

Logan and Lily were standing by a large column near the entrance when we arrived. I knew the minute Lily spotted us by the smile on her face. Lily's reaction brought Logan's attention to us.

"Now who's the late one?" he teased.

Before I could respond, Brianna's fingers began digging into my hand. When I looked down at her, all the color had drained from her face and she was staring in pure terror across the room. There was a man staring back at her with a look that told me he had more knowledge of her than he should.

"Who is that?" Logan asked. There was no way he could have missed the change in our demeanors.

"Brianna?" I asked, not taking my eyes off the man in question.

He took a step in our direction, and I felt Brianna tense. I'd only seen her react this way once before, and that was with Daren. It was all I needed to know. This man had played with her, at the very least. At most, he was one of Ian's friends who'd abused her. Either way, this needed to be dealt with.

I forced her to look at me. "You will stay right here with Lily and Logan, do you hear me?" My voice was firm and commanding. She was to do as I said. There would be no deviation. She just stared back at me, not answering. I glanced up. The man had stopped walking, but was still watching us. "Answer me," I demanded.

"Y . . . yes."

Taking her hand, I placed it in Lily's. I knew Brianna did much better with physical contact—preferably mine—but I needed to deal with the situation at hand, and there was no way she was coming with me.

The man's face began to change as I neared. It had been full of shock, then curiosity, and then maybe even a little bit of hopefulness. Now a frown pulled at his mouth and his eyes became wary. I stopped a few feet away and glared at him. He took a step back, but I matched him.

"Look, I don't want any trouble," he said.

"You should have thought about that before you put your hands on what is mine."

The man swallowed again, and took another step back. "I didn't—"

"Do *not* lie to me."

"Okay, okay. I . . . had a little fun with her. It was months ago. I haven't seen her since."

"And you will never see her again," I said continuing to glare at him. "If I ever find out that she has so much as seen you again, I will find a way to make sure you regret ever laying eyes on her. Do we understand each other?" The man looked me over then glanced over my shoulder at Brianna. "No," I snapped. "You look at *me*."

He seemed to change his tune, acting as if he was trying to shrug it off. "Yeah, whatever. It wasn't like she was that good anyway."

I took another step forward, and he frowned again, but this time he continued to backpedal as quickly as he could without tripping until he finally turned around and disappeared in the crowd.

Pent-up energy was still coursing through me. I'd not felt so out of control for years. Then again, Brianna brought out feelings in me I'd never imagined. It helped knowing they'd not had sex, but I was still dealing with the knowledge Daren had played with her. By the way that man had been eyeing her, I had little doubt that he'd been one of those who'd raped her. I just didn't know where on the abuse scale he ranked, and that didn't comfort me much.

I closed my eyes and tried to calm down before returning to Brianna. We'd drawn some attention, but once the man left most people went back to whatever they were doing. There wasn't going to be a show today, even though I wouldn't have minded putting my fist against his face.

Brianna was visibly shaking by the time I got back to her side. Lily was holding her, but it wasn't doing much. I quickly took her into my arms, letting her touch calm me as well. "Shh. He's gone."

Her tiny hands dug into my sides as she clung to me. Logan and Lily stood by in silence and watched as I comforted her. Thankfully, we were off to one side and out of the way of traffic. Although we got some looks, no one bothered us.

It took a long time for her to calm down, although I was glad she didn't go catatonic on me as she had the last time. Finally, I heard her voice float up from where she'd buried her face in my chest. "He's really gone?"

"Yes," I whispered into her hair.

She hugged me tighter, and I returned the gesture. "Thank you," she said.

"Anytime, sweetheart."

I glanced up at Logan and Lily. He was holding her, too, and I wondered if maybe we should call off this shopping trip. It seemed that every time we turned around, another obstacle was thrown in her path. No wonder she was fearful of the outside world if just going to the mall could bring with it confrontations such as this.

Another five minutes passed before Logan suggested we get something to eat. It was a good suggestion. Brianna needed to eat something, and it would help me to assess how she was doing emotionally.

She stayed glued to my side when we walked up to one of the vendors to order. I didn't bother to ask her what she wanted. I just ordered for her. When I needed to let go of her hand in order to carry the tray, she began to protest and Lily asked if she could carry it for us. I glanced over at Logan, who quickly gave his okay and nodded to Lily, handing over our food.

Lunch was quiet. Brianna picked at her food and never let go of my hand. It made eating challenging, but I was willing to make the sacrifice if it gave her what she needed. I thought back to our conversation earlier when she'd asked me to put her on a leash. I turned to Logan. "Do you know if there's a pet store here?"

He looked at Lily. She knew this mall better than either of us. "Yes. It's one of those fancy ones that sells outfits to dress up your dogs, and they have doggie treats that look like cookies you'd buy in a bakery." I nodded, and went back to eating and making sure Brianna was doing the same.

When we were finished, Lily cleaned up the wrappers and took our trash to be disposed of. "How are you feeling?" I asked Brianna.

"Okay," she said, but her voice didn't hold any confidence.

"What number?"

"Three."

I nodded. "Are you okay to continue shopping?"

"You'll stay with me?"

"Of course."

"Then, yes."

When Lily returned to the table, we all stood and exited the food court to start our shopping. I was choosing our first stop, however. Lily's shopping would have to wait. "Where is this pet store you were telling me about?"

## Brianna

I stayed as close as possible to him as we walked through the mall to the pet store. Lily and Logan stayed behind me, almost boxing me in. It made me feel better . . . safer . . . than I had earlier, even though I knew Stephan was right and he wouldn't let anyone harm me. He'd more than proven that when that man spotted me in the food court.

As soon as I saw him, I knew who he was. He was one of Ian's friends, and he was one of the worst ones. His goal was to see how loud he could get me to scream, and it had nothing to do with sex. In fact, he was the only one of Ian's friends not to have had sex with me. He was all about torture. The cigarette burns on my breasts were courtesy of him.

A shiver ran down my spine as we came to a stop inside the pet store. Lily had been right. There were outfits hanging up on tiny hangers that would fit dogs of all shapes and sizes. Bins of toys lined the middle section. The front counter held rows of dog biscuits that looked prettier than most cookies I'd eaten.

Stephan stood scanning the store for several seconds before strolling to the back wall covered with various collars. I knew why we were here. At least, I hoped I did.

He fingered several small leather collars. Some were attached to chains, some had leather leashes, and others just had a small silver ring where a leash could be attached. The collars he was looking at were much too small to fit around my neck, and I wondered if maybe I'd been wrong about why he'd wanted to come here. I continued to let my gaze roam over the collars as he scrutinized them. There were all different colors, and I found myself staring at a brown leather one that had pretty pink flowers on it. It looked more like a bracelet than a collar.

Suddenly, he picked up the collar I'd been looking at and turned it over in his hands several times. He pulled on it, twisted it, unbuckled it, and then buckled it again. "Give me your arm." I was confused, but I did what he said.

Within a few seconds, he had the collar around my wrist and secured. He then twisted my wrist left and right, examining it.

"I like it," Logan said. "Were you looking for a chain or leather for the leash?"

"I'm thinking leather. It would be more comfortable and draw less attention," he said, seeming distracted. Logan selected two simple brown leather leashes from the wall and handed them to Stephan. He tested them in his hands again before he attached the first one, and then the other to my wrist. The first was slightly wider than the second was, but other than that, they looked the same to me.

Without saying another word, he placed the wider leash back on the wall, and removed the collar from my wrist. Taking my hand, he walked to the front counter. "Did you find everything you need today, sir?" the young man asked.

"Yes, thank you."

"This is from our new designer line. I'm sure your pet will like it."

Stephan smirked. "I'm sure she will."

It didn't take long to complete the transaction. Stephan refused the man's offer of a bag, and carried the collar and leash out in his other hand. Once we were back out in the mall, he led me over to a corner and put the collar back on my wrist. After he buckled it, he slipped a single finger inside. "How does that feel? Too tight?"

"No," I said, shaking my head. Actually, it felt nice. The leather was soft against my skin. He smiled, and lifted my arm so that he could place a soft kiss on my wrist just above the cuff before attaching the leash. Even though he wasn't pulling, I could feel the slight tug on my wrist immediately. I was surprised at how much I liked the feeling.

His finger lifted my chin. "Number?"

I smiled. "Two."

He grinned, and wrapped the leash around his own wrist and then his hand. The length of leash between his hand and my wrist was only about four inches. I could move, but I wasn't going very far. It probably didn't make sense why this made me feel safer and more tied to him than holding his hand, but it did. This felt stronger somehow.

The only thing was that I did miss the warmth of his touch. Having the leash meant he wasn't holding my hand anymore. The leather was warm and comforting, but it wasn't a substitute for feeling his skin. Although this did make me feel safer, I wasn't sure how I felt about it otherwise.

Logan headed off first, with Lily close behind. Stephan and I followed. We ended up at a large department store. Everything was okay until we reached the women's clothing section. There were people everywhere, mostly women, and everyone seemed to have an armload of clothes. When I saw how crowded it was, I was glad Stephan bought the leash and collar. I knew he'd hold onto it no matter what.

Lily asked Logan if she could shop, and once he gave his permission she was off and running. She walked up and down a few aisles before stopping and motioning for me. I glanced up at Stephan. He nodded, and we walked over to where she was. She flipped through clothes, checked tags, and held some up to herself. Others she held against me. I just stood there, not sure what else to do. It reminded me a lot of the other time Lily had taken me shopping.

Slowly, a pile began to build and soon she turned to Logan. "May I try these on, Sir?"

"Yes, but you only have ten minutes."

She nodded, picked up the pile of clothes she'd accumulated, and walked quickly to the dressing rooms. The three of us walked at a much slower pace to stand a few feet away from the fitting room entrance to wait.

I watched as twenty-two different women passed us before Lily came out again, and I wondered if I'd ever be that brave. Even though they were women and not men, I wasn't sure I could do it. *Maybe.* I knew there were separate rooms, but I'd still know I was surrounded, yet alone. The women also seemed more aggressive today. I'd watched a few bump into each other in a race to get to an open fitting room.

Lily held up five dresses for Logan's approval. He looked at each and accepted all but one. She frowned, but didn't argue.

When she came back from returning the unaccepted dress, however, she had three more dresses hanging over her arm. "I thought these would look good on Brianna." She looked at Logan when she spoke, and after he nodded, she turned to Stephan. He picked up each dress one at a time. The first two he dismissed almost immediately. The third, however, he held up against me before placing it over his arm.

It took longer to check out this time since there were so many people. When it was Stephan's turn, he released the part of the leash that he'd been holding, leaving only the end around his wrist connecting us. I felt the loss of tension, but the weight was still there. A woman standing a few feet away saw the leash dangling from Stephan's wrist, but my arm was down at my side so she couldn't see anything else. Even still, I stepped closer to him and he reached down to squeeze my hand before finishing the transaction.

The rest of the afternoon was spent much the same way, going from store to store. Lily ended up finding me three other outfits: two more dresses and a pants suit. They were all nice, but I preferred pants to dresses if I had a choice. Lily seemed to be just the opposite. Even today, she was wearing a nice dress and sandals.

When we finished shopping, it was after five and Stephan suggested we all went to Tony's for pizza. I was hungry, but I wanted to get home. I needed to be close to him. He would hold me and kiss me out in public, but it wasn't the same.

I felt bad. Lily tried to talk to me all through dinner, but I didn't feel like contributing. Eventually, she gave up and listened to the men's conversation. I caught bits and pieces, but I wasn't really paying attention either. Instead, I took the opportunity to hold Stephan's hand under the table. I'd been reluctant to reach for it, but then decided if I made the wrong choice he'd let me know. Instead, he'd eagerly laced our fingers, placing our hands on his thigh and kept them there.

By the time we arrived home, I was more than ready when he told me to get my things for what was becoming our nightly shower routine. It was hard to believe this didn't frighten me anymore. I wanted to touch him, and I wanted him to touch me.

# Chapter 21

**Stephan**

*By the time Monday morning arrived, I had way too many things on my* mind. Saying goodbye to Brianna this morning had been difficult. It still seemed that every time we took two steps forward, there was always something there to push her back.

We talked about what had happened at the mall, and she told me who the man was. Her body trembled as she clung to me, speaking the words I needed to hear, but desperately didn't want to. He'd been one of the worst, she'd said, the man who'd left the burns on her breasts. Ian had allowed that. Encouraged it even, from what she'd told me.

Just thinking about it had me flexing my fingers against the steering wheel. I wanted to hurt him and every other man who'd dared touch her without her permission. They had no right. She'd been an innocent seventeen-year-old girl. It just reaffirmed my desire to see Ian get his due, one way or another.

When we took our shower last night, Brianna had begged me to continue with our exploration. I'd had my doubts, but I was finding there was little I could deny her when she looked up at me with those blue eyes of hers.

I'd gone slow, taking her to near release before pushing the boundaries farther. Once again, the moment my fingers reached her opening I could see her panic rising, so I stopped. No matter how much I wanted her, I'd never hurt her like that. She'd apologized profusely, of course, even though it wasn't her fault. I ended up drying us both off, putting her in her bed, and holding her until she fell asleep.

One thing, however, had continued to get better with our nightly showers. She no longer feared touching me to the point where she seemed almost eager when it came time to wash my body. Her hands were more liberal in their movements, and I noticed her lingering in certain areas. I was thrilled with her newfound confidence, even if it was limited.

When I pulled into my parking spot at The Coleman Foundation, I noticed movement out of the corner of my eye, and immediately went on alert. Given the confrontation yesterday in the mall with one of Brianna's abusers, Reeves actively looking for Brianna, and Karl's recent less-than-amicable departure, I wasn't taking anything for granted.

Out of the shadows, Ross appeared. His face was drawn, and there were bags under his eyes. It didn't look like he'd gotten much sleep over the weekend. I hadn't been sure how he'd end up processing the new information he'd received about Brianna. Knowing he wasn't taking the news of her past well gave me bit of sadistic satisfaction. After having to deal with his blatant immaturity these past months, he was getting a dose of hard reality. Maybe now he wouldn't be so quick to judge.

I took my time getting out of my car. The wait would do him good. He shifted his weight anxiously as I picked up my briefcase and stepped toward him. "What was it I told you about showing up unannounced?"

"I wanted to talk to you," he said, ignoring my question.

"I gathered as much since you're here waiting for me." He glanced around him, still anxious, and I wondered if there was someone else around. "Are you alone?"

"Yes," he said. "But . . . maybe your office would be better."

I nodded and began walking toward the elevator, knowing he'd follow me.

Jamie greeted us as we stepped off the elevator. "Good morning, Mr. Coleman."

"Good morning, Jamie. How was your weekend?"

"Too short, sir," she said, handing me a stack of mail.

"It always is," I said, absently flipping through the letters. There didn't seem to be anything important. "Hold my calls for the next hour, and I'm not to be disturbed."

Once inside my office, Ross couldn't seem to sit still. I sat watching him for several minutes before asking, "Are you going to say whatever it is that's on your mind in the near future, or were you planning to take up my entire day?"

He stopped his pacing. "John—Brianna's father—is here. In Minneapolis."

I sat up straighter in my seat, but kept my expression blank. This was a new development. "How do you know this?"

"He came to see me. I didn't tell him anything," he assured me. "But he asked me if I knew you."

"He asked about me by name?"

Ross nodded. "He had that picture of you and Brianna from the hospital gala a few weeks ago. He wanted to know if I knew who you were."

"And what did you tell him?"

Ross walked forward and collapsed in the chair directly across from me.

"I couldn't lie, so I told him I did, but not well." He glanced down at the floor before looking up to meet my gaze. "He's going to find her. Even if I don't say anything, he's going to find her."

"I know."

"You know? That's all you have to say?" he said, getting agitated. "I still can't believe he would do that. I can't believe he would . . . but if you're right . . ." I wasn't sure he was still talking to me anymore as his voice took on a faraway quality. After a few minutes, he stilled, but a look somewhere between defeat and confusion settled on his face.

"Thank you for letting me know," I said. Even though he was not one of my favorite people, he'd just earned some points for putting Brianna's safety first. "I won't hide her. She's been forced into seclusion too much already. I'm trying to get her used to people again, not create more fear." He looked as if he were about to argue. I raised my hand to stop him. "One way or another, he's going to find her. I can't stop that and neither can you."

"So what do we do?"

I found it rather ironic that the cocky bastard I was used to dealing with was nowhere in sight now. "*You* don't do anything."

"What?" he said, his voice rising as he stood again. "You can't mean that."

"I do," I assured him. "Anything you do is going to draw attention. That would not be helpful." He didn't seem to like that answer, but I hoped for Brianna's sake that he'd listen.

He didn't say much after that, although his mouth opened and shut like a fish several times. After a few minutes, he turned on his heel and left.

I leaned back in my chair, contemplating his visit. I was glad he appeared to be putting his attitude aside in order to protect Brianna, but I still didn't like him, and I didn't fully trust him either. I hoped that he kept his promise and didn't tell Jonathan Reeves how to find his daughter.

Glancing at the clock, I reached for the phone and dialed Oscar. My lawyer needed to know of this new development. I also wanted to find out if his private investigator had dug up any more information.

"Davis and Associates."

"This is Stephan Coleman. Is Oscar available?"

"Let me check, Mr. Coleman."

Not five seconds later, the phone clicked and Oscar was on the line. "Good morning, Mr. Coleman."

"Hello, Oscar. I wanted to see if you'd found out any new information."

He sighed. "Not much. Mr. Pierce likes to cover his tracks. I found several transactions between him and Mr. Dumas. However, they all look legit, at least on the surface. Dumas appears to be the weaker link, as we've found a few holes in his books and we're exploring them to see if they lead anywhere."

"What about Jonathan Reeves?"

"Other than some recent Internet searches and an increase in phone calls from both his residences and his office, nothing has changed. I can't find any evidence of illegal activity other than the gambling I told you about before."

"Who's he been calling?"

"Most of the calls have been to fellow law enforcement, some of which are here in Minneapolis. There have also been several calls to Cal Ross. Do you want me to look into him further?"

"Not at the moment, no. I need you to continue looking into Pierce. There has to be something there. No one is involved in human trafficking and leaves no trail. We just have to find it."

"You do know that you could get pulled into any investigation, given the rather large transaction you made with him recently?"

"I'm aware of that. We'll deal with it when it becomes necessary." There was one other thing I wanted to make sure he was aware of before I let him go. "You should also know that Jonathan Reeves is currently in town looking for Brianna. I don't know where he's staying, but I'm sure your guy could find out."

As soon as I hung up with Oscar, I called Tom. All nonresident traffic had to pass by him in order to enter my building. He was very good at denying access, but I needed more than that. If Jonathan Reeves showed up, I wanted to be notified immediately.

After my call to Tom, I walked the short distance to the window that separated my office from the Minneapolis skyline. My office was one of the taller ones in the city, affording me an unobstructed view of the tops of several other buildings. I couldn't see my condo from here, and for the first time I questioned my choice of residence. Maybe I should have found something closer, within walking distance.

I knew I was being irrational. Brianna was fine. She was safe in my condo. Tom was manning the front desk, and he was notifying security as well, just to be safe. That was his suggestion, not mine. It seemed he was also rather protective of Brianna.

Reaching into my pocket, I pulled out my phone and dialed before I could stop myself.

It rang twice before her voice came across the line. "Hello, Sir," she whispered, the happiness in her voice coming through the phone.

"Hello, Brianna. How's your morning so far?"

**Brianna**

Last night's shower was nice, until he tried to put his fingers inside me again. I'd felt a tightening in my chest and it was harder to breath. Why did this keep happening, and how did I fix it?

Stephan made sure I knew he wasn't upset with me for freezing again. I still felt bad. This was something I wanted.

As he'd held me last night in my bed, he'd assured me we'd figure it out and everything would be fine. He'd reminded me of how far we'd already come, and that it was just taking time to get there given what I'd been through, and that was okay. I could tell he was frustrated, even though he tried not to let me see. He was always taking care of me, putting my needs first. Thinking about how much he'd done for me—how he'd cared for me, guided me through my panic—brought a warm feeling like none I'd felt before.

I was happy when he called. It was hard to explain how much I missed him when he was at work, even though he always reminded me he was only a phone call away.

"Go to the window, Brianna. Look out, across the buildings. Do you see the tall one to your right? I'm right on the other side."

Even though I'd been to his office before, I'd never once thought of where it was physically in relation to where he lived. It was nice knowing. I just wished I could see his building. I could pretend that I could see him, too, and maybe he wouldn't feel so far away.

He talked to me until finally he said he had a meeting he couldn't miss. Maybe it was silly, but it made me get that tingly feeling inside knowing he didn't want to hang up with me either. It was hard to think he might be feeling the same way about me as I did about him. I mean, I was still broken in many ways. What did I really have to offer him? I couldn't even let him touch me how he wanted to.

I decided to make him a nice meal for dinner. My mom used to spend hours in the kitchen baking with me before she'd gotten sick. John seemed to enjoy my culinary skills, although he didn't comment much on anything unless it was to tell me I couldn't do something or go somewhere.

Thinking about my father brought me up short. He'd find me. I knew he would. It might take him days or weeks, but it was inevitable. I just didn't understand why he'd want to. Did he know I was free now? Is that why he was tracking me down, to make sure I went back to a master that would punish me?

All my kitchen pursuits were forgotten as I slid to the floor clutching my chest. No. Stephan wouldn't let him take me. He . . . he couldn't make me leave. He couldn't . . . Air ripped harshly through my lungs as I tried to catch my breath, but all it did was rush right back out, not giving me the oxygen I needed. Stephan. I needed Stephan.

There was no way I could stand. My legs felt heavy, and not in the good way they did after Stephan touched me. It felt as if there were weights attached to them as I crawled across the floor toward my cell phone.

I was having trouble seeing. Everything was blurred through my tears. Wiping them away did no good. My eyes just filled again with moisture, blocking my sight as quickly as I removed it.

Pain surged in my shoulder as I bumped into the end table beside the couch. I nearly gave up and just let the panic take me. It would be easy to let go and let reality fade around me, but that wasn't what I really wanted, and I knew he expected more of me, too.

My hand finally found what it was looking for, and I blindly hit the number one on the speed dial. "Brianna?" His voice allowed me to take my first haggard breath. "Tell me what's wrong, sweetheart?"

"I . . . I need you," I choked out.

"I'm on my way. You stay on the line with me. Keep talking. Where are you?"

"Home."

"Where are you at home?" he asked. I could hear him moving around, people passing by him. Then I heard the ding of an elevator, and I knew he really was on his way. He was dropping everything for me . . . again. I should feel guilty about that, but I needed him too much.

"Living room."

"Are you able to walk?"

"I don't know. My legs . . . they feel . . . heavy."

"Okay. Just stay where you are then. I want you to lie back and close your eyes." I did what he said, feeling the soft plush of the carpet against the back of my head. "Take a deep breath in and hold it." I tried, but it still felt as if I was gasping. "Now let it out." A loud gushing sound escaped my lips as I released the breath I'd been trying to hold. "Good. Again. Deep breath in, and hold it. Now release." With every word, every breath, I felt myself calming, my breathing coming back to normal. "Good girl. Keep breathing. Slow and deep. You're doing well, Brianna."

I felt that warmth again at his praise. He kept talking me through my breathing until I heard the door open and him calling my name. "Here," I said, loud enough that he could hear me.

His face came into view, and I smiled as he lowered the phone from his ear and knelt down beside me. He pulled me into his arms, rocking me. The feel of his solid arms around me was the last thing I needed to relax completely. He was here, and all was right.

After a few minutes, he began to shift us. I held on tight, not wanting to let go. "Shh. It's okay. I'm just moving us to the chair." I nodded, burying my face on his shoulder as he picked us both up enough to sit onto his chair. His hands stroked my arms, and his fingers played with my hair just the way I liked it. "Tell me what happened."

"I was going to make you a nice dinner. You've been so good to me and I can't . . . I can't give you what you want."

"All in good time," he said, kissing my forehead. "That couldn't have been what sent you into a panic, though. We've talked about this. It will happen. We just have to keep working at it."

"I know," I said, taking advantage of how safe I felt here in his arms, in his chair. "It was . . . I started thinking how I used to bake with my mom and then . . . then how it was cooking for . . . John." His arms tightened around me. "I don't know why he's looking for me. What's going to happen when he finds me?"

His mouth rested against my temple, and I could feel his breath as he spoke. "I don't know why he's looking for you either, Brianna. I don't think we're going to know until the time comes. As to what's going to happen . . . I don't know that either. We're going to have to deal with it the best we can when it occurs." He paused. "I found out today that your father is in town." A whimper escaped my lips, and my hands balled into fists, clutching the suit jacket he was still wearing. He lovingly caressed my face as he pressed me against his chest. "If you see him, even at a distance, you are to call me right away."

I nodded and continued to hold tight to him. He was my lifeline, and I was pretty sure he always would be. There was no place I felt safer than when he held me in his arms like this. Sometimes I just wanted to stay here, in his chair, and never leave. The outside world could melt away, and I wouldn't care.

"You said you'd been about to make dinner. What was on the menu?" he asked, and I knew he was trying to distract me from my thoughts.

"Chicken parmesan. I was going to try and remember the recipe my mom used to make."

"Are you feeling up to making it?"

I was torn. The original thought behind making it was a thank you to him for everything. It was a small thing, but even the small things I did for him seemed to make him happy. Another part of me wanted to stay in his chair all night. Cooking would mean leaving the perfect place we were in.

Guilt, however, won out. "Yes." I'm sure my voice didn't sound very confident.

"Come on, then," he said, patting my leg. "I'll help you. You can put me to work."

We spent the next hour and a half in the kitchen working on dinner. The area felt smaller with him working beside me, but in a good way. He always took every opportunity to touch me, in little ways, when we worked together like this. I liked it.

He was working on prepping vegetables for the salad while I began breading the chicken. Every time I glanced up, he was looking at me. I had no idea how he wasn't cutting himself with the knife since he didn't seem to be paying much attention to what he was doing. I noticed a smile pulling at his lips.

He picked up a disfigured carrot, examining it as if it would tell him some secret he didn't know. Placing the carrot on the counter, he came up behind me. He wrapped his arms around my waist, his chin resting on my shoulder. "What do you think?" he asked, nodding toward the strangely shaped vegetable.

It had one top, but two legs and they were twisted around each other. "I didn't know they could grow that way. I wonder why it has two instead of one?"

He moved my hair out of the way and kissed my neck. "It reminds me of you when you're sleeping, how your legs get tangled up in the sheets."

"It does?" I asked, looking at the odd carrot again. It did kind of look like two legs intertwined.

"Yes. You have very nice legs, Brianna."

The room suddenly felt really warm, and it had nothing to do with the heat coming from the stove. He'd helped me cook a few times in the past, and it wasn't unusual for him to kiss or hold me now and then in between. In fact, it was normal. He always seemed to go out of his way to look for excuses to touch me. This was the first time, however, that he'd taken it to a sexual place. I was anxious, but not in a bad way.

His hand slid from my waist down the front of my jeans to the apex of my thighs. "Mm. Warm," he whispered, running his hands along the inseam of my jeans.

I sank back into his chest, enjoying the feel of him behind me, around me. My earlier afternoon stress faded away as I tried to concentrate on not making a mess with my egg-covered hands. The only thing I could think about was how good he felt, and how good he made me feel.

"How are you feeling?"

"Warm," I answered honestly.

He chuckled. "Are you prepared for tonight?" His fingers followed my hipbone and then up to the top of my jeans until they were tickling my skin beneath.

"Yes," I breathed.

"Good. So am I." He stepped back then, letting go of me.

I felt the loss immediately and from the look on his face, he'd had to force himself to stop. It made me smile. I still didn't know what he saw in me and why he was willing to deal with all my issues, but I was grateful. I loved being with him.

# Chapter 22

**Brianna**

*Dinner was just as I'd hoped. He complimented me on the delicious meal* even though he'd help make it. I smiled, and blushed, under his praise. It felt good to do these small things for him.

After dinner, he told me to get my night things and meet him in his room instead of his chair. I was a little disappointed about missing time in his chair, but I was hoping that meant that we'd be doing more physical exploration tonight. It was early, though; only about seven.

When I entered his bedroom with my pajamas clasped against my chest, he stood fully clothed near his bed. He'd removed his jacket, tie, and shoes, but other than that, he was still dressed. I guessed we wouldn't be taking our shower yet.

"Come," he said, holding out his hand. I walked over to stand in front of him. He took the clothes out of my hands and placed them behind him on the nightstand. "Lie down on the bed."

I felt the beginning of my nerves start to build. This was new. His bed had always been off limits. My knees sunk into the mattress as I crawled onto the bed and lay down as instructed.

He followed, hovering over me for a second before lying beside me. "You okay?"

I nodded. Nervous, but I always was if we were trying something new.

"We're only going to go as far as you're comfortable with tonight, Brianna. I know the last time we were in a bed things didn't end well, but we've come a long way since then. For tonight, think of this as my chair. You are to speak freely. Tell me if something is bothering you, or doesn't feel right."

"Okay."

He smiled, reaching up to run his hand down my hair. "I was thinking about you today in my meeting."

"You were?" I couldn't imagine why he'd be thinking of me during one of his meetings.

"Yes. We get appeals sometimes direct from families. We usually try to connect them to the hospital that can best help them. There was one today for a little girl. She looked a lot like you with her dark brown hair and blue eyes. I wondered what you looked like when you were little." He rested his head on his hand and used his free one to continue to play with my hair.

I leaned into him, starting to relax. "I was normal, I think. I liked to play with dolls and help my mom bake cookies. For my eighth birthday, I begged Mom for a pony," I said, remembering.

"Something we have in common." His fingers brushed against my collarbone. They were distracting.

"You wanted a pony, too?" I asked, trying to concentrate on what he was saying.

"A horse, yes. I was thirteen, and a friend of mine at the time had started riding. I thought it was very cool." He shrugged. "After a lot of bargaining on my part, my parents bought me one for my fourteenth birthday. Xavier was the center of my world until my parents died." He looked down at me, his eyes serious. "He was the reason I wasn't with them when they died. I'd insisted on staying home to take care of him." His eyes got a far off look to them as he spoke. "If I'd gone with them like they'd wanted me to, I wouldn't be here."

I had a sudden need to be close to him, to comfort him as he had me so many times. My arms circled his neck as I hugged him. He held on tight.

His lips brushed against my ear, placing soft kisses along my hairline. "How is it I can tell you these things when I can't seem to talk about it with anyone else?" he mused. It came across more of an observation rather than something he was seeking the answer to, so I didn't respond. Instead, I continued to hold him, enjoying the closeness.

Lying here in his bed together did feel different. Although we weren't doing anything more than we usually did in his chair, lying next to him in his bed felt more intimate. Our bodies were completely entwined. His head rested on my shoulder. My arms were wrapped around his neck while his were securely around my torso. Even our legs had somehow managed to overlap.

"What happened? To the horse?"

He stiffened before letting out a long breath against my skin. "Richard and Diane sold him eventually. After . . . I just couldn't look at him anymore."

"I don't understand," I said, confused.

There was a long pause. I wasn't sure he was going to answer me. Then he brought his head up and looked me in the eye. "The last time I spoke to my parents I argued with them. They wanted me to go. I wanted to stay. Xavier was the reason. Every time I looked at him, I remembered." He trailed his hand down my cheek, my neck, until he was toying with the edge of my shirt just above my breasts. "I know I couldn't have saved them, even if I'd been there. I just wish the last thing I'd said to my parents was that I loved them, instead of how much I loved Xavier and that I didn't want to leave him for the week."

I traced the lines of his face with my hands. He looked much older than he normally did. I felt like I needed to say something, to give him something like he always gave me. "Thank you . . . for telling me."

He smiled, but it didn't reach his eyes. "Oh, my love, you are one of a kind. I don't know what I did without you."

That warm feeling I always got around him spread and exploded in my chest. I smiled up at him.

Suddenly, I wasn't smiling anymore as his mouth was on mine. It was slow and soft. Instead of slipping inside my mouth, his tongue licked my lips, tracing them with its tip. I moaned at the warm and wet feel, and pressed myself closer to him. He couldn't hide his excitement when we were this close, and it felt hard against my stomach as we kissed. It didn't frighten me anymore, not like this.

Instead, I held tighter to him, increasing the pressure, knowing he'd like that. Suffice it to say, he did like it. *A lot.* He gripped my waist, trying to pull me closer as his other hand twisted in my hair. I felt surrounded in a very good way.

We kissed until we were panting, but he didn't let me go, or stop. His lips just moved down to my neck and began sucking on the skin there just below the silver collar I wore. I felt the flesh beneath his mouth grow even warmer, but the feelings didn't end there. There was heat between my legs, too, and that feeling I got when he touched me was starting in my belly. I held tight to his shoulders and leaned my head back, exposing my neck more to his lips, tongue, teeth. Never in my wildest dreams did I imagine kissing could ever feel like this.

His hand snaked up my T-shirt until he found my bra-covered breasts. He palmed the soft weight in his hand, squeezing them gently before moving the fabric out of the way. My bare breasts seemed to be much more to his liking as he hummed and moaned against my neck and kneaded and pulled. It felt so good.

I was in somewhat of a daze when he raised his head and quickly removed both my shirt and bra. It happened so fast I might have missed it if not for the feel of the cool air hitting my skin seconds before the warmth of his body pressed against me again.

His tongue dipped into my mouth. It wasn't quite as gentle this time. There was an edge to it hadn't been there earlier. I knew he was aroused; his penis was pressing against me, hard and needy. His tongue moved against mine in a way that mimicked sex.

I tried not to think about the actual sex act. He'd said we wouldn't be going any farther tonight than what I was comfortable with, but I knew if I asked him for sex right now he wouldn't say no—not unless I froze or panicked, or something.

When he pulled hard on my nipple, I gasped and dug my fingers into his shoulders. My body responded in ways I didn't understand. I didn't know how his pinching me—and that's what he was doing—could be pleasurable, but it was. I felt that tingly warmth between my legs. That first time I felt it, it had scared me a little. I didn't know what was going on. Now I knew, and I embraced it, letting the feelings take hold inside me.

Wanting to make him feel good, too, I reached down between us and touched him, but as soon as my fingers made contact, his hand circled my wrist and pulled me away. "No," he said. "Tonight's about you. I'm fine."

I didn't understand. He'd let me touch him before. What was different about tonight? Didn't he want to feel good, too?

Tears must have formed in my eyes at the rejection, because suddenly his fingers were on my cheeks wiping away the moisture. "Shh. It's okay. Don't be upset."

"I don't understand. Why can't I touch you?"

He closed his eyes and sighed. "If you touch me, Brianna, it's going to be very difficult for me to take this to where I'd like to tonight. It feels far too good with your hand wrapped around me to think of much else, and having you in my bed is just increasing the problem to the point where anything other than the thought of being inside you makes it hard to hold onto my sanity. I promised you we would take this slow. I'm trying very hard to keep that promise."

*Oh.*

I glanced down at where our bodies were touching. He sighed again. "Not helping, Brianna." I giggled, and he groaned, pressing his forehead against mine. "Be a good girl and kiss me," he said gruffly as his lips descended.

As his mouth made contact with mine again, I was quickly lost in sensation overload. His mouth not only demanded my attention, but so did his hands as they slid down my torso to cup my behind. He dug his fingers into my ass, roughly grinding my lower body against his. The movement was a lot like I remembered sex, except we were still wearing clothing. This felt amazing.

He shifted our bodies slightly, lifting my leg and placing it over his hip. Then he went back to what he'd been doing before. The change in position made what he'd been doing feel even better. Sounds I'd only ever made before in the shower began escaping my lips as he continued to press and grind against me until I felt myself climbing toward the peak that I knew was there waiting for me.

Slowly, I edged closer. Kissing was nearly impossible as his movements increased and soon we were just breathing into each other's mouths harder and faster.

Then I was there, at the peak, falling off that cliff that left me feeling like a pile of mush. I arched my back and dug my fingers into his sides as I screamed.

## Stephan

Watching her orgasm had to be one of the best things in the world. I didn't think I'd ever get tired of seeing it, but she'd totally sidetracked my plans. Dry humping her in the middle of my bed had never been on the agenda for tonight. To make matters worse, I was still extremely hard. I could have let go. I should have probably let go, but then I would have just lay here with her in my arms for the rest of the night instead of pushing forward. So as difficult, and as hard, as it may be . . . I gritted my teeth and lived with the discomfort.

"Shame on you," I said, smiling so she knew I wasn't mad at her. "You sidetracked me."

Even with the smile, she seemed unsure. "I'm sorry. I didn't . . ."

My finger covered her lips. "It's all right. We both were carried away. It seems to happen a lot."

Finally, I saw a small smile appear on her lips. "I like . . . this."

I kissed her, unable to resist. She was so sweet and innocent sometimes. "So do I. It still doesn't change the fact that we have more to do. How are you feeling?"

"Relaxed," she sighed, content.

"Hm." I nuzzled her neck. "That's good, but not quite where I need you to be. Let's lose your jeans first, though."

She helped me push her jeans down her legs, and I tossed them to the floor. I kneeled at the end of the bed facing her. Her body lay spread out on my bed, naked, save her cream-colored panties. I could see the circles around her nipples from the cigarette burns that marred her flesh. Even the marks between her legs were more prominent in this position. I doubted she'd ever feel comfortable in a bathing suit out in public. The marks were low enough that they'd be visible unless she wore bottoms that went down to almost her mid-thigh.

I could tell she was getting nervous with my staring at her, and what I was going to have her do wasn't going to help. "Open your legs for me, sweetheart." Her eyes opened wide, but instead of repeating myself, I waited. She might not want to, but I was fairly sure she'd comply anyway. Sure enough, her legs slowly began to open. "Wider," I prompted when she stopped with them only a few inches apart. She gave me a few more inches. "Keep going." I saw her throat move as she swallowed. Her chest moved up and down rapidly with her nerves. When she'd opened them enough for me to sit in between them, I placed a hand on her right leg to stop her. "Good girl. How are you doing? What number?"

"Um, five?"

"Tell me why."

"I don't know what you're going to do."

"Trust me?"

She nodded. "I do. I trust you."

I smiled and moved to sit between her legs. "Good because I'm hoping you're going to enjoy what's coming next."

Leaning forward, I placed a chaste kiss on her lips before trailing kisses in a straight line down her body until I reached the top of her panties. These were ones Lily had picked out for her, and I had to say I approved. The cream color contrasted just enough with her skin, and the silky texture felt nice as I ran my nose along the top before dipping down to tease her cleft.

She sucked in a large amount of air, and I looked up, catching her gaze. Her eyes were still wide. "Tell me what has you worried."

"Will it hurt?"

I chuckled. "No. I can promise you that it won't hurt. Not at all. Why do you think it will hurt?"

"It did. Before."

I squeezed her leg comfortingly. "Do you like how I kiss you?"

"Yes."

Smiling, I bent down and placed a closed-mouth kiss on top of her panty-covered clit. "That's all I'm going to do. Kiss you."

"Kiss me?"

"Kiss you," I said, placing another kiss to her clit, adding more pressure.

"Okay," she said, seeming to have relaxed a little. My hope was for her to relax a lot more before this was finished.

Slipping my fingers inside her panties, I moved them down her legs enough for me to see what lay underneath. She was glistening, and I couldn't wait to get my mouth there. Lifting first her right and then her left leg, I worked her panties down each limb before throwing them over my shoulder to join her jeans.

She was completely bare before me except for the hair that was now starting to take over her mound. I really did prefer an unobstructed view, but she was still beyond beautiful. Her lips were the same shade as when her skin flushed as she climaxed. It guided my thoughts and my actions as I stuck out my tongue and took a long lick.

Her response was better than expected. I felt her tense at the first touch, but then she tensed in a very different way by the time I reach her bundle of nerves on the top. "Give me your hands."

It took her a moment to register what I'd said, but she reached for my hands. I clasped them together, hoping this would help her in some way. This was all about pleasuring her with my mouth. Hands were out of the equation for now.

I went back to my objective. The tip of my tongue traced the outline of her lips before sucking them into my mouth. I suckled her flesh as I would her breast before concentrating on her now-dripping entrance. Moisture was seeping out, and I eagerly devoured it.

By the time I moved my attention to back to her clit, she was holding my hands so tight I was losing feeling. I listened to her breathing hitch as my tongue circled around and pressed firmly, before backing off and repeating the same pattern. It was driving her toward the edge again, and I could tell she was close.

Pulling her right hand down between her legs, I sucked two of her fingers in my mouth to wet them before placing them on either side of her clit. My hand guided her movement and she seemed so lost in the feelings she was experiencing that she wasn't paying much attention to the details.

"Touch yourself, Brianna."

"What?" she asked, sounding groggy.

I moved our hands again, showing her what I wanted. "Touch yourself. Show me what you like, what feels good." Her hand stilled completely, but instead of repeating, I went back to what I'd been doing, hoping she'd follow my instruction.

She did. *Eventually.* Her movements were tentative at first, but grew bolder as she found enjoyment in her own touch.

When she was nearing her peak again, I readjusted her hand lower. "Put a finger inside yourself."

Slowly, cautiously, I both saw and felt her hand move. But just as the tips of her fingers were about to disappear, she cried, "I can't."

"Yes, you can," I insisted. "It's just your fingers. You control the feeling, good or bad. Would it help if I let go of your wrist?"

"No," she sobbed.

"Hey," I said, stopping. "What number?"

"S . . . seven."

"Take a deep breath and let it out." She did. "Remember how great everything has felt so far? This will feel good, too. No pain, okay?"

"Okay," she breathed. I smiled, and kissed the top of her fingers before placing them again over her opening. My tongue followed and licked around and between her fingers, encouraging her.

Then one finger, followed closely by the other, disappeared inside her.

# Chapter 23

**Stephan**

*She'd pushed two fingers in up to her first knuckle and no farther. It was* as if she was waiting on something. I could only guess the memory of pain she feared. My tongue slid in between her fingers, massaging and tasting. I was thrilled with her positive reception to oral sex. There was nothing better than feasting from a woman's pussy, but as with everything else when it came to Brianna, this experience was ranking at the top of my list of all-time favorite experiences.

"Push your fingers in a little further. You're doing well. It's such a lovely sight, seeing your fingers pushed inside you like this." I watched as her chest rose and fell with her exaggerated breathing before she slid her fingers deeper. "Good girl. How does that feel?"

"I . . . I don't know."

"Yes, you do. I've never had my fingers inside you before. Tell me how it feels."

"Puffy?"

I smiled. She was being very literal, and that was perfectly fine. "What else?"

"Really moist."

"Hm. Yes, you are very wet. I'm enjoying the view and the taste very much."

"You like it?"

I stifled my laugh. "You have no idea how much I like it, Brianna. Can you move your fingers in and out for me? I'd like to get more of those delectable juices of yours."

"Okay," she whispered.

Cautiously, her fingers began to move in and out. As her confidence increased, so did the speed of her fingers. It was an amazing sight to

Sherri Hayes

behold, and I had a front row seat. I took advantage, did as promised, and dove in to get every drop of her moisture I could from her fingers as they exited before disappearing back inside again. It took a while, but after several minutes, she started to relax and enjoy the feel of the penetration.

My hand gripped her wrist tighter, and I guided her palm so that with every motion she was bumping against her clit. Her breathing stuttered before picking up again, and I smiled, never taking my mouth from her. The joy I felt knowing I was helping her overcome this hurdle was something I could never have imagined two months ago. It also helped that I was more attracted to her than I'd ever been to another woman in my life. Even with her scars, her body was perfect. She was soft in all the right places, and she fit perfectly in my arms. Seeing her spread out before me like this, imitating the motion of me gliding in and out of her, had my groin aching, demanding attention. I ignored it.

"Brianna?"

"Yes?"

"I'm going to stick one of my fingers inside you. You'll feel fuller, but other than that it should feel very much the same."

She stopped moving for a moment and tensed, but then took a deep breath. "Okay."

"Good girl. Remember to tell me if something doesn't feel right." She nodded slightly, and her fingers began their in and out movement again.

I had to shift positions in order to remain holding onto her wrist and free my other arm enough to allow the mobility I needed. Once I rearranged myself, I began stroking my tongue along her sensitive folds again, willing her to relax. When I heard a sigh leave her lips, I knew she was ready.

Taking a single finger, I held my hand upside down and pushed it inside her, slowly trying to match the thrust and retreat of her own fingers. All the way in, I asked, "Can you feel my finger, Brianna?"

"Yes."

"Are you okay? What number?"

"T . . . two."

"You're doing great, sweetheart. Now I want you to look down here at me." She did. "Use the pillow behind you to prop your head up. I want your eyes on me." Her movement faltered as she did what I said. I waited until she was settled again before continuing. "I want you to remove your fingers."

Brianna's fingers came out warm and wet, and I latched onto them as soon as they were clear, sucking them into my mouth. "Oh," she breathed. I held her gaze as I cleaned her digits. She was flushed and looking a bit disheveled from our dry humping earlier and the show she put on for me between her legs.

I let go of her hand, kissing it, and pressed the single finger that remained inside her firmly against her wall. "Can you still feel my finger inside you?"

"Yes."

"Number?"

"Two."

I was proud of her. She was doing so well. "I'm going to add a second finger. It should feel about the same as it did with your fingers. Remember to tell me if something's wrong or doesn't feel right." She nodded and pressed her lips together. I felt her start to tense up again. "Relax. No pain, remember."

"Promise?"

"Promise."

"Okay," she said, and I felt her interior muscles begin to give.

"That's it," I encouraged. Bending down, I began stroking my tongue against her clit again, exaggerating the movement for her visual benefit.

It worked. Her pupils dilated and her lids started to close. "No, no. Eyes on me." Brianna snapped her lids open. "That's better," I said, going back to my task.

She continued to watch me as I swirled my tongue over and around her bundle of nerves. She didn't even flinch as I eased my second finger inside her. The walls of her pussy spread easily, welcoming the intrusion. Brianna seemed to be enjoying it as well, as I started to move my hand, thrusting and twisting my fingers while still pressing and circling her swollen clit with my tongue.

I knew she was getting close again when her skin began to take on that pink hue that spread from the tips of her breasts, up her neck to her face. Continuing the movement with my hand, I pressed the flat of my tongue against her cleft and made short hard motions. Her hands fisted the sheets, nearly pulling one side loose from the mattress as she arched her back and screamed her release. I was finding that Brianna was a very vocal lover, and I liked it.

**Brianna**

I did it. He had his fingers inside me, and I hadn't frozen. My jaw was beginning to hurt from the smile that was stretching my lips. When I looked down between my legs, he was smiling, too.

It hadn't been bad at all. There'd been no pain, just as he'd promised there wouldn't be, and there had been this feeling of fullness. Knowing it was him helped, too. I loved when he touched my skin, but this was more. He was literally touching me from the inside. I wanted more. At least, I wanted to try.

"Sir?"

"Yes?" he asked with a huge grin on his face.

"Will you . . . ?" I knew he had said to look at him, but I couldn't look and ask at the same time. I couldn't. "Will you have sex with me?" The words spilled forth from my mouth so fast I had no idea if he caught them. They were hard for me to understand, and I'd been the one speaking them.

The smile fell from his face, and I felt my anxiety rising. Something was wrong. What was wrong?

His hands pressed down on the mattress on either side of me as he crawled up my body. I had no idea how to read the look on his face. He didn't appear to be mad, but why wasn't he smiling anymore? I loved it when he smiled.

When his face was level with mine, he took my face in his hands, looking at me intently. I swallowed, trying to remember to breath and not to panic. There was a scent coming from his right hand that I remembered from before. It was the smell of sex. Memories started to swirl in my mind, but I forced myself to concentrate on him instead, and kept repeating his name in my head over and over again. Nothing could chase the bad away like Stephan could.

"Do you mean it? You're ready?"

He'd heard me. "Yes," I nodded, feeling his fingers digging into my scalp as I moved. I was as ready as I was ever going to be.

"Say it again, and look at me when you do."

I didn't know if I could, but I would try for him. I would try anything for him.

My gaze locked on his, and I took a deep breath. "Will you . . ." I had to take another breath before continuing. This was so hard to do. I knew what I was asking him. "Have sex . . ." Another breath. "With me?"

A hint of his smile came back, but it quickly disappeared. He leaned in to place a chaste kiss on my lips before finding my gaze again. "I want you to say it one more time, and I want you to say my name."

I had to say it again? And say his name?

It was then I realized that I'd only once called him by his name, and that was when he'd forced it out of me over the phone. But I had never called him by name to his face. I knew he was Stephan, but calling him that didn't feel right.

I must have been taking too long because he said, "Are you sure this is what you want? It shouldn't be so difficult to say again if it truly is what you desire."

At that point, I knew he was right. I needed to say it, and if he wanted me to say his name, too, I could do that. I would do that. Pressing my lips together to gather courage, I attempted saying it in my mind. *Will you have sex with me, Stephan?* After repeating the phrase in my head several more times, I felt I was as ready as I was ever going to be. "Will you have . . . sex . . . with me . . . Stephan?"

The smile was back, and I breathed a sigh of relief. His hand cupped the back of my neck and tilted my head as he gazed down into my eyes. "I would love to have sex with you, Brianna Reeves. You have no idea how badly I've wanted to make love to you." I smiled, knowing I'd made him happy. "There are a few things we need to talk about first, though."

My smile fell. What things?

"First, you are to have your eyes open and on me at all times. I don't want you panicking because you've gotten lost inside your head. Two, if at any time you need to stop, I want you to tell me. If I do something that feels wrong, I need you to tell me that as well. You have your numbers. You *always* have your numbers. Use them. And if I ask you what number you're at, I need you to respond immediately."

He gave me a pointed look, and I knew he wanted an answer. "Yes, Sir."

"And last," he said, brushing my hair out of the way and running his nose along my temple down to my ear, "I want you to relax and enjoy yourself. Sex is supposed to be fun and enjoyable."

I took a deep breath and released it as I held onto his arms, trying to do as he said and relax. This was *Stephan*. I was okay.

His mouth sought mine in a kiss that was both harsh and gentle at the same time. He plunged his tongue inside my mouth, tracing the outline of my teeth, while his lips were firm and demanding. The contrast between the two had me concentrating on what he was doing with his mouth and nothing else.

When he pulled back, we were both breathing heavily. He placed a hard kiss on my forehead before lying back on the bed beside me. "I want you to undress me, Brianna."

After undressing him for our nightly showers many times, this I knew I could do. Sitting up quickly, I knelt before him and began working on the buttons of his shirt. I always started at the top and worked my way down for some reason.

One by one, the buttons slipped from their hold around the fabric of his now-wrinkled dress shirt, revealing his chest underneath. It was a slow progression, partly because I was staring a little too long at the skin that was being uncovered. He didn't seem to mind. Every time I glanced up at him, he was watching my hands with an intensity I didn't understand.

With his shirt completely unbuttoned, I released the buttons on his cuffs and he rose to help me push the material from his shoulders and down his arms. The movement brought us very close, our naked chests brushing. I felt a shiver run through me.

He must have noticed my reaction. As he leaned back to lie on the bed once again, he was smirking, amusement danced in his eyes. I blushed, and turned to concentrate on his pants.

Stephan always wore a suit to work, and today had been no different. His pants were soft and smooth. The fabric was thin, and it didn't hide the evidence of his arousal. While the sight of him, in and of itself, didn't scare me anymore, I was nervous about having him put his penis inside me. I tried to imagine what it would feel like and I couldn't. His fingers had felt much better than I'd expected, better than how mine had felt.

"What are you thinking?" he asked.

*Oh.* I looked up and back down at my hands. They were resting on the top of his slacks, both the button and the zipper still fully in place. "I was wondering how it will feel."

"How sex will feel?"

"Yes."

"I don't know how it will feel for you, Brianna," he said, rubbing a hand comfortingly on my leg. "I imagine it will be similar to how my fingers felt for you, but I don't think it will be exactly the same."

I nodded. That made sense. I pressed my lips together and returned to my task. He'd told me to undress him, and so far, all I'd done was remove his shirt.

The button on his pants sprung easily, and the zipper helped itself halfway down before I'd even touched it with the pressure he was putting on it from underneath. I unzipped it the rest of the way, and he lifted his hips so I could push his pants down his legs. While I was down at his feet, I removed his socks, leaving him lying only in his boxers. He looked . . . handsome. Sexy? Yes, *sexy,* lying there. A warmth spread through my chest, followed by a tingly feeling in my belly.

I climbed back on the bed smiling. He smiled back.

His boxers were hung up on his penis, and it bobbed several times before it sprung free. I didn't have much time to think about it, though. "Come here," he said, as soon as I put his boxers with the rest of our clothing.

I scrambled back onto the bed, and knelt beside him. But that wasn't what he wanted. He reached out and pulled me down beside him. His bare skin against mine felt really good. He was warm and soft, yet hard at the same time, and I could feel his penis between us pressing just above the junction of my legs.

He twisted one hand in my hair, while the other slid down between our bodies and began playing with my breasts. His lips brushed against my own as he hummed. "You are so very beautiful, and I'm honored you are allowing me to make love to you, my lovely girl."

His mouth went to work, first on my mouth, and then trailing down my body. He lingered on my breasts. It was the first time he'd taken them in his mouth and the feeling wasn't like any I remembered. Even when he used his teeth on my nipple, it was pleasant in the same way his fingers were sending a surge of energy down low in my belly.

When he was once again kneeling between my legs, he licked and kissed as he had before, making my head spin. This was what it was all about, I realized. This was what people in the books I'd read craved and this was why they craved it.

The stirring of my climax began to build yet again. I couldn't believe I hadn't ever felt this way before Stephan, but in a way, I was glad. He seemed to love this and it was something I could give to him and love at the same time.

Just when I was about to reach my peak, he stopped. Before I could even think, however, he was there, lying on top of me. His weight felt good, but it was scary at the same time. I kept my eyes on him as he'd asked, and he was watching me closely.

I watched as he reached over to his nightstand and opened the drawer. His hand disappeared for a second, and reappeared with a blue square. I knew what it was. A condom.

My eyes followed his movements as he opened the package and rolled the condom down his penis. I'm not sure why, but that made it more real for me than it had been only a minute before when he'd been between my legs.

He readjusted himself on top of me. The moment I felt his penis, I jumped. "Shh. You're okay. What number?"

"Four."

"Relax and stay with me. You're really wet so he should just slide right in as long as you don't tense up, okay?"

"Okay."

"Deep breath now." I did as he said. "Again."

The breathing helped. And after a few more, I did feel more relaxed.

Instead of plunging right in, however, he took his penis and rubbed it up and down my slit. I could feel the moisture as it coated him. His knuckle kept brushing against my clit and eventually I started to feel that heat again.

Then I felt it. *Him.* His gaze was intense, his face set in a mask of concentration. I knew he probably wanted to thrust inside me hard and fast, but he didn't. Instead, he pressed in a little and stopped, waiting, before going again and stopping. It was a slow progression, but it helped me more than I would ever be able to explain to him. So far, this was worlds apart from my other experiences.

His pelvis was against my clit, and I knew he must have been all the way inside. He stilled, and searched my face for something. "Number?"

I took a breath and let it out. "Two."

He smiled and kissed me before his gaze returned to meet mine. "I'm going to start moving now."

The feel of him moving, thrusting, wasn't like anything I'd felt before either. He didn't start pounding away at me. Instead, he gradually built up to a steady rhythm and angled his hips so that with every inward movement he was pressing against my clit. The feeling wasn't something I could have ever imagined. This wasn't anything like my nightmares.

Every now and then, he'd lean down to kiss me, or his hand would slip between us so he could play with my breasts. It didn't take very long for me to feel that energy rising again. This time was more intense than before. The feeling was taking over faster. I hung onto his shoulders, digging my fingers into his skin. He was breathing hard, his chest covered in sweat.

I felt his hand move lower, brushing the skin of my stomach before reaching my clit. It was almost like an electric shock when he touched me there. "Come for me," he rasped. His fingers circled several times before pressing down hard and then pinching. My head fell back and my mouth opened to make a sound unlike any other as I fell over the edge into the most intense orgasm yet. It sounded somewhere between a scream and what a wounded animal would make.

As I came back to reality, I realized he was still moving, thrusting in and out of me. My flesh was sensitive, but it didn't hurt. His brow furrowed and he let out what sounded like a grunt as he pressed against me and held.

He was completely still, his eyes glassy and his arms shaking. I thought maybe something was wrong, but then he collapsed on top of me, wrapping me in his arms. "Thank you, my love," he whispered, kissing my neck. He was breathing hard, but I could tell he was smiling.

I did it. *We* did it. With a smile on my face, I circled my arms around him. Maybe I could do this. Maybe I could be what he needed.

# Epilogue

## Stephan

*All was right with the world. Sex with Brianna was absolute heaven.* Never in my life had sex been like that, and it was only our first time. It was much more than physical, although that was certainly there. The love I felt for her seemed to magnify when I was inside her, feeling her surrounding me. It was truly an out-of-body experience and something I'd never felt before. I couldn't wait to do it again.

We'd lain in my bed holding each other until almost ten o'clock. I couldn't let her go, though. I wasn't sure I'd ever be able to let her sleep in her own bed again.

With reluctance, I helped her out of my bed, and we took our nightly shower together. There was a lot of touching, but I kept it innocent for the most part. She was very relaxed, and I wanted to keep it that way. My own body felt heavy, and for the first time in my life, I felt satisfied.

After drying her off, I quickly changed the sheets and curled up with her in my bed. She stiffened a little when I tried to spoon her, so I rolled us over and brought her head to rest on my chest. The tension in her muscles relaxed right away, and she cuddled closer, resting her hand on my bare chest.

I didn't get much sleep, but it was purely a choice on my part. It was difficult to sleep knowing she was finally there in my arms. I'd drift off to sleep only to wake an hour or so later smiling like a schoolboy.

Brianna slept soundly throughout the night. I thought she was going to wake once when a dream seemed to take hold of her, but with some gentle caresses and whispered words, she fell back into a deep slumber. The alarm startled her a little, but as soon as she realized where she was, she smiled up at me shyly. It was adorable considering she was lying flush against me without a shred of clothing on, and that I'd gotten to know her on a most imitate level last night.

Truth be told, I didn't want to leave her this morning. Then again, I never did. I could have lain there with her all morning, even if all we did was touch and kiss, although I'd be a fool not to want to have her body again. She was perfection, and she was mine.

When we said good-bye, our normal kiss was drawn out into something that could have led to me being very late had I not stopped it. Even so, we were both quite worked up by the time I left. I had to stop outside the door for several minutes to calm down before getting in the elevator. The last thing I wanted was to give one of the other residents a show that early in the morning.

The morning went slow, but well. I conducted the final interview for Karl's replacement. Michael James was older, in his mid-fifties, and had been working in the financial world for over twenty years. One of the other executives had recommended him. They'd worked with him previously, before they came to the foundation and thought he'd be a good fit. So far, I had to agree. Mr. James had a solid resume and came across as very personable. I'd taken my time in hiring him, given what had happened with Karl. It was much better to search for the right person until I found him or her than hire the wrong person and have to deal with the likes of our former CFO again.

By the end of the interview, I was certain. He was the one. I had Jamie schedule an executive meeting for the next week and told him he should be hearing from us soon. It was one more thing I could cross off my list. And even with the loose ends hanging out there, I was feeling content with my life.

At lunch, I called Brianna. She'd been cleaning. I'd given her permission this morning to go in my room, and apparently, it had needed a deep cleaning since I'd not allowed her in there before now. By the time I hung up the phone, I was ready to dive back into the work sitting on my desk in hope I could leave early.

I was just finishing the reports I needed to approve when my direct line rang. This was the number that bypassed Jamie. Not many people had it, so it was either one of my family, Brianna, or only a handful of others. "Hello," I said, not bothering with my official greeting.

"Mr. Coleman?"

I thought I recognized the voice. "Tom?"

"Yes, sir. Mr. Coleman, we have a problem."


## Brianna

I was quite literally dancing my day away. This morning had been everything I'd read in books and more. It felt good waking up in his arms, like the chair, only better. Neither of us was wearing clothes, so I felt a little shy at first, but he'd melted my nerves away with a soft lingering kiss. Just thinking about it sent tingles through my entire body down to my toes.

After cleaning up breakfast, I started to clean. He'd told me this morning that I was no longer restricted and could go into his bedroom and bathroom at any time. Since the rest of the house was in good shape, I put on some music and decided to start in there.

It was a good thing, too. Not that Stephan was messy—because he wasn't —but I could tell no one had done more than basic cleaning in his room for a while. By the time he called me on his lunch break, I had everything almost put back in his cabinets.

He told me about his morning. Mr. James sounded like a nice man. I was glad Karl Walker was gone, and I'd never have to deal with him again.

Once I hung up the phone with Stephan, I cleaned myself up a little and made a sandwich. I wasn't hungry, but I knew if I didn't eat something Stephan would be upset. The last thing I wanted was for him to be angry with me. I was happy. He was happy. I wanted to keep it that way.

With my sandwich eaten, I went back to work. The station I'd found on the radio in Stephan's room had been set to one that played a variety of music ranging from light rock to punk. It was a little surprising. I'd never heard Stephan listen to the radio outside of his car, and even then, it was all instrumental.

I swayed my hips to the music as I stepped into the shower with the cleaner and a towel to wipe everything down. I lingered a little longer than necessary, finding my thoughts drifting to the hours we'd spent together in there. It was difficult to focus on what I was doing.

When I walked out of the shower, I was satisfied it was thoroughly clean, and I was missing Stephan terribly. I glanced at the clock on the wall, and saw that it was only two thirty. He wouldn't be home for another three hours.

The large soaker tub was next on my list. It had massage jets, and I wondered how they'd feel against my skin. I'd never been in a tub like it before, just the regular old-fashioned ones.

Bent over the tub, I was trying to reach the bottom when I thought I heard the phone ring. I stopped and listened, but all I heard was the radio. Reaching into my pocket, I pulled out my cell. There were no new messages, no missed calls. I guessed I was hearing things. Maybe it was a sound effect from the song.

Ten minutes later, I smiled as I looked over his bathroom. Everything was clean, including the floor. I hoped he would like it. He'd seemed pleased when I'd told him what I was doing over the phone. With a sense of satisfaction, I took the cleaning supplies and moved into his bedroom.

That was when I heard a knock on the door. At first I ignored it, but whomever it was continued to knock, and it was getting louder. Maybe it was Tom. If he *had* called and I hadn't answered, maybe he would come up to check on me.

Setting everything down on Stephan's dresser, I walked out into the main room and over to the front door. The knocks seemed to get louder and louder. I felt bad that I hadn't answered until now and made Tom worry for no good reason. Maybe the radio hadn't been such a good idea.

I opened the door ready to apologize to Tom, but the words died on my lips. There, standing before me, was a man I'd hoped I'd never see again.

"I'm so glad I found you. You have no idea what it took for me to find you, baby girl."

Look for the next installment in
Stephan and Brianna's story
coming Summer of 2013

# About the Author

Sherri is the author of three novels: *Hidden Threat, Slave* (*Finding Anna* Book 1) and *Behind Closed Doors* (A Daniels Brothers Novel), and a short story, *A Christmas Proposal*. She lives in central Ohio with her husband and three cats. Her mother fostered her love for books at a young age by reading to her as a child. Stories have been floating around in her head for as long as she can remember; however, she didn't start writing them down until five years ago. It has become a creative outlet that allows her to explore a wide range of emotions, while having fun taking her characters through all the twists and turns she can create. When she's not writing, she can usually be found helping her husband in his woodworking shop.

# Acknowledgments

I want to say thank you to all those who read Slave and loved it. Stephan and Brianna hold a special place in my heart, and I'm so glad you are as captivated by them as I am.

Thank you to all of my Facebook and Twitter followers who I pester with random questions from time to time. You have no idea why I'm asking, but you still chime in anyway.

And a special thank you to AB who stayed up until three o'clock in the morning on Skype with me going over a critical chapter to make sure it was worded just right. You're help was very much appreciated.